D0464562

THE
MIDNIGHT
DANCE

nikki katz

THE
MIDNIGHT
DANCE

𝒮woon READS

NEW YORK

A SWOON READS BOOK
An imprint of Feiwel and Friends and Macmillan Publishing Group, LLC
175 Fifth Avenue, New York, NY 10010

Our books may be purchased in bulk for promotional, educational, or business
use. Please contact your local bookseller or the Macmillan Corporate and
Premium Sales Department at (800) 221-7945 ext. 5442 or by e-mail at
MacmillanSpecialMarkets@macmillan.com.

Library of Congress Cataloging-in-Publication Data

Names: Katz, Nikki, author.
Title: The midnight dance / Nikki Katz.
Description: First edition. | New York : Swoon Reads, 2017. | Summary:
In 1879, seventeen-year-old Penny yearns to escape the confines of Italy's
mysterious and elite Grande Teatro and explore the flashes of memory
that suggest she once lived a very different life.
Identifiers: LCCN 2016059094 (print) | LCCN 2017029332 (ebook) |
ISBN 9781250123725 (Ebook) | ISBN 9781250123718 (hardcover)
Subjects: | CYAC: Ballet dancing—Fiction. | Schools—Fiction. |
Memory—Fiction. | Brainwashing—Fiction. | Orphans—Fiction. |
Italy—History—1870–1914—Fiction.
Classification: LCC PZ7.1.K374 (ebook) | LCC PZ7.1.K374 Mid 2017 (print) |
DDC [Fic]—dc23
LC record available at https://lccn.loc.gov/2016059094

Book design by Carol Ly

First edition, 2017

1 3 5 7 9 10 8 6 4 2

swoonreads.com

To my children:
Katelyn, Kendall, and Lincoln

CHAPTER 1

⊰ 1859 ⊱

The boy clutched a marionette to his chest and shuffled into the barn.

His best friend—his only friend—Beppe glanced up from where he was whittling a narrow piece of pine. "Oh, Cirillo, what happened now?"

Cirillo blinked back angry tears and stepped toward him. Damp hay lay strewn over the floor, covering an errant knot of wood pushing up through the dirt. He tripped over it, the puppet tumbling from his hands as his arms whirled to gain balance. The toy landed face-first in the hay, the leg bent at an awkward angle.

Not unlike his own.

"She broke it. Again." Cirillo choked out the words. "I hate her."

He could still hear his sister's laughter, tight and high-pitched as she stood in front of him. "Poor Cirillo can't catch a ball with the other boys, so he's stuck playing make-believe." Sofia threw the toy high into the air, running off with her friends as it plummeted to the ground with a loud *snap*.

He'd eased from the chair and squatted down. He fought

to keep his balance as his right leg wobbled. Scooping up the marionette, he made his way out of the expansive parlor room and through the portico. The sun soaked into his skin and eased some of the incessant pain, but his mind continued to spin hatred into a veil that clouded his thoughts.

The trek across the field and down to the barn was precarious and time-consuming, but Cirillo found Beppe in the same spot he'd left him hours before. Beppe slept in the stable loft and rarely left the outbuildings except for a hot meal or a tepid bath. Even then he preferred to swim in the lake unless it was covered in ice. An orphan, Beppe had wandered onto the estate several years before. His arrival happened to coincide with the departure of a stable hand who'd gone in search of greener pastures, so Cirillo's stepmother took Beppe in to help with the horses. What the self-centered woman didn't know was that the teen spent most hours in a hidden workshop he'd built inside the tack room. A padlock and chain kept prying eyes, and obnoxious girls, from peeking in.

Beppe put down his knife and the scrap of wood. On his table was an odd assortment of tools. A chisel, a mallet, a saw, and gouges for the wood carving, but also a liset, straight razor knives, clamps, and needles. "Come see. He's walking."

A wave of dizziness swept through Cirillo, and he clasped a hand to Beppe's shoulder for support. Was it possible?

Together they moved to the tack room, where Cirillo waited as Beppe unwound the chains and eased the door open on silent hinges.

Cirillo held a handkerchief to his nose, breathing dried lavender in the hopes of masking the scent of clotted blood that wafted from behind the door.

The room was dark, the air heavy and humid. Thin bands of

sunlight cut through cracks in the outer wall, slashing additional bars across the crates and instruments lining the shelves. Beppe lit a single lantern and the space came further into view. Cirillo leaned over to peer inside the single cage resting on the table in the center of the room. A mouse sat in a flattened bed of straw, perfectly still as if it had been stuffed. Even the whiskers remained motionless.

Beppe pulled a scrap of cheese from his pocket and handed it to Cirillo. "Put it just inside the cage."

Cirillo lowered the handkerchief, his nose acclimating to the copper smell. He pushed the bit of cheese between the bars. It fell, and he yanked his finger back before the mouse could nip his skin.

A whisker twitched. Then another. The mouse shifted and stretched its paws. It pounced on the cheese. Cirillo's mouth dropped as he took in the tiny legs. Four of them, covered in fur. Which would've been perfectly normal and unworthy of his time, if the hind leg hadn't been a scrap of metal only forty-eight hours before.

Beppe grinned at him, his mop of pale curls sticking out in all directions like a halo. "Only think of your future. You'll be able to ride horses. Spin girls around the dance floor."

Cirillo's lips smiled, but his jaw stayed tight. Those things didn't matter. What girl would want to dance with him anyway? No. He had bigger plans. A grander scheme. He'd have the biggest stage imaginable, and his sister would never laugh again.

CHAPTER 2

Penny hoped for a whisper of a compliment, at the very least.

One hand rested on a smooth wooden barre, supporting her upper body. She stood *en pointe* with her right leg stretched toward the ceiling. Every muscle strained in extension to hold the *penché*.

Not a single word of praise echoed through the drafty chamber. Madame Triolo only reprimanded with a sharp retort. "Penelope, your fingers."

Her leg sagged and disappointment wormed in to tighten her shoulders.

Madame stomped over with all the grace of an elephant. Only five years ago, she'd prevailed as the king's favorite dancer. Now she put every ounce of her petite frame into heavy steps, as if to prove her very existence.

"They go here"—Madame moved Penny's index finger a mere millimeter and twisted her thumb inward—"and here. Now do it again."

Bianca gave a delicate, but still condescending, snort from across the dance studio, where she practiced a series of *pirouettes*. She held the lead role opposite Penny in the spring equinox gala performance and relished every one of Penny's failures, of which there seemed to be many.

You did fine, Maria mouthed to Penny in the mirror. She knew how hard Penny practiced. But it was useless. Penny would never be good enough.

Not for Madame.

Madame turned away and shouted loud enough to break the thick glass windows lining the far wall. "Next week, girls. We're almost there, but not quite. I will *not* have a shoddy performance." The gala was Madame's chance to show off for Master. And his chance to put the girls on display for the public. The twelve girls made up the current student population of the Grande Teatro finishing school, and the midnight dance performance was the culmination of their extensive ballet training.

Most of the girls loved the event, the chance to be the center of attention as well as mingle with townspeople and royalty alike. It was rare they saw anyone who didn't work inside the estate boundaries.

Penny was in the minority, if not the sole minority. She disliked everything about the event. The parading and posturing. The forced small talk with strangers. It made her skin itch.

"Now for the *reverence*!" Madame Triolo ushered the girls to the center of the floor beneath the heavy crystal gasolier. At her turn, Penny stepped forward, hands dropping to her sides and a smile painted on her face. Sweeping one leg behind, she bowed low in a curtsy and waited for Bianca to join her. After Bianca repeated the same gesture, all the girls straightened in unison and grasped hands for the final bow. Penny caught their reflection in the sprawling gold-leaf-framed mirror, conscious not for the first time of how similar they all looked. Like twelve sisters.

Dark, thick hair all tied back in buns, bodies lean and sinewy. Pale muslin skirts draped from their waists to their knees. The same small symbol tattooed on their wrists to show acceptance into Master's programs. It looked like a six-pointed star, an X shape with a line running vertically through the center. And they were all so pale, like apparitions. The occasional hour of sunlight would do them good.

"Beautiful lines, Bianca," Madame purred. Bianca dug her nails into the back of Penny's hand, and she yanked her fingers away. "Dismissed! I will see you bright and early again tomorrow."

Maria led Penny into the hallway. Penny paused to lean a palm against the rough stone wall and untie her slippers. Her toes were shredded from pushing up on the toe box all afternoon. Maria stood at her side, carrying on about the book she'd finished that morning. "You really should read it. The romance"— she sighed—"do you think we'll ever have something like that?"

"A devoted, dashing, daring young man who will swoop in, brandish a sword, and defend our honor?" Penny lifted the slippers by their ribbons and strode down the hall.

"Yes." Maria failed to notice Penny's sarcasm.

Penny stopped short and Maria nearly bumped into her back. "Maria, where would we find someone like that? The only boy our age in the house is Cricket." The kitchen boy. While he was certainly cute—in a gangly, flour-dusted-hair kind of way—Penny couldn't picture him saving her from anything but a wayward fork.

Maria nudged her forward. "Cricket? I'm talking about someone like Master."

Penny chewed her lip. Master *was* only a few years older. He certainly played the part of the stoic, brooding benefactor, and he was dreamy in a tall, dark, and handsome cliché. But he had a way of unsettling her with his penetrating gaze, and he kept his guard up. Always.

Lacing her fingers through Maria's, Penny tugged her down the hall. "Perhaps you'll find a young man at the gala. Some over-zealous toff who will charm his way into your heart."

Maria grinned. "You, too. I know you'll find someone."

I will. I will find someone, Penny thought. *Only I won't meet him here.*

Of course, that would mean actually traveling beyond the borders of the estate, and then even farther to the nearest town. The manor was plopped seemingly in the middle of nowhere, a stone island surrounded by an undulating sea of woodland and fields. Master proclaimed it was to keep the girls safe and allow them to focus on their studies. Penny often wondered if, instead, it was to keep them hidden away from the outside world.

The pair swept past the closed doors that led to their study rooms and burst through heavy double doors into the foyer of the main wing of the manor. Maria pushed Penny toward the library, which opened to their immediate right. The musty vanilla smell of books greeted them as they walked into the immense space. Shelves faced one another, stretching the length of the room and two stories high. A tight, circular stairway in the corner led to a narrow loft above. Small columns, topped with odd antiques and artifacts, lined the space. A marble bust. A glass-enclosed fountain pen. A windup toy.

Long mahogany tables sat at the opposite end of the room, chairs neatly tucked beneath, waiting for the girls to grace them with their study materials. Waning afternoon sunlight poured in at an angle through high windows, flooded the shelves, and glinted off the gilded lettering of the book spines. Maria pulled out a novel and began to flip through the pages.

The wall closest to the doors held a popping hearth, topped by an enormous oil portrait of Master. His piercing green eyes seemed to follow her movements as Penny collapsed into a plush armchair near the fire. One that faced away from the painting. Something soft tickled her bare foot. She reached over and picked up Leon, the kitten who roamed the manor in spite of all Master's attempts to get rid of him. He circled three times and curled into her chest, only to hiss a second later when Ana came running into the room. She scrambled into the matching chair across from Penny and settled her sewing basket in her lap.

"What are you up to?" Maria looked over and raised an eyebrow in her direction.

"Nothing." Ana's cheeks reddened from more than the warmth of the fire.

Suddenly, Cricket appeared in the doorway, tall and broad-shouldered, with his dark blond hair mussed. "There you are." His lips lifted in a little half smile. "I didn't realize we were playing *nascondino*." Penny fought back an unladylike groan. How very much like Ana to initiate a game of hide-and-seek in order to get Cricket to chase her. Her infatuation was obvious. It was really too bad he didn't seem to notice.

He paced over, his arms supporting a silver tray heaped with pastries and cups of coffee. "I've found you, and brought the snack you requested." He spotted Penny and his smile grew larger, a dimple sinking deep in his right cheek. "Good afternoon, *mia farfallina*." His pale eyes caught hers, and she felt an odd sense of peace, strange and familiar at the same time, like she'd found something she hadn't known she was looking for.

"Good afternoon." Penny snatched a cookie before Cricket could even set the tray down.

"We can't eat those." Maria closed the book on her index finger.

Ana eyed the treats. "Why not?" As one of the newest students, she still seemed to question everything.

"You know why," Maria muttered. "Our weight."

Penny rolled her eyes and took a huge bite. *Stupid rules.* The girls were all skinny as rods. No snacks between meals. No breakfast. It was a bunch of nonsense that left Penny in a perpetual state of hunger. She chewed slowly, enjoying the rich taste of almonds and cinnamon as the flaky treat dissolved. Cricket's smile returned and he winked at her before he excused himself and backed out of the room.

Ana stared after him for a long moment and then turned to Penny. "Why does he always call you his little butterfly?"

Penny shrugged. "That's the first time I've heard him say it."

"You must be deaf, then," Maria said. "He says it nearly every time he sees you."

Penny frowned. They must be hearing things. She lifted her coffee and took a sip, watching as Ana threaded a needle with dark blue thread and began to hem a length of yellow-colored silk. A dozen stitches in and Ana gnawed on her lip in frustration.

"Here." Penny put down the mug and held out a hand. "Let me." Once Ana relinquished the fabric, Penny ripped out the loose stitches and redid them, tight and evenly spaced. "It's all in how you hold the needle."

Ana sighed and shook her head. "I'll never get it right. Mamma was so good at sewing. I guess her skill skipped a generation." She cupped her own steaming drink between both hands. "I wish she could've taught me before she passed away. I miss her."

"Me, too." Maria glanced up. "I mean, I miss my mother. Not yours."

Penny looked back and forth between the girls, her chest tightening. She'd never realized they both had deceased mothers. Penny's own mother had died from pneumonia several years ago. How odd that they were all motherless.

"She was so beautiful," Maria continued. "Long dark hair that she always kept coiled in a braid at the back of her neck."

"My mamma used to wear hers in the same style," Ana chimed in.

As did mine, Penny thought.

"She loved to cook," Maria continued, closing her eyes and inhaling deeply. "Ravioli, parmigiano risotto, and the most amazing *ribollita*. We'd purposely let the bread go stale just so she would make it."

"So did we!" Ana interrupted. "I always picked out the cabbage."

Penny jerked her gaze back down to the sash. She yanked out the last few stitches, which had gone absurdly awry. Her mother had made *ribollita* as well, a recipe handed down by Penny's grandmother. How was it possible their mothers were all so similar, their memories nearly identical?

Ana leaned in, seemingly unconcerned about the eerie coincidence. "Did your mamma ever sing you 'Ninna Nanna'?" She began to hum the melody.

Penny practically threw the sewing back at Ana. "I'm not feeling well. Sorry. I can help you again tomorrow."

She nearly tripped in her haste to flee the room before she

could hear Maria's response, to hear that all three mothers had sung the very same lullaby to their daughters.

It had to be a coincidence.

That was what she kept telling herself as she fled the library and the warmth of the hearth. The lullaby played a recurring tune through her mind as she raced down the dimly lit dormitory hall and into her barren room. Penny closed the door and threw herself into bed, willing away the nausea frothing in her abdomen.

It had to be a coincidence.

The next morning, Penny burst from her room and slid into her spot near the front of the queue of girls exactly as the second bell gonged and they began to glide forward down the hall. Bianca led the way, brushing one slipper along the frigid floor, and then the other.

"How are you feeling?" Penny nearly jumped as Maria leaned in, her lips close to Penny's ear. "Cricket said you were excused from supper with a stomachache. You did look pretty pale when you fled the library."

"Oh. Yes." Penny paused. "I'm sure it's just nerves is all. You know how jittery the gala gets me. The crowd . . ." She prattled on, all the while thinking she'd have to thank Cricket for covering for her. She'd fallen into a deep sleep, sprawled on top of her quilt, and by the time she'd awoken, the sky outside her window was stained a dark inky color, dotted with pins of starlight. An evening meal had been arranged on top of her dresser. Cricket probably needed to be thanked for that as well. The soup had helped ease the ache in her belly and her worries from the unsettling conversation in the library.

They weren't *that* uncommon, the things Maria and Ana

mentioned. . . . What mother didn't sing to her child and cook their favorite foods? Penny told herself it wasn't anything to be concerned about. All the girls at the estate had suffered some sort of tragedy. It bonded them together.

Sara, by far the demurest of the girls, tapped Penny's shoulder from behind. "You might want to do something about your hair."

With a quick nod of thanks, Penny unwound the requisite hair ribbon from her wrist, where she much preferred to wear it, and raked the snarled mess of curls back into a bun at the base of her neck. It wasn't even in the same league as Bianca's perfect knot, but it would do.

After a couple of turns through a hall lit with unevenly spaced sconces, they spilled into the servants' dining room. The girls were permitted a quick cup of coffee from the buffet and then it was straight to their studies. What few they'd be allowed to participate in today. If Madame Triolo had her way, they'd be dancing from dawn to dusk. Penny was certain they'd be called to the studio before noon.

Which meant she really needed some sustenance. She tucked two sugar cubes in her mouth and dropped a third one in her coffee. She gulped the scalding liquid only to have it nearly slosh down the front of her bodice as Ana swooped in with a squeal and grabbed her shoulders. "Did you hear? Master is due back today!"

Penny held the coffee steady at arm's distance. "No. I had *not* heard until you screamed it into my ear."

"Sorry," Ana said, looking considerably unapologetic.

Bianca's shrill voice rose above the chatter. "Come, girls, let's get moving. We don't want to be tardy." She tossed Penny a quick glare, as if somehow Penny had the ability to make everyone late. Her failure to be punctual wasn't intentional; she just wasn't so rigid in following *all* the rules. Bianca, on the other hand, obeyed every single decree as if her future depended on it.

Perhaps it did.

❧ ☙

Four hours and a quick noonday meal later, and the girls clustered outside the ballroom for an unscheduled dress rehearsal. Madame threw open the carved double doors and they spilled into the room.

The set was beautiful and simple: ornate plaster columns that scraped the high ceiling and an ethereal pastel landscape painted at the back of the stage. The girls bounded onto the raised wooden floor, jumping and leaping and dancing *entrechats* as if to test its sturdiness.

"Settle down, settle down." Madame clapped her hands, but even she couldn't seem to fight a tight smile from curving her lips. This was what they'd worked so hard for. Everyone scurried into the wings, behind thick brocade curtains that would hide them from the audience. Madame played the opening chord and the first act began. Penny danced the first scene and then exited stage left. She waited for her next entrance with her back against the wall. Her gaze was pulled to the bay window at the far side of the room, where it framed the huge expanse of lawn gracing the front of the manor. A lake took center stage, and cobblestones formed the drive that wrapped around the shoreline to stop at a roundabout near the main entrance. A coach bumped its way along the path, two beautiful Haflinger horses at the lead.

Penny felt a tug to escape, to climb aboard the coach box, scoop up the reins, and flee. Forget the gala. Forget the estate. See the world beyond their isolated existence.

With a clench of her jaw, she tore her gaze from the window and pinched her eyes shut. She pressed her fingers to her temples in an effort to relieve the piercing pain that erupted beneath her skull. She was so very tired of the migraines and their never-ending appearances. It would mean a third visit to Grandfather this week alone. As the estate physician, he'd give Penny some sort of vile tincture to drink and she'd be on the mend. But, blast, it tasted awful. And the effects of the medicine didn't seem to last very long.

"You're on." Maria shoved Penny out from behind the curtain.

Trying to pull her fingers from her temples, Penny pirouetted to center stage.

"Smile," Madame sang out in a patronizing voice.

Penny ignored her. If she made it through the routine without her head exploding, it would be a miracle. She wasn't about to force her lips into a grin.

The doors to the room were suddenly thrown open. The piano stopped midnote, and Madame startled upright. The girls bounded out from the wings and everyone scurried forward. In unison they all dropped into a curtsy. Even Madame.

Penny and Ana were the only ones left standing upright, but at least Ana realized her mistake and dipped down, a second behind the rest. Penny glanced around, her forehead creased in confusion, and wondered if someone had forgotten to tell her the rules to a game. Then her gaze slipped to the door and settled on the figure standing there.

Master.

His presence seemed to fill every inch of the doorway. He was still dressed in traveling clothes, black pants and a velvet-lined jacket cut trim to his figure. His dark hair was slicked

back, the skin above his sharp cheekbones was pricked red by
the cold, and his emerald eyes were narrowed in her direction.

As if she'd done something wrong.

Like not curtsy.

She gulped and dropped her chin. Her bodice felt tight, and
her pulse seemed to hum.

Master made Penny nervous, set her on edge. He was ex-
traordinarily dashing but guarded, his thick lips set in a straight
line while his eyes took in everything. And his voice . . . "Good
afternoon, girls." The words were low and smooth as silk. "How
have you all been faring?"

It was as if he'd released some hold on them. They leapt
from their curtsies to crowd around him, talking over one another in their haste to welcome him home and express dismay
that he'd been gone so long. Sara hung on the outer edge, but
she was still there, waiting patiently for a turn.

"We've missed you so," Bianca lamented. The whine pierced
Penny's ears. She folded her legs beneath her to sit at the edge
of the stage. Her headache still prickled at the edges, like it
needed only the slightest motivation to flare into agony again.

Even though Master seemed to acknowledge each girl, an-
swering questions and complimenting them on what he knew
was going to be an amazing performance, his gaze never left
Penny. He finally excused himself and walked over. His hand
cupped her chin, a gesture familiar yet unsettling. "You look un-
well, Penelope."

"I'm fine, sir." She croaked out the words.

"Are you upset about anything?"

She shook her head.

"Perhaps feeling a little restless?"

Her jaw tightened and she shook her head even faster. It was as if he could read her mind. But that wasn't possible.

"All right, then. Do make sure you get enough sleep and stay healthy. I'll check in with you later." He paused to tuck a stray tendril of hair behind her ear and waited for her eyes to meet his. "I expect the performance to be flawless. It will be a special day, the spring equinox, a time for rebirth."

"Yes, sir."

His fingers trailed down her bare arm. An involuntary shiver did a *bourrée* up her spine. "I must get to my office. So much work to be done."

The girls swarmed behind him as he strode toward the door. Madame clapped her hands again to rein them in, throwing a quick glare in Penny's direction. What had *she* done? It wasn't her fault Master had disturbed the rehearsal. Penny pushed herself upright and forced a smile in Madame's direction. She went straight to her spot onstage and pirouetted *en pointe*.

She would show Madame. She would show all of them.

Penny pulled the sweater even tighter around her shoulders to ward off the drafty cold saturating the far end of the dining room. A fire flickered in the hearth built into the wall near where Bianca held court, but Penny had opted to sit as far from her as possible, figuring the heat wasn't worth the price of listening to Bianca's diatribe, which today centered on the necessity that all girls learn how to sew. "Why would you ever pay to have someone else mend your undergarments?"

Maria rolled her eyes and filled Penny in on the gossip she'd overheard that afternoon. "Master has invited the prince to the gala. Can you imagine? I'm surprised he can travel. Last I heard he was cooped up in the palace, still recovering from his leg injury."

Penny shrugged, her shoulder blades rubbing against the back of the hard wooden chair. "Perhaps the distraction and entertainment would be good for him."

"Oh, so now you're okay with performing?" She lifted a fork from the knobby table and stabbed a slice of prosciutto.

"Well, as entertainers, I do think we're pretty splendid." Penny tore a pastry in half, the delicate crust shredding in thin layers. "It's the whole façade I don't particularly care for."

Cricket slipped in from the side door, a tray held aloft in one hand while the other raked his thick hair out of his face so it stood nearly upright. He made quick work of clearing off their dishes, checked the level of oil in the lamps lining the mantel, and disappeared again to return seconds later carrying bowls of steaming polenta. He moved around the table, placing a dish in front of each girl.

When he got to Penny, the tray was empty. He leaned in close, his breath a soft whisper that tickled her ear. "I'll bring your *gnocchi* in a minute."

Penny tucked her chin and smiled. He remembered she disliked the polenta. The taste was dull and the texture gritty; she rarely ate more than a few bites. "Thanks," she murmured as he rushed back into the kitchen.

Maria had barely stuck her spoon in her mouth when Master stepped into the room through the stone archway. Bianca straightened in her chair, shoulders thrown back to show off the low neckline of her blouse. The other girls grinned and jostled one another with their elbows, but Penny focused on the table, dusting at the crumbs in front of her until they formed a small pile. Master moved to stand behind Bianca, his hands resting on the sides of her shoulders.

"Good evening, girls." His tone drenched the room in a heavy warmth. Penny felt her eyes drawn toward him, resting on his full lips, imagining what it would feel like to kiss them.

Cricket entered the room again from the side, the lone bowl of *gnocchi* cupped in his hands. He placed the bowl in front of Penny, temporarily blocking her view and dislodging her thoughts. She shook her head, trying to banish the image of her lips brushing Master's. Her pulse hiccuped. What was wrong with her? She tried to focus on the scent of oregano and basil wafting from the steaming dumplings.

"Enjoy." Cricket stepped back. "I asked the saucier to add extra spice, as you like. . . ." His voice trailed off as Master jerked away from Bianca and walked toward them, sharp steps echoing through the now-silent-again room.

"I'm sorry, sir, I didn't know you were here." Cricket's gaze settled somewhere at Master's feet. "Would you like me to arrange another place setting?" He scrambled to the cabinets lining the wall behind Penny and pulled open a drawer.

Master stopped at Penny's side. His fingers reached under her heavy bun to wrap around the back of her neck. A shiver traced down her spine. The pressure of his fingers was enough to send fear dancing across the surface of her skin. His words were low. "No, that is quite all right. I will eat later."

Cricket tipped his head in deference and moved toward the kitchen. His eyes seemed to implore something as he stared at Penny, but she didn't understand.

"Penelope." Master nudged her neck so she turned from Cricket to look at him. "Come with me. There is a matter I wish to discuss with you privately." He slid his hand down her arm to grip her elbow and lift her from her seat. Even through the sweater his touch sent another chill through her body. His head tilted toward the door.

The girls all stared as they walked around the table. He stopped and nodded to them.

"Continue with your meal. I'll be back shortly."

CHAPTER 4

"Time to wake, Penny." The words sounded muffled, as if they'd been whispered to her through a long tunnel. A sharp tang burned Penny's nostrils and she coughed. Her eyes slitted and she blinked repeatedly to take in the dark furnishings and cluttered tabletops of her grandfather's quarters. She tried to sit upright.

"Don't." Grandfather held her wrist tight and reached to remove a cold compress from her forehead. "Take it easy."

"What happened?" she mumbled, the words like marbles in her mouth. Her tongue felt thick and heavy. Her entire body felt thick and heavy. She fought to remember what would have landed her on the sofa, but everything seemed hazy and vague, memories clouded in a sepia fog.

"You were brought here after supper. Apparently you didn't feel well, and I gave you medicine to help you rest." He stood, tall and thin with his head of thick, white hair.

"Oh." She remembered the headaches now, but something he said seemed off. Then again, so did the room, which tilted to the side and left Penny gulping at air.

"Here"—he handed her a cup from the buffet—"drink some water."

Penny propped herself onto her elbows and raised the glass with a shaky hand. She drank so fast the liquid dribbled down her chin and onto the blanket tucked around her torso. When she was done, Grandfather took the empty glass and smoothed back damp tendrils of hair that stuck to her forehead.

"Thank you." She shifted higher so her back rested against a plum-colored satin pillow. It was new. As were the amethyst silk blanket and heavy emerald curtains. Her nose wrinkled. "Did someone redecorate your room?" Her grandfather rarely stayed at the manor; he had his own residence near the edge of the estate property. On the occasions he did spend the night, he slept here, in his chamber on the second floor. But these bright accents were a stark contrast to his rustic home.

He shrugged. "They're moving me into the estate. I told them to do with it what they wanted."

"It's horrible."

"Oh, Penelope." He closed his eyes and shook his head. "What am I to do with you?"

She raked the hair back from her temples and into a loose braid over her shoulder. Grandfather winced and reached over, nudging the braid so it covered her ear and the side of her neck. Then he glanced away, his eyes seeming to flit off every surface of the room before landing on the large clock ticking in the corner.

"You should be getting back to your room." He opened his cracked leather bag and handed her a stoppered vial. "One last dose, so you can sleep through the night."

She took the glass container and kissed his cheek. "I'm not tired."

"I know." He turned his back and walked over to place the bag on the dark maple sideboard running the length of the wall. "But just in case."

⚜ ⚜

The next morning Penny awoke and reached for her photograph album. It was a daily ritual of hers, to flip through the photographs of her mother. The images were imprinted on her brain.

Or so she thought. Because, at that very moment, she didn't recognize anyone.

Not a soul.

Did I wander into another girl's room last night? It had been late when Grandfather had walked her back to the dormitory quarters. And the tincture he'd given her had tasted even more potent than normal. Perhaps she'd gotten confused.

She glanced up from the leather-bound book resting on the faded quilt pooling in her lap. Her gaze skidded past the sterile stone walls toward the few personal belongings she kept on top of her dresser. The lopsided rag doll with a missing button eye was something she knew she'd brought to the estate. A stack of books sat precariously near the edge of her shelf, and her favorite pink sweater hung on a hook near the door.

Pink? My favorite color isn't pink.

The words came unbidden and unexpected, falling fast through her mind as if they weren't really her own. And yet she knew instinctively it was true. Pink was too feminine, a false color used to stain their cheeks and paste their nails. She preferred blue, pale blue. The color of a cloudless sky or the lake just after dawn. Or Cricket's eyes.

This was definitely Penny's room, but it couldn't be her leather-bound album. The toddler in the photographs was unfamiliar, even with her dark mop of spiral curls and dark eyes. The stoic woman standing at her side, unsmiling for the camera, didn't spark any sort of maternal recognition in Penny's mind. Her chest tightened both in dismay and a sudden burst of fear. With a racing pulse and a sense of urgency, she kept flipping the album pages, trying to find something that struck her as . . . her.

"Ouch!" Penny slipped her fingertip into her mouth, sucking at a paper cut. The copper taste of blood dotted her tongue and she threw the album against the wall. It fell with an unsatisfying *plop* onto the patchwork quilt.

She closed her eyes and took a deep breath, unsure what was going on. Her thoughts felt fuzzy. Like pages in a book had been ripped out, leaving unfinished sentences and gaps in a story. She knew some things with crystal clarity, like the fact that their entire morning would be spent in ballet. So why couldn't she recognize these pictures? And why was everything in her wardrobe the color pink?

A bell gonged, echoing through the walls of the dormitory. Only three minutes until a second bell would ring. No time to think this through. Penny scrambled to her feet, rising immediately on tiptoe to avoid the frigid floor. She pulled on a clean skirt that had been draped over the bed frame and was still crisp from yesterday's wash.

Pink, of course.

❧ ❧

The practice room felt warm for once. A fire popped in the hearth, the sweet scent of hickory wafting from the corner. "We need to keep your muscles limber today," Madame said. "Now line up at the barre. First position."

The girls glided into place, heads held high, toes pointed outward, arms sweeping above their heads as Madame barked her way through the positions. The stark winter sunlight streamed in the windows, pooling at their feet like an oblong limelight.

After they'd warmed up, Madame directed the girls to form a queue in the corner. She nodded at each student in turn and shouted a move. Bianca leapt a series of perfect *grands jetés* across the floor to the opposite corner. Maria whirled through her *soutenus*, and Sara followed with a sequence of *pas de chat*.

"Penelope, second *arabesque*."

Penny's foot elevated behind her, pointing toward the window, but her hands flapped like a wounded bird. She couldn't remember their positions. Eyes wide, Penny looked around the room for help, but the girls only stared at her. She forced a smile to mask her unease.

The echo of Madame's footsteps resounded off the walls, accosting Penny from all directions. She yanked Penny's right arm forward and her left arm to the side. "Are you trying to anger me?"

"No, M-M-Madame," Penny stammered. Her fingers flexed outward, and she held the pose until suddenly her stomach rumbled. Madame sighed, her tiny chest rising like a bloated parakeet. "Penelope, please excuse yourself to the kitchen and grab some food before you ruin the entire rehearsal." Her nostrils flared. "And may I suggest that tonight you find time to eat your meal? I can only make this exception once."

"Thank you." Penny dipped into a quick curtsy and raced out the door.

She stopped right outside the door and leaned her head against the wall. Tears of frustration built behind her eyelids, but she refused to let them flow. The clouds filling her mind would clear soon. She would return to normal. She would remember her mother. She would remember the dance steps.

Or so she kept telling herself.

She pushed away and headed toward the kitchen. It bustled already with the frenzied preparation of the midday meal. Marble slab countertops held an array of bowls and utensils, spices and floured breasts of fowl. She waited at the entranceway, not daring to cross the threshold until someone invited her in. The chef finally strode over and stood before her, hands on his aproned hips. "What do you want already?"

"A snack, sir." Penny focused her eyes on a small red dot of sauce marring the stark white material at his waist.

With a low groan and a large number of expletives, he yelled at the *pasticcere* to give her a loaf of *ciabatta*. "Now go. We are far too busy for such nonsense." He lifted his hands as if to turn her around and then stopped, his palms a mere inch from her arms. Not touching. Never touching. Master's rules. The male staff was allowed no physical contact with the girls, except for Penny's grandfather and only when needed. "Out. Now."

Penny gripped the *ciabatta* and dashed out of the kitchen, bits of flour sailing into the air behind her. Once she'd cleared the doorway, she skidded to a stop. She wasn't exactly in a rush to return to Madame's tirade.

Picking off bits of the crisp crust and shoving them in her mouth, Penny opted to take the long way back to the studio, via the enclosed portico that stretched the length of the dormitory wing. It was one of her favorite rooms, bright and airy, with immense arched windows looking out over the lawn and pond. The view always put her mind at ease.

Except today.

Voices erupted from the other end of the hallway, and she launched herself into one of the many alcoves tucked into the interior wall. Squatting, she willed her pounding heart not to betray her presence as the voices carried to where she hid.

"How is she?" Master. Her chest tightened.

"Fine. She's almost ready," Grandfather responded, his words sounding distant and clipped. Penny nearly stepped into the open, wanting to confide in him all the oddities that had transpired that morning. He certainly would have an explanation.

But something held her in place, weighing her feet to the ground.

"Good. Speak to Primo today. He will prepare everything to your specifications, although perhaps it's time to incorporate new mementos?"

Penny scratched at the starburst symbol marring her wrist. *They must be talking about a new student.*

"Are you certain we should go through with this?" Grandfather asked. "It's not too late."

"Of course I'm certain. You continue to doubt me, but this is important." Their footsteps grew closer. Penny shrank as far into the shadowed corner as she could, burying her cheek against the wall. "Her youth is to our benefit. She seems to have responded very well thus far."

"Too well . . ." Grandfather's voice trailed off. "How's your leg?"

"Fine. Better with the new treatments."

"I'm glad." There was a rustle of movement. "Well, I must finish packing. The carriage is picking up my equipment tomorrow."

"I presume the new space will be adequate," Master said, his tone suggesting the words were a statement, not a question. The echo of footsteps veered off down a more distant hallway.

It was her chance to flee.

Penny launched from her hiding spot and nearly smacked into Master's chest. "Oh. I'm sorry." Her heart hammered a discordant beat. She'd assumed they'd both gone off together.

He reached out and gripped her bare shoulders. Warmth spread at his touch while a cool shiver set her on edge. Always a conflict. But his eyes. Those lips when they opened to speak. She felt herself leaning into him. "Were you eavesdropping on us, Penelope?"

"No, Master."

His eyes searched hers, and Penny forced herself to look down at her slippers. The spell broke, and her thoughts cleared. She remembered her grandfather. Their words. His new quarters. "Why is Grandfather moving into a room at the estate? He doesn't like it much here, you know." She didn't know where the question came from, only that she regretted it as soon as she said it.

"It's not any of your business." He squeezed her shoulders and leaned in. "And I don't think you know as much about your grandfather as you presume."

Master slid his fingers down to her wrists, circled them tight with his thumb and forefinger, and then released her. He straightened and ran his palms over the front of his lapel, smoothing out nonexistent wrinkles. Penny swallowed hard and fought the urge to run.

"I imagine Madame Triolo is wondering where you've disappeared to." He reached out and touched the ribbon in her hair. "Enjoy the rest of your morning, Penelope."

CHAPTER 5

$\mathcal{P}$enny's thighs quivered and her toes felt numb as she staggered to the dining room for the midday meal. The morning had passed with nearly nonstop movement and Penny collapsed into her chair, pink muslin skirt rustling. Bianca's hand shot out to grab the latest newspaper clippings lying in the middle of the table. "Look, it's us!" She sorted through various articles and columns featuring the gala.

The side door flew open and Cricket burst through. His smile brightened the room like sunlight, warmer than the fire in the hearth. "Sorry I'm late." Cricket made his way to the table, somehow managing to keep the food dishes he carried from colliding and tumbling to the floor. He placed their *antipasto*—an array of olives, cheese, and little quiches—in the middle of the long wooden table. A lone bruschetta sat on the edge of the tray, and Cricket whisked it in front of Penny. "Your favorite, *mia farfallina*," he said, pink staining the skin not already dotted by freckles on his cheeks.

Penny stared at the toasted bread topped with prosciutto and olive oil. Her mouth opened and words tumbled out. "That's my favorite?"

She suddenly had no *idea* what she liked to eat, unable even to imagine the taste of the *ciabatta* from only a few hours ago. The only thing she could conjure was the tang of blood from the paper cut that morning. And that certainly wasn't her favorite.

So what was?

With shaking hands, Penny poured steaming coffee into the fragile china cup resting near her silverware.

"Let me." Cricket finished pouring the drink before he added several teaspoons of sugar. "That's how you like it, right?"

Penny swallowed. "I'm . . . I'm not certain." Her tongue felt heavy, dead in her mouth, as if her taste buds had shriveled into chunks of solid stone. She couldn't breathe, couldn't get enough air into her lungs.

A look of panic must have crossed her face because Cricket crouched next to her, grabbing her hands. "Calm down. Look at me."

Shock vibrated through her skin. He wasn't allowed to touch her. He wasn't . . . And then it didn't matter as a series of thoughts flooded her mind.

Someone stands behind me . . . a deep breath near my ear . . . cold fingers brush the skin of my bare shoulder and pull my braid to the side . . . a soft touch of lips on my neck . . . followed by both hands circling around like a noose . . . fingers reach to nudge my chin up . . . a whisper . . . "Stand proud, darling, you're mine, always mine."

Penny shoved at Cricket and skittered away. Her knee banged the underside of the table, sloshing pale brown liquid across the pristine white cloth. She stood, the chair pushed sideways, and she retreated until her lower back hit the cabinets behind her.

"Penny, what's going on?" Bianca frowned, the concern of her words not quite reflected in her voice.

Maria's eyes widened, and she made as if to stand. "Are you all right?"

"I . . . I . . ." She didn't know what to say. That twisted memory. The whisper in her ear. It had been Master.

Cricket answered the girls, his eyes never leaving Penny. "It's my fault. I spilled coffee on her arm." He pulled a dish towel from the pocket of his jacket and began to mop up the stain.

Penny stood motionless, tremors racking her body as she tried to fight back the terror and force her brain to make sense of what was going on. First the confusion with the album that morning, then forgetting dance steps and her favorite foods. Now she'd had glimpses of memories she didn't understand. Master's touch had seemed loving, sensual almost. She flushed just thinking of it. It was enticing and yet wrong in so many ways.

She rested the back of her head against the maple cabinet and closed her eyes, trying to get control of her breath.

The other girls dismissed Penny's outburst, moving on to topics they found more interesting—like the remaining scraps of society notes, delivered from Rome and already outdated. And Master. Always Master.

Cricket tucked her chair back against the table and continued to move around the room, clearing away dishes and serving the *primo* and *secondo* courses. He circled wide around her, and for that Penny was grateful.

With a last dab of her napkin to the corners of her mouth, Bianca stood. "You heard Madame: only thirty minutes. It's time to return." Penny forced herself away from the cabinet. Her breathing had finally returned to normal, the invisible corset of fear no longer strangling her although it still gripped tight.

"Penny." Cricket called her name as she stepped near the threshold. He held out her pink hair ribbon. "You dropped this."

Penny grasped the satin strip of material without touching his fingers. "Thank you."

He leaned close, not releasing the ribbon. His pale eyes sought hers, compassion and comfort swirling in their depths. "We need to talk later. Be ready." His voice was soft and quiet.

She blinked. "What?"

Cricket put his fingers to his lips. "Please. Trust me. I'm one of the few people here you *can* trust. I'll find you, but for now you must go. You can't be late."

With a half smile, he shut the door between them. His dimple was the last thing she saw before she turned and fled down the hallway.

❧ ❧

The afternoon passed by in a blur of dance, literature lectures, a lesson on Renaissance sculptures, and a small discourse on the High Middle Ages for history. The girls were given instruction in any subjects that might prove useful in conversation with guests. Unfortunately, the discussions were as bland and dry as the white chalk their few select tutors wrote with on the blackboard. On a normal day Penny would find herself frustrated, raising her hand in an attempt to debate the realism of Donatello's *Penitent Magdalene*, but this wasn't a normal day.

Her mind hurt, her heart ached, and her bottom lip burned from chewing it as she worried over what was going on, what had happened to her. It was obvious *something* had, or Cricket wouldn't have reacted the way he did. He'd asked her to trust him. To meet with him later.

She was debating asking Maria, or Ana even, if they were

experiencing the same things. But she decided to keep quiet until she spoke to Cricket. She imagined she'd come off as downright crazy if she told the girls she was having strange visions and had somehow forgotten what her own mother looked like.

Dismissed for the day, Penny and her friends split up. Penny hoped the quiet relief of her chamber would fuse her brain back together. She waved to Maria and Ana, who were off to the library, and walked the length of hallway back toward the dormitory.

"Penelope."

Her own name startled her, and she almost tripped.

Not again.

She turned around, eyes downcast.

Master loomed over her. "I'd like to speak to you. Alone." Penny could only stare at Master's fingers, feel the weight of them around her neck and wonder if it was really a memory, that flash of thought she'd had when Cricket touched her.

What had Master been doing?

Tremors traipsed down her arms, and she crossed them in front of her chest to keep still.

"Master, if you don't mind, I'm really not feeling well."

He stood in silence, as if weighing her words. She dared to glance at his eyes and almost reeled back at the strength of his seemingly contrasting emotions. Anger and excitement flashed like beacons of light. He towered over her, broad shoulders filling the width of the hall. "I'm sorry to hear that," he finally spoke. "I'm rather a busy man, and I think now is the best time. Let's move this into my quarters."

He strode away, his gait long and quiet, without even a backward glance. Penny couldn't refuse Master's request, as much as she desperately wanted to. She dashed to keep up, her skirt swishing at her ankles. Her chest heaved, and she tried to fight the panic that had threatened to suffocate her since morning. But she was doomed to lose that battle. This felt wrong. Whispers of memories tugged at her mind, as if they were pieces meant for a different puzzle. One of an entirely different existence.

She'd walked this path before, gone to his quarters, danced for him even.

Penny clenched her jaw tight.

It couldn't be.

The stone floor changed to plush carpet, the barren walls replaced with rich tapestries and heavy silk drapes. Deep sofas and chairs, dark mahogany end tables, and gold-and-glass gasoliers filled the sitting room and salon. Master threw open the carved double doors leading to his private quarters. The immense room was familiar in an intimate way, and suddenly the memories were real. She knew the cream-colored rug near the hearth would feel thick between her bare toes. She knew the bathroom held an oval gilded bath and a marble basin in the corner. She knew the open doorway to her left led to a large bedroom, where she would spot an ornate four-poster bed filling much of the space. She knew the lounge chair grew uncomfortable after lying on it for hours, her head pulsing with the pain.

Hours. Pain.

Cool sweat beaded in the small of Penny's back. She had the sudden urge to scream at him, to beat at his chest with her hands and ask him what he was doing to her. Yet, somehow she knew she'd be punished for speaking out.

Master motioned her into the center of the room before he turned and eased the door closed. All the curtains had been drawn, leaving only the flames in the fireplace to cast a flickering light on his face. He stepped in front of her, darkened eyes searching hers. His hand wrapped lightly around her wrist, his fingers resting against her tattoo. Her pulse leapt, against her will. "I thought for certain the treatment last night would have taken care of your insolence. But it seems to have only made it stronger."

Penny stiffened and tore her gaze from his. She wanted to ask what he meant. She hadn't seen him the night before. But she knew she couldn't question him. Her mouth was so dry she probably couldn't have spoken anyway. She stood perfectly still, her focus on the flames as Master made a slow, appraising circle around her.

"Penelope." The word was a sigh. He released her and reached his palm toward her chin. She winced. Anger furrowed his eyebrows together, and he dug his fingers into her jaw. Tears burned into her eyes at the pain. "Come. Let's get started, shall we?"

His hand whipped away and he pointed at the lounge chair at the far side of the room. Dark wood cabinets rose behind it, the shelves neatly lined with strange contraptions and metallic equipment. Long poking utensils that looked like daggers. A cluster of wires coiled around a silver box.

Terror seized Penny's chest. She didn't know what Master had planned, but it couldn't be good. She fought to remember, sure that the memories were lodged somewhere in her brain. But could she trust them? A part of her wanted to run before Master hurt her. She feared what he'd do, how far he would go. *How far he'd already gone.* But, just as she readied to flee the room, her mind shifted, telling her she could trust Master. That he was gentle and kind and stunning. He was trying to make things better. Make her better.

It was difficult to reconcile the contrary viewpoints.

It was difficult to reconcile any of this.

Her feet shuffled toward the chaise as if pulled by an invisible string.

"That's my girl." Master stepped beside her as she sat down, a stiff statue. His deft fingers made quick work undoing her hair ribbon and freeing the mass of hair from the bun. He wrapped a strand around his index finger and pulled.

Penny bit back a yelp.

Master released the curl and squatted next to her. He reached behind the chair and began to twist and turn at something on the cabinet.

"Hold still for a moment, Penelope. I'm going to try a new procedure today."

She held her breath, knowing instinctively that a new procedure could not be a good thing. But perhaps it would ease the discord in her mind, make her thoughts whole again. That would be a welcome solution, wouldn't it?

Bang!

A loud rap erupted from the other side of the door. Penny's heart nearly did a *jeté* out of her chest.

Master turned toward the sound and snapped, "This is not a good time."

"Sir, there was an accident in the kitchen." Penny recognized Cricket's voice, the words frantic even though they were muffled through the thick wood. "Hot oil spilled and one of the stoves caught flame."

Master strode across the room, hands balled into fists. Penny jumped to her feet and followed, smoothing her skirt as she went.

With a violent tug on the handle, Master threw open the door, slamming it against the wall. "Is the fire out?" His tone was deceptively void of anger.

"Yes, sir," Cricket said. "But there is damage to a portion of the wall and flooring. And one of the scullery maids was burned."

Master inhaled deeply and then, without warning, swung his fist at Cricket's jaw. Penny stifled a gasp as Cricket's head smashed sideways against the door frame. He bent at the waist, his hands cradling his chin. Master leaned over him, teeth clenched. "Next time, do not disturb me unless the fire is beating a path straight for my door. Do you understand?"

Cricket lifted his head and nodded. A string of bloody saliva dripped through his fingers.

Master straightened and shrugged his shoulders back. He glanced in Penny's direction, as if suddenly remembering she was in the room. "Wait here. I'll return in a few moments."

With that, Master turned and paced toward the main wing. He called out for his steward, Primo, and left Cricket and Penny slack-jawed and staring after him.

CHAPTER 6

$\mathcal{P}$enny raced to Cricket's side and crouched next to him. "Are you all right?"

Ignoring the mandate of no physical contact, Penny grabbed his sleeve and tried to pull him into the room. Helping to clean his wound was the least she could do, considering his knocking had saved her from . . . something. She already felt better in his presence. Calm. Safe.

"I'm fine," he muttered. He flexed his jaw and closed it again with a wince. "I'm more concerned about you, *mia farfallina*."

His pale eyes searched hers, anxious and hopeful.

A thought hovered at the edge of her mind. *My little butterfly.* A smile pulled at her lips, and his eyes widened. "I knew it! We have to go see your grandfather. Tonight. In the meantime, go to your room and stay there. I'll distract Master further if needed."

"The fire?"

A quick, lopsided grin pulled at the swelling on his bottom lip. "I started it."

"Why?"

"Isn't it obvious?" He tipped his head toward the room. "I

couldn't let him experiment on you anymore. Come. Let's go before he returns."

Cricket reached his hand toward Penny. She flinched and pulled away. She knew he would never hurt her. But when he'd touched her before, she'd had that memory. She couldn't chance a new one surfacing. Not now.

He tensed, his focus on the floor. Then he turned from Master's chambers, long strides carrying him forward. Penny followed close behind.

Back in the servants' wing, shouts echoed down the hall from the kitchen. Cricket stopped. "Go to your quarters—quickly, before someone sees you. I'll find you tonight." He swallowed hard and rushed off toward the smoky tendrils snaking from the kitchen.

"There you are." Maria suddenly pulled Penny into the dark corridor that led to their rooms. "I peeked in your chamber earlier, but it was empty. Were you sneaking around with Cricket?" Her nose wrinkled.

"No! It wasn't that at all." Penny's pulse hiccuped. At least not yet. She had, after all, promised him to do just that. Sneak off with him.

"Well." Maria shrugged. "That's good. Did you hear about the fire? Primo ushered me out of the library as if the books would burst into flame. Can you imagine?"

"I'm sure he only wanted to keep everyone safe." Penny inched farther into the cool recess of the hall. "Maria, when was the last time you went to Master's wing? I mean, what did you do there?"

Perhaps she'd only imagined the chair and the gears and the gadgets. Maybe he'd only wanted to discuss her studies. Or have her practice her solo portion of the gala.

Maria cocked her head to the side as if the answer was only just off the center of her mind. "It's been a while. He definitely prefers to have you or Bianca visit. Ana sometimes, too." She tapped a fingernail to her lip. "We talk. About classwork, the arts, my future." A blush darkened her cheeks. "He's such a charmer, and ravishing as well. I can't imagine ever leaving. We are so very fortunate he allowed us into this school. Only the best for the students."

Penny cringed. It sounded as if Maria was reading from a brochure.

But even more eerie was that Maria's memories of Master's chamber didn't involve anything out of the ordinary. There was definitely something unnatural happening at the estate.

Maria clutched a thick novel to her chest. "It's nearing supper; we should probably be seated."

"I'm really not hungry," Penny said.

"Oh, posh. You have to join us. This would be the third night in a row you've missed." She linked her arm through Penny's. "Let me drop this in my room and we can walk over together."

Penny wanted to pull away, but Maria was right. She couldn't miss supper again. She'd be safe with the girls, and Cricket would keep Master occupied so he couldn't come search her out.

Or so she hoped.

❧ ❧

It must've been well past eight o'clock that evening. Penny sat cross-legged on her bed. Leon pawed at the piece of string she dragged back and forth across the patched blanket. He pounced forward and she yanked it away. For the hundredth time, Penny thought she heard the whisper of a footstep and her gaze flicked to the door.

Her nerves were stretched thinner than a spider's silk. Cricket hadn't served their food as usual; it had been more of a hodgepodge affair, a buffet of dishes brought in as soon as the head chef churned them out in the kitchen. At first she thought Cricket had merely been too busy, but with each passing moment she feared Master had learned he was the culprit behind the fire and punished him. Not that a fist to his jaw wasn't enough of a punishment. She'd never seen that side of Master, his temper getting the best of him.

Suddenly, her bedroom door eased open to let in a draft of cool air from the hall. She froze, only able to exhale when Cricket's face came into view. And it was more than just relief that settled over her. Her heart stuttered a little as she drank him in: his dark blond hair and slate-colored eyes, freckles and dimpled cheek, and painfully bruised jaw. She flinched. The skin was now a dark blue stain, tinged violet on the edges. He brushed the back of his hand up and over his chin as if to hide it. With his other arm, he motioned her over. "Are you ready?"

Penny jumped up, unceremoniously dumping the cat to the side. She most certainly was ready. Ready for answers and ready to escape the constraints of the manor walls. Determination coursed through her veins, nudging at the fear and terror she'd felt all day.

After pulling tight the laces of her boots, Penny followed Cricket as he slipped back through her open door and toward the kitchen. The lingering smell of smoke tickled Penny's nose. A cacophony of sounds reached her ears—the whine of voices, a *clink* of dishes, running water. The kitchen staff would be busy through the night as they ended one day of meals and prepared for the next. That room was never empty of staff.

Cricket veered to the left into a darkened corridor lit by a single sconce near a heavy door leading outside. She stepped closer while he worked to unlatch the bolts, so close she detected the scent of cinnamon and honey caught in the fabric of his shirt, as if he'd been helping bake *panforte* before he'd come to her room.

With a last *click*, the lock unfastened and the door slid open. A stone path, meant for delivery carts and servants' wagons, extended for several yards in front of them before veering off and around the main building, where it would eventually join the immense cobblestone driveway at the front entrance of the manor. The woods stretched across the horizon, leafless tree branches knotted tight together. A dirt trail began in a narrow gap in the tree line. It was the fastest way to her grandfather's cottage.

Cricket took the lead, shoving aside the errant branch daring to jut into their path. The only lights to see by were the faint glimmer cast by the waxing moon and the twinkling of glow flies playing tag in the distance. They kept up a good pace, despite the uneven terrain and Penny's intermittent tripping over wayward roots and loose rocks. She wasn't a fan of this stretch of woodland, of the forest in general really, but at least during the day she could see more clearly through the maze of gnarled trunks. Her chest tightened as an owl hooted a lonely note somewhere in the distance and a bat beat its leather wings above her head.

"Why exactly are you taking me to Grandfather?" Penny asked Cricket, the words shriller than she'd intended. She hoped the conversation would serve as a distraction, and perhaps their voices would keep any animals at bay.

"He can tell you what's going on. With your memories. The thoughts you're having." The sentences were stilted, as if he didn't quite know how to describe the strange visions she'd been having.

She hesitated, wondering how Cricket knew this. Although he'd seen her reaction, she had never told him about the memories. But before she could ask how he'd known what was going on, before a single word tumbled from her mouth, a piercing pain slammed into her forehead. A nail hammered into the center of her skull, and the ache splintered out in all directions.

With none of the grace of her ballet training, Penny fell to her knees, her palms pressed into the skin above her eyes. She was vaguely aware of the mud soaking into her skirt and cooling her shins, and she couldn't fight Cricket when he rested his hand on her shoulder and leaned in. His voice was an echo down a long tunnel. "Are you all right?" He shook her gently. "Penny?"

She moaned, the only answer she could give.

"What can I do?"

Penny knew he was only trying to help, but the words felt like needles stabbing her eardrums. Her entire head throbbed, a pounding that spread to her heart, her limbs, her fingertips and toes.

Mercifully, it was mere seconds later that she blacked out.

CHAPTER 7

$\mathcal{P}$enny's eyes squinted against the harsh light of a lantern as she tried to get her bearings. She lay sprawled on a narrow bed, a thin quilt wound tight between her ice-cold fingers.

"What happened to her? And what happened to your face?" The voice was sharp but muffled, as if it came from another room.

Penny recognized Cricket's voice in response. "Master. He punched me for interrupting before he could begin another treatment."

The other voice, sounding very familiar now, swore. "He's quick to anger lately."

"She's getting worse," Cricket continued. "At *il pranzo*, she seemed to have a vision that left her nearly crippled with distress. It's like Rosaura."

Rosaura. Penny didn't recognize the name.

"Then, just now, I think he tried to manipulate her thoughts from the manor. Is that even possible? She collapsed in the forest, gripping her head. I had to carry her here." Cricket's voice dropped. "I thought you were working on a countermeasure."

"I am. But he keeps overriding everything, testing his limits. I fear I'm only accelerating his control." Something scraped across the floor.

With a low groan, Penny pushed herself to a sitting position and looked around. She recognized the room instantly. The soft yellow walls, the pale blue rug on the floor, the dresser top overflowing with leather-bound novels. Her room. They were at her grandfather's home. Cricket was speaking with him now.

But why are we here?

Based on the charcoal sky out the window, it had to be well after supper. Master would be angry at her disappearance, and Penny needed to squeeze in further dance practice before bedtime. She glanced in dismay at the ruined skirt tangled around her legs. The pink taffeta had ripped up one seam, and the entire front was covered in drying mud. Signora Moretti would exhaust her knowledge of foreign curse words when she saw the garment. Penny walked barefoot through the room and down the creaking, narrow flight of stairs.

Grandfather and Cricket turned in unison and rose from where they sat around the knotted maple kitchen table. "How are you feeling?" Grandfather stepped closer.

"Very well, albeit a little confused." She brushed her hands across the skirt. "Was I kidnapped by bandits and dragged through the mud?"

They paused, expressions suspended in disbelief. Cricket sprinted over, skidding to a stop in front of her. "You don't remember?"

She shook her head and swallowed. He looked shocked and angry. His teeth ground together, which couldn't have been easy considering his jaw was marred an unsightly blue color and a cut slashed his lip. Penny tried to remember. "I was working on my gown in the sewing room. But that must have been hours ago. . . ." She frowned, distracted. "Do you need something for your wound?"

Cricket dragged his fingers through his thick hair, making it stand on end. "No, I'm fine, thank you."

"Shouldn't we be getting back?" Penny wondered aloud. A flicker of light flashed in her peripheral vision. She turned toward the window, where she could vaguely discern torches in the distance. "Never mind; it appears they are coming for us." The words were monotone, seemingly unlike her, and yet they came from her mouth.

Cricket turned to her grandfather. "Where can we hide?"

"Hide?" Penny crossed her arms over her chest. "I'm not hiding."

Grandfather pointed upstairs. "I'll distract them. Flee as soon as they are gone. Push past the wolves." He bent over and looked Penny in the eye. "You can do it; I know you can. Get to the Azul Apothecary Shoppe in Ravinni. Tatiana will provide shelter. I'll call on you as soon as I can." He wrapped his arms around Penny in a tight embrace. "Be safe, Penny. Listen to Cricket. He's always taken care of you."

"I told you, I'm not hiding," Penny said. "And I need my boots." While they continued their crazed behavior, Penny planned to go outside and wait for Master.

Without warning, Cricket's hand shot toward hers. He grabbed her wrist where the bare skin peeked from the cuff of her blouse. Penny tripped forward. Her mind tumbled and spun, memories shifting and splintering.

I sit on the sofa downstairs with a cup of tea clasped in my hands . . . asking Beppe how many more times I have to do this . . . scared because I don't remember my family . . . asking so many questions . . . sobbing because I feel so alone. "I'll be your family, Penelope." He pauses and pulls my head to his shoulder. "If you'll have me."

She yanked away, gasping for breath, and turned to Beppe. Burning tears threatened to escape.

"You're . . . you're not my grandfather. Why have you been lying to me?"

❧ ☙

Cricket and Penny squished under the bed, legs not touching, arms not touching, eyes squinting into the darkness.

Penny focused on keeping her breaths as calm and quiet as possible, even though she desperately wanted to scream with panic and confusion. Her thoughts circled inward: Cricket helping her escape from Master's quarters, the pounding headache in the woods. She remembered her confusion earlier in the day, and how Cricket's touch had sparked strange memories of Master. But with each of these recollections, she felt like others were failing her. She couldn't remember the color of Maria's eyes, even though she knew her name and that they were the best of friends. The more Penny struggled to focus, the more the images faded into nonexistence. A feeling of loss swept through her. She had no family to speak of. A photograph album full of pictures of a woman she didn't recognize as her mother. A man masquerading as her grandfather.

She had no idea where she'd come from.

She had no idea who she belonged to.

She'd never felt so completely, utterly alone.

The front door downstairs burst open like it had been hit with a battering ram.

"It's time to go." A low baritone echoed through the house.

"I'm rather busy here, Primo. Surely whatever it is can wait until morning."

"Master needs you at the manor now. You have sixty seconds to gather your things."

"I don't see what the rush is. I was there this afternoon. Is someone dying?"

"Forty-five seconds."

"Fine. Fine. Let me put on my coat."

Shuffles and creaks and then the door slammed shut again. A cloak of silence blanketed them.

Penny relaxed and turned her head, ever so slowly, in Cricket's direction. He shook his head, held a finger to his lips and mouthed, *Wait*.

Minutes passed and then they heard the *screech* of the door and footsteps again. Stomps echoed through the house as someone marched around downstairs. Then the distinct *clomp* of boots against the wooden stairs. Penny's chest constricted. Her shoulders hunched up near her ears, and she drew into herself, curling as far as she could under the bed. She squeezed her eyes tight and wrapped her arms over her head.

The door practically bounced off the wall. She stopped breathing altogether.

Cracked leather boots were visible as they stepped in and stopped near a shelf. "This better be what he wants. Crazy old kook." Primo's voice echoed through the room and then suddenly an array of glass jars were swept off a shelf. They cracked and shattered, fragments splintering and shooting in all directions. One shard cut across Penny's bare forearm, and she bit down hard on her lower lip to prevent a yelp from escaping.

She could feel Cricket tense beside her and wondered if he'd been hurt as well.

Primo kicked something that went flying into the wall with a *thump*. Heavy footsteps faded back down the hall, down the stairs, and then there was silence.

Cricket didn't move.

Penny didn't move.

They waited. Penny counted each inhale and exhale until finally Cricket began to worm his way out from under the bed. "I think they're gone."

She pressed her toes into the hardwood and wriggled free, trying not to use her arm. The cut stung something fierce. As soon as she could kneel, she ripped a piece of fabric from the back of her skirt—the cleanest part, surprisingly. She handed it to Cricket and held her arm in his direction. "Can you please wrap it?"

Doing his best not to touch her, Cricket wound the fabric several times and tied it in a tight knot. "We should get going. Beppe suggested Ravinni."

"Stop." Penny stepped in front of him, careful to avoid the glass. She blocked his way out the door. "I'm not going anywhere until you give me answers. I need to know what's going on, why I have these thoughts and new memories of my past. And how are you involved?"

His long lashes rested on his cheeks as he closed his eyes and took a deep breath. When his eyes opened again, they sought hers, the pale gray-blue a magnet of truth. His arms reached out as if he wanted to touch her, offer comfort, but then fell to his sides again. "Master has been tampering with your mind. That equipment you saw in his room, what I was trying to prevent from happening when I started the fire, it's all a part of it."

She almost laughed. "That's ridiculous. It's not possible."

Cricket rubbed at his jaw and she felt a longing to touch him, to feel his warm skin beneath her palm. He stepped toward her. A small amount of space separated her toes from the tip of his boot, but it might as well have been the universe. "Take a look at yourself, Penny. Think about your *sorelle*. You are proof that it is, in fact, possible. Very possible."

"No." The word stretched into a hollow note as it tore her vocal cords, shredding them with the pain of Cricket's words. Because she knew, somehow, in the memories of her mind, that he spoke the truth. And it wasn't just Master who'd been working on her . . . the equipment arranged in his quarters.

She'd seen it before.

She could picture a room. Dark and humid with a table in the middle.

It came more into focus as she shoved past Cricket. Her bare feet padded down the stairs and into the abnormally short hallway that led to a small guest chamber off to the side.

Reaching the end of the hall, Penny pressed her palm against the stones, pushing at the corner seam until the false rock gave way and she nearly tripped forward into an empty space.

She sank to her knees, fingers fluttering at her mouth to try to capture the silent scream.

It was as she'd imagined. The windowless room dimly lit by sconces placed at regular intervals along the dark gray walls. A skylight cut into the ceiling would let in the sun's rays come morning. Wooden tables butted against the walls, various tools lined in an orderly fashion. Scalpels, scissors, needles, forceps, metal instruments, all waiting patiently to be used.

In the center sat the narrow table, a bed in the barest sense of the word.

And there, resting on top, a young girl lay, her eyes staring, unseeing, at the ceiling.

※ 1861 ※

The wolf snarled at Beppe, snatching at his fingers from between the rusted bars.

"Isn't he perfect?" Beppe stood back and stared at the creature.

Cirillo nodded. He was perfect, but not in the way Beppe thought. No, Beppe was proud of the wolf's movements, of the fur covering its newly crafted jaw, the hinges opening smoothly only to slam shut again. It was the first time they'd tried something other than a limb. Something necessary to survival. They'd found the wolf a couple of weeks ago, alone and near death, deep in the woods. Its mouth had been destroyed, the lower jaw nearly removed, a gaping hole in its cheek.

Beppe had immediately set to creating a new jaw.

Cirillo had worked at cleaning the wounds, soothing the animal, and feeding it with a spoon.

Beppe focused on the craft.

Cirillo focused on the control.

"Down." Cirillo snapped his fingers and pointed at the ground.

The wolf whined, dipped its chin into the dirt, and slid its haunches back until it lay flat against the packed floor.

Beppe didn't even notice. Instead, he changed the subject back to one Cirillo wasn't quite ready to discuss. "You have nearly enough skin to cover the machinery. Your right leg is slightly smaller, but we can stretch the flesh tight."

Cirillo glanced toward the corner, where the implement rested, glinting in the few rays of sunlight able to pierce the mud-caked window. It looked like a mass of silver snakes twining along vertical rods. Wires protruded from both ends, ready to be attached to his knee and ankle. A book sat propped open beneath the apparatus, the pages displaying a two-dimensional version of the leg. They had spent hours poring over the details, discussing how to work around the arteries, what pieces of anatomy they needed to remove. What they could keep.

"We should schedule a time." Beppe glanced at the metal leg. "We risk damage leaving it exposed to the elements."

"I know. Tomorrow. We'll decide tomorrow." He wiped a handkerchief across his brow and scooted out of the workshop. *Coward*, he berated himself.

The idea of pain didn't bother him. Much. He was in pain every day. But he knew this would be worse, his skin cut apart, his bones broken, his tendons severed, only to be replaced with steel rods and cables. The tinctures they'd concocted would keep him sedated, though. It wasn't the pain that caused his fear. No, that stemmed from the potential for failure. The potential for his leg to be worse than before. Even though they had done the surgery multiple times on animals, it seemed more intimate and dangerous on a human. On himself.

What if the leg had to be amputated?

He inched his way up the grassy slope to the house. Music and laughter echoed from the open window upstairs. His sister was having a grand time, no doubt.

The front door had barely shut behind him when his step-mother stormed into the foyer. "Where have you been?" She didn't bother to wait for a response. "Playing in the mud? Look at you, all covered in dust and sweat." She grabbed his shoulders and shook him. "You are a disgrace."

With a sudden jerk, she released him. He fell back and landed on his tailbone. A sharp pain raced up his spine. He crossed his arms and dug his fingernails into his skin so he wouldn't strike back.

She leaned over him. Her eyes narrowed into slits and her mouth split wider as she continued her tirade. "It is bad enough you are unable to help around the house. You will forever live off the good graces of your father. But to embarrass us by acting like a farm animal?"

Cirillo sat on the cold marble floor. His eyes never left hers. He hoped she could see the hatred there, even if he couldn't act on it.

She swallowed and straightened. Her voice settled back somewhere into the range of normal. "Your sister has been upstairs all afternoon studying and packing. Your father sent word that we're to meet him in Rome. He has a few days' leave and wants to see us." Her head tilted to the side and her mouth turned down in a fake little frown. "It is rather unfortunate that you will not be able to join in the festivities. I will let him know that your illness has taken a cruel turn, leaving you bedridden for the next two weeks. Such wretched timing."

"That's . . . that's not fair." Cirillo fought to stand. He hadn't seen his father in months. "You have to take me. I'm his son."

"I am his wife. And I shall not have you tarnishing his name. *Our name.*" She spun, her skirt nearly knocking him over. "Now go get cleaned up for supper, or I will send you off to eat with the servants. Perhaps *that* is where you belong."

Cirillo struggled to stand. Just as he got his balance, his sister bounded down the staircase, her best friend Teresa on her heels.

"You'll have such a splendid time. I'm dying of jealousy." Teresa clasped her hands at her chest and sighed. "What if you meet a boy there?"

"A man," Sofia said with a grin. She pointed at Cirillo. "*That* is a boy." They squealed in laughter. Cirillo felt his face begin to flame.

Sofia ushered her friend out the door to the waiting carriage.

He stood shaking with anger.

Tomorrow. Tomorrow he would tell Beppe. Tomorrow they would get started.

And two weeks from now, when his stepmother returned . . . when his sister returned, he would show them. Show them what he was really made of.

And there would be no more laughter at his expense.

❧ 1879 ❧

$\mathcal{P}$enny inched closer to the girl on the table.

She was perhaps twelve years old, younger than any of the girls at the estate by several years. Stunning. Perfect porcelain skin, dark eyelashes, full lips, and layers of dark hair fanned across the table. Her body was covered by a white cotton sheet, pulled up and neatly tucked under her armpits. A long black line of stitches ran behind her ear and down to her neck. The skin beneath oozed yellowish fluid, as if it had only recently been sutured closed.

Penny shuddered and crossed her arms over her chest.

The girl's pale arms lay flush at her sides, palms facing upward. On the inside of her left wrist was the same small starburst symbol Penny had on her own arm. Just above the marking, a tube protruded from the large vein on the girl's wrist. The tubing looped down off the table and up into a stoppered glass urn on the table, where a pump compressed a bloody mix of liquid. Wires were attached to the sides of her temples, the opposite ends disappearing inside a small, foreign device, a metal box with dials on the side that clicked and spun of their own accord.

"What is this?" Cricket stayed close to the door.

Penny rubbed at her arms, trying to ease her shaking. Her voice was raw when she spoke. "It's his workshop. I can remember being in here. She must be the new girl. I heard Master and Beppe talking about her earlier today."

Acid swirled in Penny's stomach as she wondered what Master had planned for the girl. She looked so young, so innocent. And Beppe had obviously been involved. He was the science behind the operation. The physician at the estate, he must be the one to . . . what? Alter them? Create them?

Penny ran over to the line of cupboards along the back wall and yanked them open one by one. Terrified that unanimated bodies might topple on her, she exhaled when she saw they contained only clothes: dresses, overcoats, tutus, undergarments, stockings, and shoes, all in hideous shades of pink. She spun back toward Cricket. Her fingers flapped at her sides like terrified moths. She clasped them together in front of her in an attempt to calm her nerves.

"Cricket, I don't understand. This girl, she came from somewhere. But where? How did this happen?" Penny couldn't wrap her mind around it. She and her *sorelle*, they all looked so similar, had similar memories, similar mannerisms. She had no idea if they were human or something else. Something mystical or magical or terrifying at best. Tears burned at the backs of her eyes, and she dashed away the few that dared to leak out. Her voice was a harsh whisper. "If you know what's going on, why haven't you stopped it?"

Cricket shook his head, his lips pursed in apology. "There's not much I can do, Penny. I don't know where she came from. I don't know where any of you came from. Beppe tells me very little, only what he says will help you girls. He tasked me to look after you all while he works on a countermeasure. That's the only thing I can do at this point. Master holds the power."

Penny wanted out of the room. She wanted out of the house with the memories threatening to seep from the walls and flood her thoughts. She didn't know if she trusted Cricket, but she had to trust her instincts. They were telling her to flee now and get answers later. With long strides, she raced through the stone doorway, down the hall, only stopping at the entranceway to search for her boots.

"We need to go." She hated that her voice sounded small and tired. So . . . doll-like. "Cricket, we need to . . ." She spun around and stopped, the words left unspoken and tumbling back into the knot lodged in her throat. He held a pile of clothing in his arms: a clean, heavy knit dress, a wool jacket, and a pair of boots. He'd taken the time to gather them from the other room. For her. Thinking of her.

"I thought you might want to change first. It's going to be a long walk."

"Thank you," she whispered. She took them, careful not to touch his hand with her own.

He grabbed a knapsack from a stand near the door and opened several cupboards. "Get dressed and I'll gather provisions to take with us."

"What about the girl?"

"Beppe will return and care for her. We can't exactly take her with us; she's in no condition to travel. Those machines may very well be keeping her alive."

She swallowed hard, hating herself for even considering leaving the girl behind, knowing what might be in store for her. And her *sorelle*. "What about Maria? Sara? The other girls? I can't just leave them."

He stopped, his hand wrapped around a jar. "Penny, we can't return to the manor. Think of what Master will do to you. The girls are safe right now. You, however, are not."

"I know. But still. I feel horrible leaving."

"We will send help. But please, we have to go now."

Penny took a deep breath. There was something holding her back, something on the fringes of her memories, something Beppe had said. But it flitted away and she hurried to the bedroom to change.

✳ ✳

The moon had fallen beneath the horizon when Penny and Cricket started their trek away from the cottage. Her headache had returned, and she pressed her fingers to her forehead, willing the pain away.

Cricket held a lantern that cast a dim light on the packed dirt path. On her back, Penny carried a small knapsack filled with a blanket and a spare change of clothing. Cricket managed to carry everything else.

Penny hoisted her dress until the hem brushed the tops of her boots. The trees closed in from both sides and a wind whistled eerily through the canopy above. She scooted close to Cricket, his cinnamon scent somehow still noticeable among the damp and musty smells of pine and cedar. She braced herself for more answers. "Can you start at the beginning? Tell me what you know?"

He paused to push a jutting branch out of the way. "Your memories have been altered. At least that's what Beppe says. Childhood ones have been completely replaced and some events in the more recent past have been modified, depending on what Master *wants* you to think. It's some strange notion he has of molding the perfect student. The perfect dancer. I have no idea how it actually works." A tremor of fear shook Penny's shoulders and she shrank into the jacket, as if it could somehow protect her from Master accessing her mind. "Ever since last year, when Rosaura's false memories began to break down, Master has been working to further the science behind the manipulations."

"Rosaura?" She remembered Cricket saying the name earlier. It tickled the edge of a memory. A girl at the estate. In her classes. A dance prodigy.

Rosaura.

Penny gasped and nearly stumbled. Horror clenched her heart as she remembered. Rosaura had been her friend. An eccentric girl who loved to wear bangles on her ankles and rings on every finger. She was petite, an extraordinary dancer with beautiful lines and extensions, always the lead role in the gala, until the previous year. Mere weeks before the performance, she'd been whisked off to the hospital late in the evening while everyone slept. She'd never returned.

"Cricket, I didn't remember her until now. Master must've wiped her existence from my mind." His stricken look mirrored the panic seeping into her pores. Master could do the same to Penny. He could delete her from her *sorelle*'s memories.

"But you did remember. And other ones are returning." Cricket's eyes searched hers, asking questions she didn't have the answers to.

She had no idea how many other people had been removed from her thoughts. Her family for sure. Her fingers clenched into fists and she dug her nails into her palms. She had to get to the bottom of this. "What exactly happened to Rosaura?"

They started walking again. "Her true memories kept

returning, just as yours seem to be doing. Master's control over her weakened. She was confused and constantly in fear. Her rantings were too much of a risk, so he had her removed from the estate altogether. Beppe pulled me into his confidence and had me look for the same symptoms in the rest of you. He figured it would happen to Bianca, you, or Maria next. And today . . . yesterday?" He glanced skyward as if the stars above might tell him the time. "I saw your panic when you didn't remember what foods you liked. And your reaction when I touched you—it had to be a memory."

She flinched as she recalled the image of Master's fingers around her neck. The forest closed in around her, the cold air seeping down the back of her jacket and turning her to ice. Her chest tightened and she fought to focus on her surroundings. The circle of lantern illumination surrounded by the pitch-dark forest. Light and dark. Black and white. Truths and lies. Repulsion and attraction.

A study of contrasts.

Penny knew next to nothing about herself. Not her history, not her likes or dislikes, not even her childhood, if she'd even had one.

But she *did* know some things. She clung to these notions, these ideas that seemed to oppose the ones implanted in her mind. Pink was most certainly not her favorite color, and she didn't particularly care for dance. She knew this through every part of her still-aching bones and tendons. Penny laughed, an angry, impulsive, horrified, choking sound. All this time she thought she'd adored dance, but that was a lie. It didn't matter how well she performed, or how easily the steps came, Penny despised it.

She kicked a rock with as much force as she could muster, only to hop on one foot with an aching big toe.

Beppe can fix it.

The thought came unbidden. Beppe fixed everything. He was the expert at healing their wounds. It had always seemed effortless, uncanny even, how he could mend lacerations and fuse bones in nearly no time at all. Now she understood why. With all the advanced machinery and equipment she'd seen, he surely could alter more than their minds. It made her itch, made her skin feel foreign and tight. She didn't understand how he did it, how he could even be a part of all this. Master seemed to be the one in control, but Beppe conceded to all of his requests. Even though he'd asked Cricket to watch over them, Beppe had lied to her. Repeatedly. His betrayal stung worse than the cut on her arm.

"I'm sorry for all this, all that's happened to you." Cricket's voice rippled through the ominous quiet that had descended.

Penny wanted to believe him, wanted to trust him, but it was difficult not to wonder if he'd told her the entire truth. He seemed to be holding something back. But he'd spent all this time looking out for her, caring for her, even stepping in that afternoon when Master had taken her to his chambers.

"How is your jaw?"

He rubbed it with the back of the hand holding the lantern, causing a swinging arc of light to sweep the forest. The trees glared down on them, their branches glowing burnt orange. "It hurts, but it's certainly not the worst pain he's handed me."

Penny wondered about Cricket. Truly wondered how he'd ended up at the estate and whether he aspired to be something more than a kitchen boy. The other girls whispered rumors he'd attended an elite boarding school. He had to dream of some-thing bigger.

He had to. Why else would he be running away with her?

Before she could ask, her focus was yanked toward a pair of yellow eyes buried in the tree line to her right. "Cricket," she whispered.

With a flick of his fingers, he hooded the lantern, and they stood frozen. The only sound was their muted breath. Each exhale ended with a pale puff of fog that dissipated in the net of branches above.

"What is it? Do you see something?"

"Some sort of animal." With that, another pair of eyes appeared, a few feet away. A howl erupted, raising the hairs on Penny's arms and the back of her neck. Another yelp echoed it, this time from behind them. She whirled around, spotting more eyes. "What do we do?"

Cricket lifted the lantern hood and light once again pooled at their feet. "Penny, I don't see anything."

"There and there." She pointed in the direction of each of the animals.

He squinted. "I see only trees."

Another howl sounded—as if in warning. She covered her ears. "Don't you hear them?" She took off at a sprint, running ahead into the woods, but stopped in horror as the animals crept out into the light. They were huge, larger than any wolf she'd ever seen. Dark fur was matted down over the well-defined muscles on their flanks. Their yellow eyes glowed, and their bare teeth were blinding white against dark gums.

Penny shrank back toward Cricket. "We have to go back. Now."

"What do you mean? Penny, there's nothing there. I promise you. Whatever you see, it's not real."

She grabbed his arm and pulled him back the way they'd just come. "They're real." Penny glanced up at him, terror gripping her heart. "And they'll kill me."

CHAPTER
10

As soon as Penny and Cricket raced back several yards, the wolves retreated into the trees and the howls died down.

Cricket slowed to a stop. "Penny, what did you see?"

She fought to regain her breath. "Wolves. They were massive."

"But I saw nothing."

"They were there, Cricket." She almost screamed the words but feared it would only attract the beasts. She had to convince him. She knew without a doubt they would rip her to shreds. "Last winter they attacked Sara. I remember her screams. She crested the hill on the side of the manor with red ribbons of blood trailing behind her. Bite marks and claw slashes along her arms."

"Penny." He leaned forward so he could look her in the eyes. "That's not true. It's a false memory. Like others Master has embedded."

"How do you know?" Her voice rose and she took a step back. A branch tugged her hair. "You weren't there. How can you possibly know everything that happens at the estate in your absence?" The last words were a snarl. She could see the pain her words inflicted, see the crease in his eyebrows.

"You're right. I don't know everything." Cricket inched toward her. His voice was still soft, as if he were talking to a wounded animal. "But Beppe mentioned it before, to push through the wolves. This must be what he meant. He tried to explain it to me once, that Master had started tampering with more than just memories. He wanted to be able to edit your perception of the world around you. Make you think you see and feel things that aren't really there."

Penny shuddered at the thought. If that was true, then this could all be an altered perception. Cricket might not be here. Penny might not be in the woods. It was like a living nightmare. Except that didn't make sense. Cricket had to be real. He was her compass in this mad situation. Master wouldn't program thoughts or situations in direct conflict with his control. So this was real. But the wolves . . .

Cricket urged her to continue onward. "Let's fight through this. We can circle around the animals. You keep your eyes closed, and I'll lead. You won't see them and they can't frighten you again." He pointed to the left. "We'll head off in that direction."

Penny took a deep breath and nodded. "I'll try." She owed him that much.

Cricket shoved past the overgrowth, and they hiked away from the path. She tried to keep quiet, but it was near impossible with all the dry branches in their way and under their feet.

"Do you see them?" Cricket put out his arm to stop her. She peered through the wall of trees and shook her head. "All right. Close your eyes."

Her eyelids fluttered closed, and Penny waited for Cricket to grip her sleeve. He wrapped one arm around her shoulders and shuffled her forward. Warmth spread down her arm and she tried to concentrate on the pressure of Cricket's fingers instead of the darkness of the forest.

They'd gone several yards at least when Penny sensed the animals. The temperature dropped several degrees, the air an icy blast against her cheeks. It carried a sour sort of smell—blood and sweat. A growl erupted, so close to her face she could feel the steam of hot breath bathe her skin. Penny shrieked and her eyes flew open. The animal loomed in front of her, massive and covered in dark fur. Its teeth ground together, saliva beading in the corners of its mouth.

"Keep your eyes closed!" Cricket's voice sounded muffled over the panicked thundering of her pulse in her ears.

She squeezed her eyes shut. Cricket pushed her forward. She felt the air around her shift, and suddenly pain erupted from her arm. Fangs pierced the skin, slicing like the sharpest of blades. The teeth slid down toward her wrist, tearing the make-shift bandage from her previous cut with it.

Penny screamed and yanked herself from Cricket's grasp. Her eyes opened again and she bolted. Her fingers wrapped around the wound, staunching the thick, sticky blood, as she ran back through the woods, following their path of broken branches. Cricket hurried to catch her, lifting the lantern so she could see.

"Penny, stop!" His shout bounced around the trees in an eerie echo. "What happened?"

She slowed to a walk, her lungs near to bursting. The wolves had stayed back and the woods fell silent again.

"One attacked me." Penny clenched her jaw at the pain and fought back frustrated tears. Cricket caught up to her and she stopped to show him. She eased her hand away from her arm and winced. The gash was angry, red, and gaping. There wasn't nearly as much blood as she would've thought, but the wound sat right over the glass cut from before.

"That's your scrape from earlier. Where's the wrapping?" He tried to take her hand, but she yanked away.

"The wolf tore it off." She looked through the trees as if she might see the pale fabric on the ground.

"You must have lost it when you pulled away from me." He took a deep breath and followed her gaze. "I didn't see anything. There were no wolves. No howling. No movement. Your wound looks the same as when I wrapped it. We have to push forward. You can do it."

"No." It wasn't possible. She could see the teeth marks, feel the shredding of her skin. "I can't do it again."

"But Master—"

"Cricket, why don't you believe me?" The tears finally broke free. She'd been holding back for so long she felt she would drown in them. They coursed down her cheeks, hot and ugly. "The wolf attacked me." She shoved her arm in front of his eyes again. "I don't care if you can't see it. It is excruciating." Her jaw tightened. "And if my brain can conjure up this much pain, what's to say the animal won't puncture my heart and it will cease to beat completely? Can you risk that? Because I can't."

Her chest heaved. She swiped at her tears and glared at him. "I can't risk it. I'm going back to the estate. I'm going to get answers. I'm going to figure this out. I'm going to free the girls. With or without you."

He grasped her shoulders before she could pull away, and tucked her, shaking with angry sobs, against his chest. She fought to break free, but he held her tight until she relented. Her shoulders fell and she buried her face, snot and tears and all, into his shirt. He finally murmured into her hair, "I'm not leaving without you."

❦   ❦

When it seemed like they must've gotten lost in the woods, that they'd been circling for far too long and Penny's legs ached and her eyes had nearly closed with exhaustion, they suddenly burst out of the tree line onto the manicured estate grounds. Penny held her breath as she and Cricket made a mad dash across the drive to the door.

She hated that they were forced to return. Master held all the control and could change her mind on a whim. Perhaps he'd edit her memories of this very night. The thought stopped her in her tracks. Fear swept through her again, rooting her to the ground like one of the trees in the forest they'd just left. "Cricket." Penny grabbed the edge of his sleeve to stop him.

"Yes?" He was all shadows and puffs of breath in the cool air, but his eyes still made her pulse stutter.

Her voice dropped to a hoarse whisper. "If Master reverts my memories again, makes me forget all that I learned today, will you please find a way to tell me? I—" She choked on the word. "I can't bear to think of myself going forward, unknowing, letting him manipulate me. I have to know what's going on, and we have to find a way out."

Cricket nodded. "Of course. I promise."

They stepped up to the door and he pulled on the handle. A crack of light brightened the stone patio a pale yellow at their feet.

Clinks and clangs and the smell of sugary dough greeted them as they snuck down the hallway. Preparation for the morning meal was already under way. Cricket held his hand out to stop Penny from walking farther, and peeked his head around the corner. With a sharp inhale, his head ducked backward like a turtle retreating into its shell.

Master, he mouthed at Penny in the flickering light of the sconces. They waited, breath held, to see if he'd turn into the kitchen or walk past them. Penny couldn't hear anything save her pulse drumming. Her chest constricted tight, just as her body wanted to do. She wondered what Master was doing in the servants' wing this late at night.

His voice was smooth as satin and barely raised enough to be heard. It carried to them above the din of the chefs. "Primo. Stop sampling the plum tarts and come with me." He waited a mere second. "The cargo is ready to be transported."

"Now?" Primo's response was drawn out, as if he'd been partaking of more spirits than pastries.

"Yes. Now." A sigh and the sound of feet scuffling. "After you're done, you may take the rest of the night off. I have returned Ana to her room, and the rest of the girls have been asleep for hours. Stay in town. Enjoy any pleasure you wish. Only be back by morning."

"Yes, sir." Primo sounded chipper at the instructions.

Cricket grabbed Penny's elbow and ushered her forward. She tried to keep her boots from slapping on the hard floor. They turned the corner and plunged into the darkness of the hall, only stopping when they had slipped around into the dormitory corridor.

"Quick." Cricket pointed at the closed door to her room. "Get inside. He may check on you girls again before retiring for the evening."

A shiver trickled down Penny's spine at the thought of Master entering their rooms while they slept.

"I'll see you in the morning," Cricket whispered, releasing the grip he still had on her sleeve. "Sleep well."

Penny nearly snorted, and even in the dim lighting cast by the sconces, she could see his cheeks redden.

"As well as you can, considering." He leaned close, his mouth a mere, very distracting, inch from hers. "I will do everything in my power to keep him from changing your true memories."

"Thank you," she said, hoping he knew how much she meant it. "Good night, Cricket."

It wasn't until she shut the door behind her and her shoulders slumped forward that she realized she still carried the knapsack from Beppe's home. Not knowing what else to do, she shoved it in the back of the armoire, behind the wall of pink.

Where nobody would find it.

CHAPTER 11

$\mathcal{P}$enny awoke to Leon swatting at her hair. She lifted the kitten and stared into his flat face. "Let. Me. Sleep."

Exhaustion made her words crack and her arm heavy as she lowered him back onto the quilt. She'd only been in bed a few hours and had hardly slept, not with the revelations and fear heavy in her mind.

Even now, the thoughts consumed her. Master had molded her into this person and she had no idea what parts were real, what memories were true, and what had been fabricated. She was no closer to knowing who she was. No closer to knowing how to leave the estate boundaries.

The bells began their low gong, and Penny pulled the pillow over her head. The last thing she wanted to do was go to dance. Make that the second-to-last. The *last* thing she wanted was to be confronted by Master and have him discover she'd learned some of his truths. And that was exactly what would happen if she didn't go along with the pretense of her daily routine. She couldn't wallow any longer. The brightness of daybreak pushed away some of the dreary fog of the night before, and she felt marginally better. Stronger. Ready.

She jumped out of bed and with long, fluid motions she peeled off her nightgown and pulled on her practice bodice and skirt. Her ballet slippers clasped in one hand, a brush and hair ribbon in the other, she threw open her door and followed the last of the girls down the hall.

Hopping on one leg, she put on one slipper and then the other. The brush caught on a multitude of snarls in her attempt to pull her hair back into a bun. She'd barely tied the ribbon before they walked into the dining area. The smell of coffee made her want to guzzle it down by the pitcherful.

"What happened to your arm?" Bianca sidled up next to her.

Penny froze and glanced down at the gash tracing a line nearly from her elbow to her wrist. She had cleaned it before going to sleep the night before, but it still looked red and angry. The teeth marks were visible to her, but would Bianca even see them? Or did she see a smaller scratch from the glass? "Scissors. I was sewing last night."

Bianca raised a delicate eyebrow and drawled, "Really?"

What did that mean? "I know. It seems nearly impossible. I don't even recall what happened. One minute I'm cutting fabric; the next minute I'm bleeding." She mentally berated herself. She was horrible at this. The lying and deceit.

The side door opened and Cricket stepped halfway through. His hair was dusted in flour and stood in all directions. Even so, Penny felt drawn to him. He spotted her, his compassionate eyes searching hers. She smiled and nodded, letting him know that her memories were solid. He grinned back, his dimple deepening, before Bianca stepped forward, disrupting their line of sight.

"More sugar. Please," she demanded. He apologized and slipped away.

Penny shifted away from Bianca and rested her head against the wall. She sipped the coffee and closed her eyes, letting the girls' chatter meld together into a soft harmony she could ignore.

They were oblivious to everything. To Master's manipulations. To their own heritage and history. Sadness and frustration built in Penny's mind. She desperately wanted to tell them the truth, but she knew she couldn't yet. Not until she talked to Beppe and got answers.

For now, she had to go along with it. She didn't have a choice. So she gulped the last of her drink, forced herself to smile sweetly at Bianca's grimacing frown, and followed the girls off to the studio.

❧ ⸙

"Pe-nel-o-pe." The word was drawn into a four-syllable song as Madame Triolo tried to get Penny's attention. Her elbow slammed onto the piano keys, a discordant groan echoing through the room and piercing Penny's ears.

Penny rushed forward into position, muttering apologies. She'd forgotten her cue again, but she was beyond tired. Her eyelids felt heavier with each *pas de chat*. It didn't help that she'd realized mere hours before that she detested dancing. It made every step, every pointed toe, every *pirouette*, a chore.

"I'm so sorry." Penny knew she was only making Madame Triolo's job more difficult. It wasn't her teacher's fault, after all, even though the woman could afford to be a bit nicer to the girls. Penny wondered if Madame knew what was going on, if she reported back to Master what transpired during dance class, telling him of Penny's missteps so he could correct them. Cricket knew about the false memories, so maybe all the servants were aware of the extent of Master's control.

But if they knew, why would they go along with it? Unless Master threatened them. Or perhaps—Penny thought back on the scar lining the *pasticcere*'s arm—perhaps the staff was indebted to Master.

She glanced sidelong at Madame, wondering if Master had helped her in some way. Penny forced her feet to sweep across the floor, preparing for her *grand jeté à la seconde*. She leapt, her torso facing the front as her legs kicked to either side. As she landed, her right ankle twisted and rolled her foot beneath her. She crumpled, protecting her leg and fighting back an angry sob.

"Oh, good gracious." Madame Triolo stomped her way over, her forehead tightening in slashes of angry wrinkles. "If I didn't know any better, I would say you were purposely trying to get out of performing next week."

Penny bit her lip against the pain, and her fingers tightened around her ankle as if they alone could fight the swelling. "It wasn't intentional. I swear."

Ana rushed to her side. "You should get that wrapped right away."

"My grandfather." The word felt foreign on her tongue, but Penny knew she had to keep up the pretense. She couldn't suddenly call him Beppe without someone wondering what had changed. "He can help."

And it would be the perfect way to talk to him. She'd be alone, without fear of interruption.

"No."

Penny jerked her gaze up to Madame Triolo. "But you know he can mend it. If it's swollen, how can I practice?"

Madame Triolo turned toward the window, her fingers laced together behind her back. "I'm afraid Beppe isn't available to assist you and your myriad injuries. He left this very morning to go on an important trip. Master told me over breakfast." Penny caught the faint smile that lifted Madame's lips as she turned. "He's unsure when Beppe will return. If at all."

Penny wanted to scream. Her fingers tightened even more and she dug her nails into her skin. It wasn't possible. Beppe was supposed to be there. Today. She needed to talk to him. She needed answers that only he could provide. And those answers were her way to escape.

Madame broke into Penny's thoughts, her smile now a sneer. "I suggest you get back into first position and learn to work through the pain." She walked over and leaned in until their noses nearly touched. "This performance will be impeccable. With or without you."

Then why not without me? Penny forced herself not to shout the words. The walls closed in on her, suffocating and claustrophobic, pushing until she couldn't move.

Maria reached out a hand. It was a lifeline and Penny clasped it with her fingers. She pushed down with her good foot and hobbled into a stand.

"Stretch your ankle and get back in line." Madame turned back to the piano.

Penny shuffled over to the barre, where she flexed and pointed her toe, rotated her ankle, and tried a few *entrechats*.

She didn't know what else to do.

⚜ ⚜

"I have something that can help the pain. It will probably help your arm heal faster, too. That cut looks awful," Ana said. She glanced around to make sure everyone had gone on ahead. "Your grandfather gave me extra vials to keep in my room, what with all the headaches I've had recently."

"Oh, that would be lovely." Penny hopped another step forward.

The others had raced off to eat the noonday meal. Penny didn't blame them; she was famished herself. But it seemed to take her a bit longer than normal to limp down the hall toward the dining room.

Maria came skipping back toward them, a cloth napkin held in her palm. "Here. Cricket sent me with this. It's prosciutto and fig."

Penny unwrapped the pale green fabric to find a small piece of *crostata*. She lifted a bite to her lips, savoring the taste of honey as she chewed and swallowed. "Thanks," she called to Maria, who was already halfway back down the corridor. Penny held out the slice to Ana. "Have a bite."

Ana pinched off a bit of crust and ate it. "Cricket is darling, isn't he?" The words might as well have been a sigh. They came to a bend in the hall. Ana scurried off to the left. "I'll run and get the tincture. You go on ahead."

With her hand tracing a line along the cool stones bulging from the wall, Penny continued her hop, shuffle, limp until she reached the dining room. The girls were already arranged around the table, their forks somewhere between their plates and their mouths, depending on whether they preferred to eat or gossip.

Cricket had barely burst in through the opposite doors, the hinges groaning their distress at being opened so fast, when Penny motioned at him. He set down two porcelain pitchers in the middle of the table and came to where she rested against the door frame. His fingers brushed her sleeve, and her entire arm tingled.

"Are you all right?" His bruised jaw tightened. "Maria said you twisted your ankle."

Penny nodded. "It's fine." She lowered her voice. "But it seems *my grandfather* has gone away—some urgent trip. Have you heard anything?"

Cricket frowned. "No, but I haven't set foot out of the kitchen."

"I fear he's in trouble. And if he is, so am I. How will I get out of here?"

"Cricket, where is my cappuccino?" Bianca's voice shoved them apart.

"I'm getting it now." He grimaced and leaned in next to Penny's ear. His warm breath sent a shiver down her back. "I'll see what I can find out from the kitchen staff. Maybe they know where he's gone to."

Penny put a bit of her weight onto her foot, testing the pain, before easing into a chair at the table.

"Serves you right," Bianca said, her neck stretching as she stuck her nose in the air.

"Really?" Penny stared at her. "Serves me right? I dance, twist my ankle, and it serves me right? That doesn't make sense."

Bianca stuffed a bite of *antipasto* into her mouth.

But Penny wasn't done. "If I had twisted my ankle while running away from the dance studio . . . or playing outside when I was supposed to be in rehearsal . . . that would serve me right. That would almost be ironic."

"I don't need a lesson," Bianca muttered.

"And I don't need to be told I deserve to be in pain," Penny muttered back.

Ana came bounding in, her loosened ribbon flying behind her. She sank into the chair next to Penny and uncurled her fingers to release the vial grasped in her palm.

With a murmur of thanks, Penny drank the pale liquid,

grimacing at the bitter taste. She reached for a goblet of water and chugged until it was empty, then dug into her lasagna. Only a few bites remained before Cricket finally reappeared.

"Seriously, boy, how long does it take to make a drink?" Bianca nearly grabbed the steaming cup of milky espresso from his hands.

"He has a name, you know," Ana said.

"And a guardian, too?" Bianca snapped.

"Good grief." Penny slammed her palms onto the table and pushed away. "I'd rather help clear the table than listen to you anymore." She nearly laughed. Bianca's tirade was the perfect excuse to ask Cricket what he'd discovered.

"What about your ankle?" Bianca called as Penny grabbed a stack of empty dishes and walked around the table.

"Madame Triolo suggested I work through the pain. So I'm working." Her ankle was already feeling better from the medicine, but Bianca didn't need to know that. Penny pushed through the open door and Cricket let it shut behind her. They were in a small, narrow room lined with cabinets containing fresh napery, extra glassware, silverware, and table spices. Penny rested a platter on the countertop and tried to refrain from running her fingers through the dregs of sauce along the edges.

She was still hungry.

Cricket slipped past her, his hip brushing her waist in the confined space. Her breath hitched slightly as a flush of heat bloomed over her. "Well?" she asked when she could breathe again.

"Nobody has heard anything." He reached up and pulled fresh tablecloths from a high shelf.

Penny closed her eyes and drummed her fingertips against her chin. She needed to think. Beppe had all the answers and could very well be in danger. She had to find him. But Madame had insinuated he'd left the estate, and Penny was unable to pass the borders. That was the first hurdle. But how . . .

"What if I ask the girls? I'm certain someone has left the estate, to go into town . . . or somewhere." She pushed harder against her temples. Surely she'd left the manor in the past couple of years. Her mind pulled up memories of excursions and parades and parties. Could it be that she'd been able to leave the boundaries of the estate because she'd been in the company of Master and her *sorelle*? Or were they false thoughts, implanted to make her feel she was at liberty to leave whenever she desired?

Cricket's long fingers toyed with the corner of one of the tablecloths. "I fear involving the other girls. They won't know anything different from you. They're conditioned to believe their false memories."

"What about Sara? I can ask her for more details about the wolf mauling her, see if there's something there that we can use."

"Penny . . ." He gnawed on his lower lip and his eyes seemed to look everywhere but at her. Finally, they landed on her own and she fell into their slate depths. "Is there a chance you feel differently this morning? Could you try again to escape? Perhaps during the day the wolves would fail to appear."

Panic bloomed in her chest and flooded her entire body. "I don't know." She stared at her arm again.

"Okay. Okay." He seemed to sense her alarm. "Talk to Sara. You're right; she might have answers. But please be discreet. If she mentions to Master that you've been asking odd questions, he will most likely escalate treatment to keep you from discovering the truth. I can't let him do to you what he did to Rosaura. I swore never again would he take one of you away."

His eyes darkened to a stone color. She couldn't imagine what he was going through, tasked to watch over them, analyzing their behavior and every move.

"Now get back in there and let *me* gather the dishes." He placed his hand on the small of her back and nudged her toward the dining room. "I'll find you this afternoon."

She took a deep breath and pulled the door open. The girls were all rising and shuffling out into the hall. She was just in time to go conjugate verbs in French class.

And see if she could interrogate Sara.

CHAPTER 12

"*Qui sait la réponse?*" Madame Desrochers asked, her fingernail tapping at a sentence on the blackboard at the front of the narrow room. Their small wooden desks were crowded together and the sun poured in from high windows, warming the room to a stifling degree.

Bianca waved her hand and began speaking without being called on. "It's the wrong verb choice."

"*En français, mademoiselle.*" Madame heaved a sigh, her bosom trembling.

Bianca slouched down in her hard-backed chair. "*C'est le mauvais verbe.*" She paused, creases lining her forehead. "*Il devrait être avoir au lieu d'être.*"

"*Bien,*" Madame said with a nod. Her updo looked like it might topple over with the slightest shift, but Penny knew the elaborate braids were very secure. They twisted and curved over one another to cover the jagged scar stretching over the top of Madame's head. Penny had seen it only once, when Madame had come to Beppe for some ointment to ease the itching.

Most likely another one of Master's indebted employees.

Madame turned back to the blackboard and began scribbling

out more uses of *avoir*. Penny found it difficult to focus and spent the hour running her finger along the edge of the slate board resting on her desk. Finally, they were dismissed. Everyone began to file out of the classroom amid loud chatter and giggling.

Penny rose quickly and slid next to Sara. "How are you feeling?"

Sara pulled her braid to the side so it hid most of her face. "Fine. Why?"

"I wanted to ask about something. The wolves. Last winter."

Sara tensed and froze. "What about them?"

"I'm sorry to even bring it up, but is there anything you can tell me about that day? I know you've explained it before. I just thought perhaps you may have remembered more details since? I hope to speak to Master about getting rid of them. There must be a way to remove them from the estate grounds." This lie came more easily than the one she'd spun that morning about the cut on her arm. "I'd hate for someone else to get hurt."

Sara's eyes glazed and she chewed at the cuticle on her index finger. "I was on a walk, looking for wolfsbane for Beppe. I'd been following the tree line, but then wandered inside the woods, hoping to find an errant patch of sun. It was late afternoon, and I must've gotten lost."

Penny nodded. She knew all this; it was the story they'd all been told. "And the wolves?"

"Suddenly, they were there, howling and scratching, their eyes yellow." The words were fast and frustrated. "I tried to run, but I wasn't quick enough. One jumped at me from the side, its teeth gnashing." She pushed up her sleeve to show the silvered lines across her forearm and wrist, crossing right above her marking. They both stared for a second, until Sara yanked the hem of her sleeve down again. Her fingers brushed across the back of her neck, where Penny knew other scars lined up like chains of a necklace. "It bit me. I couldn't breathe. I couldn't move. It was as if I'd been paralyzed. Master saved me. He said I should never go that close to the border again. I haven't. Why would I want to . . . We should get going." Sara halted the conversation and ran toward Bianca.

Penny slowed her steps and let them pull ahead. She didn't blame Sara for not wanting to talk about it. The encounter still terrified Penny, and her arm throbbed from the bite marks. Sara's memory further confirmed Penny's inability to cross the border.

Was there truly no way to escape?

A dull pain pulsed in Penny's temples, and she gulped back fear. It wasn't like the previous night, the pain that had slammed into her temples as they'd walked through the woods, but it made her nervous. Master had the ability to tamper with her thoughts at any time, reverting her back to unknowing.

He could do it now.

With French, Latin, and another exhausting hour of dance complete, Penny made her meandering way back to her chamber. Madame Triolo had suggested all the girls stretch their muscles and spend a bit of time relaxing before supper.

Penny had no intention of doing any such thing.

At the last second, with all the girls in front of her, she slipped into the corridor leading to the kitchen.

A shadow eased off the wall, and Penny nearly shrieked.

"Shh." Cricket stepped into the light of a sconce and she

found herself able to breathe again, although her pulse still raced at the sight of him.

"You scared me near to the grave."

"Sorry." Cricket's mouth tugged into a grin and his dimple flashed. Penny knew her smile grew and matched his own, and she ducked her head. "Did you talk to Sara?"

"Briefly. I had heard most of it before, although she went into a little more detail." Penny took a deep and steadying breath. "The wolf attacked her much the same as me, mauling her and biting her neck. She said it paralyzed her. The scars look painful."

"Scars?"

"You know, on her neck and wrist." Penny rubbed her own arm.

Cricket's eyebrows knit together. "She doesn't have any scars."

"Of course she does. You don't see them because her shirt covers them."

"Penny, I've seen Sara in a costume without any sleeves. There is absolutely nothing wrong with her skin. Perhaps a few freckles on her arm, and her marking, but certainly no wounds."

Penny braced a hand against the rough stone wall. "Are you certain?"

"I'm more than certain."

"But I just saw them. . . ." Penny swallowed and let the words trail off. It was another discrepancy between her visions and what Cricket saw. Another way that Master might have altered her perceptions. Bianca hadn't seen the bite marks on Penny's arm. So it was entirely possible that Sara's scars didn't exist. That the entire situation hadn't occurred and was instead implanted in all the girls' minds as a deterrent. But still. Sara had felt paralyzed, unable to move in the forest. Penny couldn't risk it. They needed answers from Beppe. "Were you able to discover anything?"

Laughter spilled in from the dormitory, the high-pitched giggles echoing off the walls and into their small alcove.

His fingers brushed her waist, pressing briefly before letting go. He leaned in close, his lips near hers as he dropped his voice to a murmur. "Let's talk later. Meet me outside, after supper, at the badminton lawn." Before she could press him further, Cricket disappeared back into the shadows.

"Penny." Ana rushed toward her. "We're off to the library to study. Would you like to join us?"

She didn't want to study, but the library might hold answers she needed. Cecilia and Maria crowded close and swept her along into the main hall. The library was awash with the warmth of the afternoon sunlight. The girls separated, Cecilia searching the shelves for a book written by a particular French author she loved, Ana settling at one of the tables with a history textbook, and Maria working beside her in her journal.

Penny took in the library, the sprawling shelves with books on every topic imaginable. She wondered if there was something that would speak to mind tampering or thought control. She walked the length of the room, her eyes scanning the titles, but nothing seemed to hold the information she sought.

Come on. Think. She doubted Master would casually shelve the books he needed on the first floor, but perhaps there was something in the loft. Those oddities on display must have had significance.

She ascended the circular staircase and walked along the balcony. The space was narrow and the railing low, creating a dizzying effect as she glanced down at the girls. Along with the display columns, a series of boxed shelves lined the wall. Inside one a wooden marionette dangled from a ring at the top. Its crossbars were folded together and the toy hung with its head slumped down.

Another box held a strange carving that seemed to be made of metal. Iron or steel, she couldn't tell. Upon further inspection, it seemed the shape of a bone. It was as long as her forearm, and skinny, flexible rods extended from both ends. Penny had bent over to take a closer look when she felt a presence behind her.

She whirled around to find Master mere inches away. Her eyes were at chest level, and she had to lift her chin to look at him.

"Anything of interest?"

Penny willed her pulse to stop its galloping pace and shook her head. "I was only looking."

His emerald eyes searched hers, and she feared for a moment that he could look directly into her mind. Time stood still. She felt pulled to him, like a moth to fire. Her entire balance seemed off, and she nearly fell against him. At the last moment his hands lifted to gently grip her arms. She steadied herself and blinked hard to break his gaze. There was something about him, the lines of his cheekbones, the strength of his shoulders, the thick black hair that curled at his neck, that was intoxicating. It was no wonder the girls seemed willing to throw themselves at his feet.

And yet, so much of it was a façade. Penny couldn't separate the reality from the memories from the manipulations.

Master turned her around slowly and stepped in close until

his chest was flush against her back. He released one arm to point at the glass. "That was designed to mimic a child's tibia."

Penny swallowed, wondering who had created it, and to what purpose, although she had a feeling she knew the scientist behind such a device.

"It worked, for a time. The child could move freely, without pain and discomfort." His voice was strangely flat. "It was life-changing."

His fingers slipped down her arm and brushed the scrape below her elbow. She sucked in a breath and flinched. He turned her back to face him and lifted her arm to examine it. "What happened?"

Penny fought back the fear threatening to overcome her. She had no idea what he saw when he looked at her wound. Whether it was bite marks or a cut from the glass. But surely he'd know she tried to escape if it was anything unusual. "It's nothing. I cut myself earlier. Cricket bound it right away. I'm sure it will heal fine. . . ." Her voice trailed off as his teeth ground together.

"Cricket. Why was he with you? Did he do this?"

"No!" Penny shook her head vehemently. She couldn't have Master blaming Cricket for any of this. "I was sewing. In my room. By myself. I reached for my basket and caught my arm on the scissors. I went straight to the dining room to get a rag." She knew she rambled, talking over herself in her hurry to explain. "Cricket was there and he helped. He's always willing to help."

Master's eyes flashed ebony and Penny willed herself to stop talking. Her voice fell. "It will heal by the gala. I'm sure of it."

"That's not the concern, Penelope. I don't ever want harm to come to you." He raised her palm to his cheek. Her breath caught. They stood motionless for a minute and then he let go. "I imagine you and the girls should get ready for supper."

He walked the opposite way and into an opening in the wall she'd never seen before.

She paused, wondering if she should follow, but no. She'd done enough damage for the day.

CHAPTER 13

$\mathcal{P}$enny slipped out the servants' exit and into the plum-colored haze of evenfall. A yawn stretched her mouth as she fought against the exhaustion from a day of constant second-guessing and fear of being caught knowing things she shouldn't. Not to mention the lack of sleep from the night before. She favored her sore ankle as she skirted the edge of the building and stepped onto the worn dirt trail leading to the badminton court. She'd traveled the path many times before, although not very often this winter.

The ground inclined to a hill, darkened in shadow, and Penny lifted the hem of her skirt above her boots so she wouldn't slip on a loose stone. The last thing she needed was to twist her ankle again.

She cast intermittent glances behind her, back at the brightly lit, yellow-eyed windows of the main building, to make sure she wasn't being followed.

Or watched.

The skin on the back of her neck prickled, and she wondered what Master would do if he caught her on the grounds, rushing off to speak to Cricket. Nothing good, that was for certain.

Her pace picked up as a stilt circled overhead, and she burst onto the flat, grassy stretch of badminton field that was out of view of the manor.

"What's wrong? Did someone see you?" Cricket appeared at the opposite side of the plateau, a dark smudge of rumpled hair and cropped wool jacket. He came more into focus as his long strides carried him closer.

"No." She forced herself not to look behind her. "I think we're in the clear."

He held out a racquet.

Her eyebrows arched as she took it. "We're actually going to play?"

"Why not? It's a good excuse if anyone happens to come upon us. I'll say I'm teaching you to serve."

"In the dark?" She edged away from the slope and onto the shorn grass. "Oh, never mind." Let him think he could help. She'd perfected her backhand serve months ago.

They walked side by side, arms almost brushing but not quite. It felt like pulses of lightning leapt between her skin and his. She wanted to touch him, lean against him, feel his arms around her, and revel in the safety of his embrace. But she didn't want to risk another memory. They needed to focus and make a plan.

Cricket stopped at the net. "I have a note." He reached into his pocket and pulled out a loose sheet of paper. It already looked worn; the folds had obviously been creased and uncreased several times.

Penny squinted at the page. She recognized the looping penmanship as Beppe's, but there was something hurried in the slant of his letters and in his curt tone.

C—

I've been sent on an urgent trip to Rome for a client. I don't know when I will return. If you need anything, I urge you to visit Tatiana at the Azul Apothecary Shoppe.

Remain cautious and keep the girls safe.

—B

Her teeth worried at her lower lip as she read and reread the words. "It doesn't make sense. He'd never be sent away this close to the gala. Master needs him at the estate in case one of us is injured. He wouldn't risk it. It must be a ruse."

"I agree." Cricket pulled a shuttlecock from his pocket. He tossed it in the air once, twice, and tapped it with his racquet. He caught it in outstretched fingers and glanced at Penny. "As soon as I received the note, I went to his cottage to check on the girl."

Penny stiffened. "Is she all right?"

"She wasn't there. The workshop had already been ransacked, broken glass covering the floor. I imagine Master took her."

"We should've gone back for her." Penny tipped her head back and stared at the expanse of stars above. She'd never felt so insignificant and incapable. "We should never have left."

"There was no way for us to know that Beppe would leave the estate."

"It's obvious he didn't leave on his own terms. They wouldn't barge into his home and move the girl. If he was planning to come back, I'm sure they would've let him continue to do . . ."

whatever it was he was doing." She lowered her chin and stared at him. "You should go to the apothecary."

"We should go together."

"I can't. You know that." She willed him not to fight her.

He stepped in close to lay his palm against the outside of her shoulder. Heat flooded down her arm and across her chest. "Maybe the wolves won't attack a second time. We'll take the cabriolet instead of going on foot."

She shrugged away and shoved down the dread clawing its way up her throat. "I can't risk it. You can travel much faster and in secret if I'm not beside you shrieking in agony as we try to leave the grounds. You visit the apothecary and see what answers you can get. I'll go to Beppe's cottage and search there."

"We'll need a couple of hours to sneak away. Can you feign an injury tomorrow morning?"

"I'll pretend my ankle is worse. It's their fault Beppe isn't around to fix it."

"I'll get out of kitchen duty and we can sneak away after breakfast."

"I have to get answers soon, Cricket." She felt as if the last grains of sand in an hourglass were ready to fall through. Time was up.

"I know—"

Suddenly, a piercing headache shoved nails into her skull. She whimpered, the racquet slipping from her grasp as she collapsed in a heap on the ground. Sobs racked her chest as she curled into a ball and mercifully fainted.

Again.

Penny groaned and lifted her hand to brush something wet off her cheek. Her eyes opened to a nighttime canvas of starlight and charcoal. With a heave, she sat up, flinching as she spotted the kitchen boy squatting in front of her. The moon painted him in streaks of white light and dark shadows. His hair spiked in all directions, as if he'd run his fingers through it repeatedly. His eyes were narrow slits, and his lips were pursed into a pale streak.

Is he going to harm me?

The thought came unbidden. But once it entered her mind, she couldn't unthink it, couldn't stop analyzing the calculating look in his eyes.

Penny scooted away, not caring that her skirt was getting more muddied. "Where are we?" She squinted, trying to get her bearings.

"At the badminton court." He settled back on his heels. "Don't you remember?"

Penny shook her head. The court was yards away from the manor, out of view and bordering the woods. He must have brought her there so the other girls wouldn't hear her screams. Could she make a run for it? He had such long legs; he'd surely catch her.

Cricket stood and took a step closer. Her pulse scampered and she fought the urge to scream. "Why did I have a feeling this was going to happen?" he said as if to himself.

"Wh-wh-what?" Penny stuttered.

He crouched next to her, light on the balls of his feet, as if he knew she was about to flee.

Penny took a deep breath and placed her hands flat on the damp grass, readying to push herself to standing. Before she could muster the courage to dash away, Cricket reached out and grabbed her hand.

"What are you . . . Oh." The memories flooded back, the wolves, Beppe, the girl in the room, and images of Master . . . his fingers around her neck.

And Cricket's promise.

He yanked away before she could. "Sorry. I wish I knew why my touch brings your memories back."

That it did, and some other ones as well. It seemed with every contact further binds were broken. New memories leaked from where they were locked in her brain.

I run through a field . . . chasing a butterfly . . . the grass is bare beneath my feet, the sun bright overhead . . . a laugh echoes from behind . . . "Wait!" . . . I see the butterfly land on a fence . . . horses graze on the other side, tails flicking . . . I inch toward the butterfly . . . I signal the boy behind me to be quiet . . . I reach out a finger toward the blue wings but it flits away . . . I sigh and frown . . . "Next time," he says . . . always an optimist.

Penny rubbed at her wrist and pulled down the sleeve. She looked at Cricket with unclouded thoughts, but her mind was tangled in the memory. The boy. Was he her brother? She had no memory of his appearance, only his words. But it could have been a family member, someone who missed her and might, at that very moment, be looking for her.

Cricket still squatted next to her, looking at her as if she were a skittish animal. "Do you feel all right? You fell pretty hard. I tried to catch you, but you sort of collapsed."

"I feel fine." She yanked out several blades of grass and gripped them tight in her hand. "I mean other than my memories being ripped away." She pushed herself up and paced away. Her fingers slowly released the grass. What if Cricket hadn't been there? What if he couldn't bring her out of the spell Master had cast? The what-ifs were getting to be too much.

She needed to get control of the situation. She needed to stop Master.

Penny turned back to Cricket. "Do you know how he does it?"

"I don't know the science behind it, but it seems he's accelerated the equipment so he can access your mind from afar." Cricket stood and stepped closer. "Beppe says he alters your thoughts depending on the level of control he wishes to exert. Some of the girls bend to his will a lot easier. I don't think you were ever one of them."

"No, I imagine not."

Something else tugged at Penny's thoughts, something about her memories, about awakening on the ground a few minutes ago. "Were you going to hurt me?"

"What?" His eyes narrowed and his jaw tightened. "Of course not. Penny, I would never harm you."

"But"—she pulled her gaze away—"when I opened my eyes, I had this sense that you brought me here for that very reason."

"Damn him," Cricket nearly growled. "He must've placed the idea in your mind."

But had he? Could she trust Cricket?

Penny started shaking and crossed her arms across her chest. Her teeth chattered as a chill settled deep in her bones, caused by something more menacing than the winter air.

Cricket seemed to realize this, and reached an arm around her back to pull her close. "I promise you. I know you must struggle to believe me. I know you must question everything. I wish there were a way to prove to you I speak the truth."

She rested her cheek against his chest and willed herself to believe him. He had done nothing but help her thus far. If he had ulterior motives, she had yet to see them. She desperately needed someone to trust.

It still unnerved her how easy it had been for Master to turn her against Cricket. She wondered if Master had chosen this manipulation because of the comments she'd made that afternoon, saying that Cricket had helped her clean the wound on her arm.

"I'm sorry," she said. The words were soft, wrapping around them like the fog that had started to creep in and mask the stars. "I shouldn't have asked. I know you'd never hurt me."

"You have no need to apologize. None of this is your fault."

"Nor yours," she added.

Cricket squeezed once and released her. He bent down to grab the racquets, tucked them under one arm, and nodded toward the manor. "Let's get you back. Tomorrow, we will get answers."

They took their time walking down the hill, their boots crunching in the frost that had begun to coat the blades of grass. They'd barely reached the servants' entrance when the door swung open. Cricket yanked Penny into the darkness of an alcove just as Primo clomped outside.

"Watch the damned girl," he muttered. "That's all I hear. All day long. First it was 'find out what's wrong,' and then it was 'make it go away,' and now it's 'watch the girl.'"

Cricket stood behind Penny, his arm curved around her waist and stomach as she leaned against his chest. She could feel his heart beat erratically and the release of air when he exhaled slowly. Primo had disappeared around the side of the building, toward the stable. Bits of words and sentences still streamed toward them. ". . . not my job . . . someone else . . ."

It was silent for a minute.

"Quick. Before he comes back." Cricket nudged Penny out, and together they raced toward the door.

At Penny's room, she bid Cricket farewell.

"Until tomorrow," he said.

Penny shut the door and leaned her head back against it. She could still feel his arm around her waist, the pressure of his fingers, the strength of his chest behind her. It felt disconcerting to be away from him. He was her anchor in this stormy sea.

"Until tomorrow," she whispered.

CHAPTER

14

The frigid water dripped down her cheeks and back into the basin. Penny had woken early to get ready. She washed her face and dipped her fingers into the liquid to smooth her hair back into a tight bun. Sorting through her wardrobe, she found a clean skirt and pulled it on. She laced her slippers and sat on the edge of her bed, willing her nerves to settle.

Today would be a test of her acting skills. She had to be immaculate, polite, and gracious, giving nobody a chance to question her motives when her ankle began hurting even more and she asked for a day of rest. Madame already seemed furious with the interruptions. It would be difficult to persuade her.

The second she heard the first bell begin its toll, Penny leapt into the hall. Bianca made an odd sort of choking, retching sound when she whisked out her door and found she was second. She tried to elbow her way past Penny.

Penny, being in a congenial mood that morning, allowed herself to be nudged backward. "Good morning, Bianca," she trilled.

"Hmph."

Cecilia and Sara burst from their doors across the hall. Maria glided out, eyes widening to find Penny already there. "You're up early."

"I couldn't help it," Penny said. "I'm so excited for the performance." The words were torture, each syllable a knife to her throat.

"I know. I'm so excited to perform for Master again." Maria nearly swooned and Penny fought not to gag.

Bianca led the way to the dining room. As everyone rushed to fill the void of silence, Penny chomped on sugar cubes. She wondered if her personality might absorb some of the sweetness so she could keep up her cheery demeanor for the next couple of hours.

"Good morning, girls. Is everything okay in here?" Cricket poked his head in, his gaze settling on Penny for the briefest of moments. Her heart leapt at the sight of him.

"Yes, divine, absolutely perfect, splendid, thank you," Ana chirped. Her forehead furrowed and she sucked down her drink as if somehow the hot liquid would stem the flow of words.

He nodded in Penny's direction, and she tipped her head in return. They were ready to do this. The quest for answers would start, and hopefully end, today.

When they arrived at the dance studio, Penny positioned herself at the center of the barre. She smiled at Madame, who looked at her as if she'd sprouted thorns from her eyeballs. Perhaps she was laying it on with a trowel. She didn't want to draw too much attention to herself. Penny dropped the grin and stared at her reflection in the spotless mirror.

For the next thirty minutes she concentrated on stretching, bending, molding her body into whatever shape Madame requested. "*Brava*, Penny!"

Then, during a *jeté en avant*, Penny collapsed onto the ground with a wail that quickly receded into a whimper. She clutched her ankle and bent over her leg, letting false sobs rack her body.

"What happened?" Ana raced to her side, several of the other girls right behind.

"I . . . my ankle . . . I hurt it again." Penny spoke through fake shudders. She couldn't seem to work up any tears, so she bit on her lip, hard, until her eyes watered.

Madame clomped her way across the room and stood over Penny. "Let me look."

Penny slowly released her grasp and lifted her head. Madame squatted at her side. She pushed into Penny's ankle with the tip of her index finger. Penny yelped and yanked her foot back.

Madame sighed. "And you were doing so well today."

"Has Grandfather returned?" Penny asked, knowing full well that Beppe was nowhere on the estate grounds.

Madame shook her head.

"But what am I to do?" Penny wailed. "This is the second time I've hurt my ankle in the same number of days. If it happens again, I fear I won't be able to dance at the gala!" She dared a glance in Maria's direction, hoping her *sorelle* believed her lies. Based on the haunted expression pulling Maria's face all inward on itself, it seemed Penny's fake fall had worked.

"As I said before," Madame said with a frown, "dancing through the pain is the best way—"

"No!" Penny interrupted, and then swallowed. "I mean, I really do think that rest is the best medicine, without Grandfather around to mend it, that is."

Madame's frown deepened.

Penny waved Ana over. "If Ana could help me to my room, I'll keep my foot elevated for the rest of the day. Tomorrow it will most certainly be healed."

"Since when are you the reigning physician?" Bianca asked with a sneer. "Your grandfather leaves and suddenly you're dispensing advice?"

Penny's eyes widened and she feigned dismay. "I didn't mean to imply that I was an expert on such things."

"Oh, leave her alone, Bianca." Maria stepped forward, ever the defender. "She's in pain and wants to rest."

Penny flashed her a relieved smile.

Madame settled her fists on her hips, her stance wide as a bull. "We're wasting time. Penelope, go back to your quarters and prop your ankle on some pillows. But as soon as you feel better, I want you back in this room to practice your performance."

"Thank you." Penny tried to hide a grin as she hobbled to standing and leaned on Ana's arm. "I promise I'll be better in the morning, at the very latest."

Penny wanted to skip through the hallway, but instead she shuffled and stopped and moaned her way away from the studio. It took forever, but they finally reached the dark and dank corridor of their dormitory hall.

The door closest to them swung open and Master stepped out. Ana skidded to a stop and tilted her chin in deference while Penny tried to peer over his shoulder into the room. It was an unoccupied chamber, at least before today. Now furniture filled the space. Penny caught glimpses of a pale quilt draped over the footboard and a wardrobe stuffed with shades of pink.

With a gust of air, Master slammed the door shut.

He stood in front of them, his hair in disarray. The crisp white shirt he always wore was now a little rumpled, and his cuffs were rolled up at his wrists instead of clasped neatly with silver links. The top two buttons at his throat were open, revealing a thin black cord that hung around his neck and dipped beneath the shirt. It was disconcerting to see him this way. He seemed less austere and more human.

"Why are you girls not in class?" he asked them both but looked only at Penny.

"I hurt my ankle," Penny said, her mind reeling. The girl. The one in Beppe's workshop. The room must be meant for her. At least that meant she was okay, but Penny shivered, knowing what was in store for her.

The silence grew stifling, and Ana finally dared to lift her chin. "I was taking Penny to her room so she might rest."

Master finally tore his gaze from Penny. "Thank you, Ana. Your assistance is much appreciated." Ana blushed a faint peach color. "I will take it from here. You can get back to rehearsal." He grasped Penny's arm, and she had no choice but to lean against him as she had Ana. His shoulder was solid and firm beneath her fingers where she clutched it to hold some of her weight. He tucked an arm tight around her waist and escorted her farther down the hall.

Whispers of footsteps echoed behind her, the only sound of Ana's departure.

"Madame Triolo said you injured yourself yesterday." His fingers tightened slightly, pushing against the skin just above her hip bone. "Is it the same ankle?"

She nodded and tried not to lean in too close. It was intoxicating being near him, but she couldn't let herself fall under his spell.

"You should have mentioned it yesterday afternoon. You keep hiding your distress from me, Penelope. There's no reason for it." He opened the door and ushered her into her room.

"I didn't want to bother you," she said quickly. "It wasn't hurting much then anyway."

"And how is the cut on your arm?"

Penny knew he was baiting her, seeing if she'd mention Cricket.

"It doesn't hurt at all. Thank you for asking."

With a fluid and unexpected movement, he tucked his arm below her knees and lifted her onto the bed. She couldn't stop the flush of heat that flooded her cheeks. It felt too personal, him being so close and her sprawled on her quilt in her chamber.

His palm smoothed out a wrinkle on the blanket and he glanced at the open door. "I must go, but I will return later." His lips lifted into a shy smile and his eyes, dark green and endless, caught hers. "I know a bit of rudimentary medicine, a way to ease your pain. You might forget you were even uncomfortable."

Penny gulped. She focused on his fingers, still splayed on her quilt, unable to meet his gaze for fear he would see the terror in her eyes. "I thought I might try to get some rest first. Perhaps this evening would be a good time?" She had to stall him, prevent him from coming back to her room anytime soon.

He patted her leg, his hand lingering only a second past comfortable, and stood. "I will return after the dinner hour. I have a . . . some guests to attend to. Until then, rest well, Penelope. Call on me if you need anything."

Master hesitated in the open doorway, his mouth parted as if he wished to say something more. Then he slipped off into the darkness of the corridor.

Penny counted to fifty until she was certain he would be gone. There was no time to spare. One of the girls might return to bring her some snacks or her schoolwork. She needed to find Cricket and get out of the manor.

And back again before Master discovered her missing.

Penny grabbed a bundle of sweaters from the wardrobe shelf and bunched them together under the quilt, hoping it looked enough like a body that someone peeking in might leave her alone. The more time she could buy, the better. After yanking off her practice skirt, she stepped into a riding dress and laced brown leather boots tight against her calf. She found her riding gloves in the drawer and pulled them on.

Silence greeted her as she edged along the length of the hall and dashed into the kitchen. She spotted the *pasticcere* and waved him over. He looked torn between wanting to help and not wishing to get in trouble. "Please?" she hissed, and he scooted over.

"If you see Cricket, can you let him know I'm waiting? He was tasked with accompanying me on a walk. Fresh air and all that." She waved her hand, dismissing the notion as if it were something unnecessary. "I'll . . ." The chef emerged from the arched entrance that led down to the cellar, a sour expression on his face. "I'll wait for him at the servants' exit."

She backed out of the kitchen and waited.

And waited.

Her pulse hiccuped, and she distracted herself by removing her hair from its bun and braiding it over her shoulder.

Finally, Cricket appeared, apologizing profusely. Penny's fears dissipated as she drank him in. Pale eyes, strong jaw, and the freckles that dusted his nose and cheeks. His broad shoulders stretched at the white shirt he'd tucked into his breeches. She wanted to curl into his chest and feel his arms wrap around her. He raised an eyebrow at her silent appraisal and nodded toward the door. "Shall we?"

She turned the handle and they spilled out into a day filled with dull, gray clouds and heavy air. By the time they arrived at the stable, sprinting the entire way, her dress clung tightly to her back and arms. The sweet scent of damp hay tickled her nose as they approached the stalls. The horses neighed softly, as if begging her for a treat.

Cricket made fast time saddling one of the mares. "We'll ride together to Beppe's home, and I will go to Ravinni from there."

He held out a hand to help her up. Penny glanced down at her gloves and then grasped his fingers tight. She settled into the saddle while Cricket closed the stall door and led the horse outside. He pulled himself up behind her. His thighs gripped the outside of her legs, and his chest rested against her back. His arms reached around her to grab the reins. Every nerve tingled, and her entire body was on alert as he shifted and brushed up against her. He couldn't be touching more of her if he tried.

They wound out along the main lane and Cricket urged the horse into a trot. A cool breeze pulled at Penny's braid. The clopping of hooves was the only sound for several minutes, and Penny found herself leaning farther into Cricket. Only a few minutes passed before they came upon the smaller drive that opened up to the left, winding off into the woods, leading to Beppe's home.

Before they turned, Penny's gaze settled on the horizon, her eyes squinting to detect any movement, any flicker of sunlight or shifting of shadow. A low wooden fence lined both sides of the street and tall, dry grass spread out to either side. She bit her lip and fought back a shudder, wondering at what point the wolves were set to attack.

They slipped onto the narrow path and the trees closed in

around them. Shadows built, and the temperature cooled by several degrees.

The cottage came into view, dark and empty, the front door open. "I don't know if this is a good idea," Cricket said as he slid one leg away from hers and prepared to dismount. Penny missed his touch as soon as it was gone.

"They won't return. They've already taken everything they needed." Beppe. The girl. "I'll be safe." She reached out a hand and gripped his tightly. "I promise, at the first sign of danger I'll head back to the manor via the trail."

He helped her down from the mare and they walked to the porch. Silence descended, deep and heavy as they crossed the threshold. The parlor was undisturbed, other than the layer of dirt and dried leaves coating the floor and furniture like bits of potpourri.

"Stay inside. Lock the door. I'll be back shortly." With a half smile and a blush that dotted his cheeks, Cricket shut the door between them.

❦ 1866 ❦

Cirillo stood at the edge of his desk, staring down at the notes he'd meticulously taken earlier that day. He couldn't sit. The skin on his right calf still stretched tight and itched like mad. The third, and final, surgery had lengthened the rods to match his left leg, but it bothered him frequently. He tried to ignore the distraction and focus.

Today, he and Beppe had met with a world-renowned physicist, who had taken the train in from Germany. They had talked at length about electricity, wavelengths, and energy pulses. The physicist thought they were working with magnets.

In actuality, they were working with brains.

But they'd never let the scientist know that. Just as the surgeon they'd spoken to the week before thought Cirillo was interested in curing diseases. It was all a ruse. They sought out key professionals in each industry, asked specific questions, and then manipulated the knowledge to suit their own needs. They'd been slowly gathering clients, helping an equestrian accident victim with a severe limp, a burn victim with visible scarring—the list went on.

Cirillo dropped the fountain pen on the desk. With a slow

stride, he paced the room, flexing his knee and then his ankle with each step.

Beppe walked through the door, his hair a mass of unruly curls. Cirillo was struck at how white it had turned.

"Is Röntgen gone?" Cirillo glanced out the window. A coach kicked up a cloud of dust as it traveled on the long path around the lake.

With a nod, Beppe collapsed into a chair, one leg hooked over the arm. Cirillo grabbed the cane leaning against his desk and knocked at Beppe's foot. No longer needed as a walking device, the cane could at least be used to teach his friend some manners. Beppe straightened and sighed, his palm reaching to his lower back like an old man.

Cirillo shook his head. "You need to stop experimenting on yourself. You're aging faster by the minute."

Beppe shrugged, the movement tight in his shoulders. "I prefer to be the test subject before inflicting new procedures on others."

"Have you looked in the mirror, though? You could be my father."

Beppe laughed, the light in his eyes the only indication of his youth. "I will never be your father. God rest his soul. And don't worry about me—I'll be fine."

Cirillo continued his pacing, stopping only to grab the journal from his desk. He placed the open page on the table in front of Beppe. "Do you think it will work?"

Beppe leaned forward, taking in the sketches and notations. "It will take a while. I'll need to build the control system first. But Röntgen gave me an idea for mapping the pulses to specific brain functions. . . ." He continued on, but Cirillo tuned him out. He trusted Beppe implicitly. And Beppe trusted him.

Perhaps he shouldn't. Beppe didn't know yet how Cirillo planned to use the completed engineering. In their earlier discussions, Cirillo had alluded to eradicating disease. Helping others.

That was what they'd been doing all this time. Creating. Fixing.

Now Cirillo wanted to add one final element.

Controlling.

He already had his test subject in mind.

As if on cue, there was a loud rap on the door.

Primo, his valet, stood on the other side. "Sir, your sister and her husband have arrived."

"Very well." Cirillo crooked his finger, inviting Beppe to join him. "We shall be right down."

CHAPTER 16

Cricket's absence felt heavy, weighing down Penny's shoulders.

She paced the main living room of Beppe's cottage. Her fingers danced along the back of the sofa, the knotted wooden table, and the stack of books piled high in the corner. She brushed off dust with her thumb. A series of shelves lined one wall, full of bits of mechanical odds and ends. Gears and windup toys that weren't really toys, more like misshapen metal people. Most likely devices he'd worked with in the past. While certainly interesting, none of them provided her with answers and a way past the estate borders.

She pulled open the drawers in the kitchen and glanced through the cupboards, unsurprised to find nothing more than utensils, silverware, pots, and pans.

Upstairs, Penny stepped into the first bedroom, the one she'd once considered hers. She knew its every nook and cranny, so, after a cursory glance, she moved on to Beppe's chamber. There was nothing much to distinguish it from the first. The size and furniture were the same, although masculine clothes filled the armoire. A large book rested on the nightstand, its pages open to a drawing of a heart. Charcoal notes, in Beppe's handwriting, lined the margins. She sat on the edge of the hard mattress and pulled the book onto her lap. Each page contained a detailed anatomical illustration. She spent at least thirty minutes poring over the notes, hoping Beppe had made any comments that would clue her in to the manipulations he had conducted. Words like *neuron* and *electrotherapy* and *bimetallic energy* filled the pages, but nothing made sense in terms of helping her escape.

Frustrated at the waste of time, Penny carried the book downstairs and dropped it on the table. She took a deep breath and turned toward the hallway that led to the secret chamber, the place she least wanted to visit.

The corridor was thick with shadows. She paused briefly in the guest room. The bed was neatly made, a quilt tucked in at the corners. The armoire doors were flung open and clothing— pink skirts, white chemises, a pale nightgown—spilled out of the sides. A vanity held a mirror, pitcher, and basin. Penny ran her hands down the inside of the armoire, hoping for a letter or something of note.

Nothing.

Back in the hall, she stopped at the false wall and traced her fingers along the corner seam to unlock the door. It swung open and she stepped just inside the workshop. Nearly all the equipment had been removed. The shelves were bare, except for a few errant jars tipped on their sides. Broken glass dotted the floor. She walked along the perimeter to the desk. The surface was empty save for an overturned inkwell and pen. The drawers were cleared out as well. The bottom one stuck, and she yanked twice before it came tumbling open. Papers were stacked in a haphazard pile.

She pulled them out and laid them on the desktop. The pages were of a similar format, labeled with a subject number and then two columns below. One held dates. One held notes.

SUBJECT #2

10 DECEMBER	Childhood memories tied to holidays removed.
	5 milliliters serum.
12 DECEMBER	Docile behavior continues. Suggestion to wean off serum.

Penny riffled to another page.

SUBJECT #4

8 JANUARY	Combative with C. Increased electrotherapy.
10 JANUARY	Thought waves indicate desire to leave estate.
	Selective neuro pulses.
	Complains of headache.
	10 milliliters serum.
11 JANUARY	~~Combative again~~.

The words were scratched through. Dark slashes of lines.

Dozens of papers lay underneath. Multiple pages for some of the subjects. And the final one, *Subject #14*. It was blank.

Penny swallowed hard and gathered them into a pile. She knew they had to refer to her and her *sorelle* and their treatments.

The thought of all this analysis, the medications and serums, made her nauseated.

They weren't dolls.

She felt no closer to finding anything. Frustration at the constant dead ends, and fear of forever being trapped at the estate, circled like caged animals in her chest. She closed her eyes and took a deep breath. Her fingers drummed on her lips as she forced herself to focus, to clear her thoughts and try to remember when she'd been in this workshop. She hoped some memory would surface. If she could only remember the specifics of waking up on the table, she might be able to push further back and see what she'd been like . . . before.

Recall any family, her personality and likes and dislikes, picture where she'd come from. Discover something, anything, about her identity.

"Penny?"

She nearly fell over, she spun around so fast.

"Cricket?" She raced back toward the front room.

Penny skidded to a stop, her mouth falling open.

"Who . . . who are you?"

Standing in front of her was a wisp of a woman, nearly dwarfed by Cricket's height as he shut the door behind them. She was beautiful, fair-skinned, with bright lips, brown eyes, and a shock of turquoise hair. Penny had never seen anything like it. It fell in soft waves over her shoulders and down her back, a solid sheen of color.

"I'm Tatiana," the woman said, although Penny had already assumed as much. "It's nice to meet you, Penny, although I wish the circumstances were a little different." She walked over. "Beppe has spoken fondly of you and all the other girls."

"You . . . you know him well." It was another dagger, another secret. The way Tatiana's pale cheeks flushed a soft pink told Penny that this woman meant much to Beppe, and yet he'd never told Penny about her.

But then, why bother? Penny wasn't really his family.

She clutched the papers tight to her chest. Her eyes sought out Cricket, needing some familiarity in this world of the increasingly unknown. As if he knew, a smile lifted his lips and he stepped closer from where he leaned against the door frame.

Tatiana lowered a large leather bag to the ground. "Beppe and I have known each other for several years."

"So he's told you what he's done to us?"

Tatiana shook her head, her expression a not-quite-readable mix of frustration, understanding, and anger. "I actually know very little of what has transpired at the estate. Beppe kept his life here a secret as much as he kept me a secret from you all. Mostly for my safety. Cirillo has used me as leverage with Beppe since the beginning."

Penny winced at the thought of Master holding Beppe's relationship in such disregard, but really it only seemed to fit with everything else she'd learned.

Tatiana frowned as she took in the dirt and dust and disarray of the front room. "Cricket showed me Beppe's note. I wanted to see if he left a message for me as well."

"Do you think he's in danger?"

"I don't know." Tatiana walked to the shelves and stared at the objects, her back to Penny and Cricket. Her fingers danced over several of the mechanical trinkets. "When Cirillo is involved, anything is possible. Beppe could have been sent to look after a patient, as his letter indicated, or he may have been tasked with conducting research in a remote location. But I would be very surprised to find that he left willingly, considering his desire to keep watch over Rosaura."

"Rosaura?" Penny stepped closer.

Tatiana reached for a wooden box on the shelf. With deft fingers, she tilted it, twisted the top once, and pushed something on the side until the lid popped open. "As I figured." She pulled a folded piece of paper from within. Her gaze tripped over the words, and her mouth pursed together in a thin line. "*Dannazione.*" She cursed and crumpled the page. "He's always so cryptic. I realize the need for secrecy, but for once, a straight answer would really be beneficial."

Penny cast a quick glance at Cricket. He looked as surprised as she felt. "What does it say?"

"'Cirillo holds the key.'" She placed the balled-up note in her pocket and the box back on the shelf. "Honestly, I don't even know when he stashed the note here."

"What does it mean?" Penny dropped the loose pages on top of the book from Beppe's room and sank into a chair. Her head dropped into her hands. She was finding no answers, just more questions. "And what did you mean about Rosaura?"

Tatiana walked to the sofa across from Penny and sat on the edge of the arm. "Last year, Cirillo removed her from the estate and placed her in an asylum, where nobody would believe her ramblings could possibly be the truth. Then Cirillo approached Beppe a fortnight ago. He had some new experiments in mind and wanted to test them on Rosaura."

Penny shuddered and a chill swept over her arms. *New experiments.*

"Beppe couldn't let that happen. It was bad enough Rosaura had been kept a prisoner all this time. He freed her from the asylum, using his authority as physician for the estate. He kept her hidden at an inn on the outskirts of town and then moved her into my residence the day before his disappearance. We had to wait until after Cirillo questioned Beppe's involvement and checked my shop. It didn't take long."

"I talked to Rosaura briefly, this morning." Cricket crouched next to Penny, his eyes level with hers. "She wanted me to tell you to be careful. You can't react to any memories in front of the others, no matter how horrific they are, or Master is bound to lock you away as well."

And conduct experiments on me. Her throat tightened and she couldn't swallow. If Master saw Rosaura as a liability and an easy subject for testing, surely Penny faced the same risk.

She was unable to tear away from Cricket's gaze, from the depth of his pale eyes and the way they implored her to stay safe.

"We have to find a way out." Penny choked out the words and turned to Tatiana. "Did Beppe tell you how to get past the border?"

"I'm sorry." She shook her head in resignation.

Penny rose and paced across the room, frustration mounting. At the end of the shelves a lone doll head sat on its ear, stitching undone across the back. She shuddered and turned back. "Is there *anything* you can tell me? Why he and Master did this or how I can reverse what's been done?"

"In all the years I've known him, Beppe only ever told me what I needed to know. I wish I had pushed him for more information. But it's always been this way. Cirillo forbade him from telling me anything. Beppe came to me for salves and medication when his own resources failed, but he refused to tell me what they were for." She opened the flap to her bag and rummaged inside, finally pulling out four vials full of a clear liquid. Tatiana motioned Penny forward and placed them in her palm. "I did bring these to help with your headaches. I know they've been increasing in frequency."

"Thank you," Penny said. And she *was* thankful, but also disheartened and disappointed that Tatiana had nothing more to share.

Tatiana must have seen it in Penny's expression, because she reached across the table and folded her hands around Penny's fingers. "I'm so sorry for everything that's been done to you girls. Beppe cares for you all deeply and regrets ever having been involved with this program. But he's too involved and Cirillo has threatened him several times if he leaves."

Penny gripped the vials tight. She wanted to fling them across the room and let them shatter on the floor. What good were more tinctures for a headache when her life was in jeopardy?

5 milliliters.

She remembered the loose pages, grabbed them, and handed them to Tatiana. "Does this make sense to you? Is there a chance the numbers refer to your tinctures? Or perhaps something else?"

Tatiana flipped through the papers. "Perhaps. I've made a variety of formulas." She paused and read. "I can take these back to the shop and compare them to my records. I don't know that it will tell us much, but it's a place to start."

"This might be of help, too." Penny handed her the book. "You will let us know if you find anything?"

Tatiana nodded. "Of course. And I will look into Beppe's absence as well. I'm fearing more and more that it wasn't voluntary."

Penny stared out the window at the forest nudging against the cottage. She desperately wanted to flee, but not until she knew she could pass without the wolves attacking her. She had smelled them. Felt her skin tear. Seen the blood. If her mind could do that, it could certainly feel an animal rip out her organs and let her pulse slowly fade.

She couldn't take the chance, even though she hated to return to the manor. Hated feeling trapped. Trapped within the borders. Trapped with a man who was capable of erasing all her memories, all her thoughts.

Penny took a deep breath and willed herself to be strong. She would get through this. She would get answers. She would save herself and her *sorelle*. She turned to Cricket. "We need to return before my absence is noticed."

"I will stay a bit longer and look around." Tatiana pulled Penny into an embrace. "Stay safe. Run at the first sign of danger. Run and keep running."

Danger.

The first sign of danger had already passed.

She could only hope she didn't run out of signs.

CHAPTER 17

The ride back to the manor seemed to take mere minutes. They skirted the edge of the building and led the mare into the stable. Cricket slid off the saddle first and reached his hands to grip Penny's waist and help her down. A wave of heat raced through her body. Her heart slammed in her chest. "Shall we groom the horse?" Her voice came out breathy, as if she'd run to the badminton courts and back.

"I'd normally say yes, but I fear time is against us," Cricket said.

"Or perhaps time has run out altogether."

Their heads whipped in unison to see Primo standing in the stable entrance, his long, black overcoat brushing the ground behind him.

"Where have you two been?"

Penny's heart began to beat a different, more terrified rhythm. She glanced back and forth between the mare and Primo. There was no getting out of this, no way they could say they'd only come into the stable to feed the horses or prepare for a leisurely afternoon ride. Not when the animal behind them was covered in a sheen of sweat and in desperate need of a brushing.

"I took Penny for a ride." Cricket stepped forward so he mostly blocked her from Primo's view. "She twisted her ankle, and instead of keeping her cooped up, I thought fresh air would do her good."

"You failed to get permission." Primo's boots crunched on the dirt floor as he stepped closer.

"Master wasn't available, and I'm not allowed to interrupt him when he's busy." Cricket pointed at his bruised jaw, as if that were explanation enough.

Penny stayed as still as possible, her eyes trained on the ground at Primo's feet. His boots were black leather, worn in, but still shined and spotless.

The silence grew heavier and clogged her throat. Finally, Primo spoke. "I suggest you get back to the pantry, steward. I'll make sure the girl gets safely back to her room."

"I can take her," Cricket interjected.

"Just go," Penny whispered. She didn't want him to get in trouble on her account. "I'll come find you later."

Cricket straightened and walked toward Primo. "If you hurt her, I will sprinkle monkshood on your food." He leaned in close to Primo's ear. "You'll fall dead before you even taste it."

Primo's nostrils flared as if he wanted to tackle Cricket to the ground. Instead, he stalked over to Penny and pointed a finger toward the manor. She knew he wouldn't touch her, wouldn't forcefully drag her away, but there was no chance of escape. He was an ox, but he was fast.

She brushed past him and limped quickly toward the servants' entrance. Cool air whipped her face and tugged at her hair. She pulled her jacket together, tightening it over her chest, trying to hide.

Minutes later, they stood in the doorway to Master's private library. "I found her." Primo stood right behind Penny. His breath sent shivers down her spine.

Master stood in the center of the room, facing them. He nodded at Primo. "Thank you."

A grunt of acknowledgment and the door closed on her heels.

Master motioned for Penny to sit in a chair. She sat stiffly on the edge of the leather seat. The warmth of the wood furniture belied the coldness of the atmosphere. He pulled a second chair closer, directly across from her, and sat so his knees were on either side of hers. He leaned in close, a swath of dark hair falling over his eyebrow. His bright green eyes drew her into their depths. "Where were you, Penelope?"

Her mind fought to push through a fog of panic to come up with an excuse. Cricket had already told Primo they'd gone out for some fresh air. Master wouldn't believe it. But he also knew she couldn't have left the estate grounds. Not if he controlled the thoughts that kept her prisoner.

"To Grandfather's home." She stumbled on the word, nearly calling him Beppe. She rushed to speak further. "Cricket brought me some food for the noonday meal. When I told him the pain wasn't improving, he asked why Grandfather hadn't treated it. I said he'd been called away and Cricket suggested I go visit Grandfather's cabin, that surely he kept medicine stocked in the cupboards. I remembered I kept several vials in my chamber there." Penny reached into her pocket and pulled out the glass containers Tatiana had given her. "Cricket offered to saddle the horse so I wouldn't further injure my ankle. We were only gone a short time."

Penny swallowed the bitter taste that accompanied the lies. She fervently hoped he believed her, that it made sense. Who knew when Master had discovered her absence and sent Primo to hunt her? He had to believe her.

Silence filled the room, cloying and claustrophobic. Master's gaze had caught on the vials. She waited for more questions, for him to spin a web to further trap her in her own deceit. Instead, his question caught her off guard. "How is your ankle feeling now?"

"Better. Much better." She froze, her entire body on edge.

He exhaled slowly. "I told you I would treat it this evening." He sounded petulant. His knees tipped in, trapping hers between them. "I, too, have medicine at my disposal. If only you'd come to me, you could have avoided traipsing around the grounds. It's not always safe." His gaze focused on the wrist she'd covered unconsciously with her other hand.

"I . . . I apologize," she said. "I knew you were busy and I didn't want to bother you. Cricket was with me. . . ."

His jaw tightened.

"Cricket is merely a kitchen steward," Master spat. "I would suggest putting your faith in more capable hands next time." He leaned over and grasped her shoulders in his long fingers. His hands slid down along the length of her sleeves to her wrists. "I hate to think of anything happening to you."

She swallowed past the lump of confusion lodged in her throat. His behavior seemed so erratic. She'd expected a stoic and cruel punishment, and instead he was acting compassionate. It was disconcerting, and she could feel herself losing some of her drive to escape.

"You're under my care. I'm all you have left. Your family . . ."

Penny didn't hear the next few words. *Family*. What did he mean, he was all she had left? What had happened to them?

Or were the words yet further manipulation spilling from Master's mouth? Her desire to flee the estate sharpened to a needle point again.

"You will come to me first next time."

"Of course." Another lie.

He leaned back into the chair. "Oh, I don't need your assurance, Penelope. I can guarantee this won't happen again."

There it was.

She forced her lips into a smile, even as a band of fear gripped her chest. Master was done with benevolence. His words were a threat. And a promise. He was sure to change her thoughts that night, perhaps even erase what had happened the entire day so she wouldn't remember going to Cricket for help.

She needed to find Cricket.

Master broke into her desperate thoughts. "Let me walk you back to your room."

"I'm fine, sir." Penny stood. "Really. I'm certain you're very busy, and I've already taken up too much of your time."

Master ignored her. He rose and took her elbow. A flood of heat raced to her toes. Penny felt her body betray her as she leaned into his side, some sort of reflex that drew her to him. Was it the changes he'd made to her brain or something about Master himself?

Penny suddenly remembered to feign a limp. Master shifted one arm around her lower back, his fingers splayed on her waist to help her along. His hip brushed her side as they inched down the hall, through the main wing, and into the dormitory wing.

"I expect you to stay off your foot for the remainder of the afternoon." Master opened the door to her room. Penny quickly stepped in front of him, hoping to hide his view of her unmade bed and the pile of clothes beneath the quilt. It was to no avail. Master stood inches taller, and a single eyebrow rose at the sight.

She was doomed.

He knew everything. All of this lying and deceit was getting her nowhere closer to the truth. To her family. To escape. And there was a good chance she wouldn't remember anything the next morning. Master lifted a finger and tilted her chin so she was staring into his eyes. She felt her mind spinning, her body weightless. His face dipped closer, his lips nearing hers until they seemed to share breath. Her eyelashes fluttered closed, and then she felt the briefest touch as his lips pressed against her forehead.

He pulled away. "I must get back to my research."

The door closed behind him and Penny leaned against the cool wood. An ensemble of emotions battled for center stage. Desire and intrigue swelled her heart, warring with the fear and disgust that permeated her brain. The latter won because it all boiled down to one thing.

He was controlling her mind.

Her fingers closed into a fist and she raised it, ready to slam her knuckles into the door. She stopped as sobs shook her chest. She had to find Cricket before Master did something horrific. Before he pushed his experimentation any further.

Penny opened the door and peeked through the narrow slit to make sure the hall was empty. She dashed down the hall and began her search.

But he wasn't in the kitchen.

He wasn't in the dining hall.

He didn't serve them supper.

He was nowhere to be found.

❧ — ❧

Night had fallen and Penny lay in bed, the quilt pulled up to her shoulders. She faced the wall and counted, up to one hundred and back down to zero. The clock had barely chimed the eleventh hour when the door to her chamber opened and light from the hall sliced across the floor of her room.

Penny felt her entire body tense, but she forced her breaths to stay long and even. Master's shadow fell across the bed briefly, and then the door closed and the light disappeared.

It was several more counts to one hundred before Penny shoved the quilt off and stood. Her feet bare, she padded down the hall toward the main wing. The servants' quarters were in a separate wing of the manor, and she hoped she might find Cricket there. Worry knotted into a pit in her stomach. She feared Master had harmed Cricket again.

Or worse.

The stone floor was frigid beneath her soles and a cool breeze seemed to whistle along the corridor, the sconces casting a dancing orange glow on the walls. Penny hurried, running nearly on tiptoe, until she got to the end of the narrow hall and paused. A glance in either direction, and she darted into the smaller hallway that led to the kitchen. She snuck past the entrance-way and down another passage. It was darker here, lamps lit only occasionally. Her steps slowed and then stopped alto-gether as she found herself turning to face a door, ornate and firmly closed.

A fog dampened her thoughts, the walls around her turning hazy and pale. Everything seemed softer, the edges blurred. Her fingers reached of their own volition toward the doorknob, and she twisted it open. She knew instinctively that it led to a set of stairs, descending deep beneath the building. Her feet glided forward and her head smacked something hard. She jerked back, rubbing at the now-tender spot on her forehead.

The trance lifted, confusion rushing in to take its place. Penny frowned. It wasn't a staircase at all, but a wall. A gray, rough brick wall.

Penny looked around and back again, wondering how there could be a door leading to nowhere. She backtracked and turned down another corridor. This one she knew was the entrance to the servants' wing.

At least she thought she knew.

It was entirely possible she'd gotten turned around in this maze of a manor.

Penny paused, shifting her weight from foot to foot as she pulled on a lock of hair. She couldn't exactly knock on random doors, waking the servants to ask for Cricket's room. That would be rather scandalous. But she couldn't quite remember which was his, either.

She needed to see him, now more than ever. "Cricket," she called in a high-pitched sort of whisper. She stopped outside each door, trying to listen for movement inside.

At the fifth door, a rustling sound emerged. She held her breath.

"Cricket?" She whispered his name again and the door flew open.

He stood there, hair rumpled and broad shoulders blocking her view of the room. He peered past her as if to check to see if she'd been followed and then motioned for her to come inside. He shut the door and she relaxed infinitesimally.

"What are you doing here?" He rubbed at his arms and she realized he wore only a thin cotton shirt and loose pants. Her cheeks warmed at the intimacy of being in his chamber and seeing him dressed so casually.

A single lamp burned on the wall near his headboard. His room was much like hers, barren except for a narrow bed, a dresser, and an armoire. The space was neat and tidy, no errant clothing piled on the floor, and it smelled of Cricket. Cinnamon and honey.

"Are you all right?" Penny turned back to him, suddenly remembering why she was there. "Did anyone harm you?" She took a visual inventory, looking for further bruises on his face, or a black eye, or some sort of bandage.

Nothing.

Cricket shook his head, and she exhaled in relief. "Where were you at supper, then?"

"Mucking the stalls. That was my punishment. I think Primo came up with that one on his own. Master certainly would've prescribed something worse. I only came back to the manor an hour ago to bathe." He stepped closer, and the room felt significantly smaller. "Why are you here?"

"I needed you." She shifted her weight, feeling suddenly nervous. Heat raced up her spine and spread to her fingers and toes. "I mean, I wanted to make sure you were okay. But—" Fear swelled her throat and nearly choked her.

"Penny, what's going on?" He led her to the mattress and she sat on the edge. She leaned forward, swallowing and gasping for breath. "Did he hurt you?"

She shook her head. "He might. He will. He's definitely going to change my thoughts again." She recounted the afternoon with Master.

"I can't stop thinking he must do this all the time." Penny stood and paced the short length of the room. "Whenever I disobey him, or do something he doesn't like, he changes my memory like that." She snapped her fingers. Her pacing stopped short and she rubbed at the goose pimples erupting on her arms. Anger shoved aside any fear of Master's control. "What a horrible, twisted power to have over someone."

The words were bitter.

"Penny, I'm here for you. I won't let it happen again. I know my touch seems to somehow invoke the truth. . . ." He glanced at the bed, and even in the dim lighting, Penny could see his cheeks redden. "Do you . . . would you feel more comfortable . . ." He rubbed at his jaw. "Would you like to stay here? Tonight? In case he changes your thoughts. That way I'd be here to pull you out of it."

Penny wanted to hug him, if only they weren't wearing so very little clothing. Now it was her turn to blush. "Thank you so much."

An awkward silence descended, and then they both spoke at the same time. "I'll take the floor."

"You can't possibly," Penny said. "It's your room."

"I insist." Cricket pulled an extra quilt from out of the armoire.

And so it happened that they both stretched out on the floor, ignoring the comfort of the bed altogether. Cricket lay on his side, angled so he faced the window. Penny curled alongside him, leaving a couple of inches of space between them.

She lifted her hand. "Stay still."

He froze as she put her palm flat against his bare arm and wrapped her fingers loosely around his bicep. He took several shallow breaths and then relaxed back into the quilt.

"Are you sure you'll be comfortable down here?" He twisted his head to look at her.

She nodded and synced her breathing with the rise and fall of Cricket's chest. Soon enough she fell asleep.

※ ※

Penny's eyelids flew open and her fingers reached to press into her temples, trying to shove away the remnants of pain. She rolled away from Cricket, so as not to wake him, and crouched near the door with her forehead resting against the cool wood.

The searing pain hadn't been nearly as bad as the last time. It faded quickly, and in its place was another memory.

My satin gown swishes at my feet as I'm whirled around the ballroom. . . . The orchestra plays a waltz. . . . Master's grip on me is tight enough to break my bones. . . . "You are mine." His jaw is clenched and the words barely escape his lips. "You are not like the other girls. I will not let anyone else have you." . . . I fight not to look across the dance floor, at the gentleman watching me. . . . Master yanks me in the opposite direction. "You are done here."

Penny slid up the door, stretching to standing. Pale light tinted the room through the window, and she guessed it was nearing dawn. She needed to get back to her room before her *sorelle* awoke.

Before anyone caught her out and about in the manor.

With a last glance at Cricket, and a whisper of thanks, she slipped away.

Penny's pulse tripled as she raced from shadow to shadow down the corridors back to her room. Once she was safely inside, she dared to breathe again. It was only by good fortune that she'd escaped notice during the trek back to the dormitory quarters.

Even though she'd slept on a hard floor all night, and woken early with the pain of nails piercing her forehead, Penny knew she couldn't fall asleep again. She felt strangely refreshed and decided to ready herself early. After she had combed her hair and twisted it into a high bun, she paced the small room, her thoughts all awhirl. She couldn't keep up this dishonesty and sneaking around much longer. But she didn't have much of a choice. She couldn't leave the estate boundaries. She was as much a prisoner as Rosaura had been in the asylum.

She hoped Tatiana would send news regarding Beppe, or something that might help Penny escape. And in the meantime, she was determined to solve the mystery of her past. Master had mentioned her family. But how to get more information?

The pacing continued. Penny tapped at her forehead with her fingernails, willing her brain to think. There must be something she could do, somewhere she could search for information.

She assumed any family members would still remember her, that Master's mind control didn't extend outside the estate. So either they thought she had disappeared or they knew she attended the school. Perhaps they encouraged it and had been sending her correspondence all this time. She had to find out, had to look around. She tapped harder, wondering where Master would keep such private items.

In his private library.

Cupboards and panels lined an entire wall of the room. She'd been there only yesterday. She would sneak in.

At the first possible chance.

❧ ❧

Penny sucked in her stomach so Signora Moretti could shove a pin through the basque at her waist. After their normal morning coffee, the girls had been rushed to a final costume fitting. Somehow, despite all the sugar cubes Penny chewed at every opportunity, she'd lost weight since the last time she'd donned the tutu. Signora muttered to herself, "It's a wonder I get anything done around here with alterations you all are needing. But things *have to be perfect.*" The final four words were said with a flawless imitation of Madame Triolo's nasally inflection.

Penny snorted.

With her hands on Penny's hips, Signora gently spun her so she faced the mirror propped against the wall. The tutu was made of several stiff layers of itchy muslin and buckram in a sickly shade of green and pale pink. The bodice was green and embroidered with ivy that wound up to the neckline and over to the bell cap sleeves.

She looked like a dying tulip.

Signora reached nimble fingers to tuck a loose tendril of hair behind Penny's ear. "You are to be wearing a flower garland in your hair, no?"

Penny nodded. Then shook her head. She wasn't sure. Her chest tightened, straining against the costume. She couldn't remember whether she and Bianca were to wear garlands like the other girls or an ornamental headpiece.

It was trivial, something easily forgotten in all the madness of the past few days, but Penny felt a wave of panic threatening to overtake her. This wasn't something Master would have changed, so was she possibly losing memories as she gained new ones? She feared her mind was a sieve, arbitrary thoughts pushing others out until she would find herself with nothing. An empty shell of a person.

She sank down onto the dais. The rough fabric scratched her legs, and her eyes burned with unshed, scalding tears. She hated this, hated Master.

"What is wrong?" Signora looked worried, her olive skin lined with wrinkles as she dipped down to look into Penny's eyes. "You are tired, no?" Long fingers patted Penny's own. "The gala is causing much stress. Only three more days and then you sleep for a month."

Penny nodded and forced a quivering smile.

"What's going on over here?" Bianca swept in, her tutu rustling and nearly poking Penny in the eye.

Signora narrowed her eyes at Bianca. "Nothing. We are just finishing."

Bianca collapsed on the dais and tucked her head near Penny's, as if the two were the best of friends and Penny would spill all her secrets. Penny scooted away and took a deep breath. "It's only a headache."

"You know . . . all these headaches . . . and drama . . ."

Bianca drawled out the word. "This reminds me of something. Or someone . . ."

Penny braced herself.

"Yes . . . this reminds me of . . ." Bianca leaned in and whispered, "Rosaura." She shifted away, staring at Penny as if to gauge her reaction. "She acted much the same way as you are. Forgetting things. Blinding headaches." She bounced to her feet. "I wonder if Master knows. This is important; I must tell him."

Penny grabbed Bianca's wrist and yanked her back down. "You will do nothing of the sort." She had no idea why Bianca retained memories of Rosaura, but Penny couldn't let on that she knew anything about her. Not Rosaura's time at the estate, her being taken away, or her recent nonsanctioned release. If this was a test, she couldn't fail it. Not now. "We've never had a girl here by that name. Perhaps you're the one with a problem." She hissed the words. "But I won't bother Master now with such nonsense. It is a wretched idea, what with the gala so close. Leave well enough alone."

Bianca's eyes pierced hers, as if she could berate her with only a glance. "Interesting. I wonder why you've forgotten your friend so easily."

Penny could only mask her expression and shrug. "I don't know what you're talking about."

"Yes, well, it's probably for the best." Bianca inched her arm from Penny's grasp. "I hope you don't succumb to the same malady. I'd hate to see you escorted from the manor so close to the performance."

Penny wiped her palm on her skirt, dismissing Bianca and letting her have the last word. With a false grin, Bianca rose to her feet and stalked away just as Ana bounded over, Maria in tow. "Did you hear? Master is hosting a dinner tomorrow evening! The prince will be here! And we're to attend!"

Penny wondered if Ana would forever talk in exclamations.

"It's a chance to show us off before the gala," Maria said. "And we're to miss afternoon classes to get ready."

Penny's pulse beat out a discordant rhythm as she slipped her housedress back on over her underclothes. The posturing itself was enough to make her nervous, but now she had to feign innocence and dote on Master. Any slipup could clue him into what she knew, could make him tamper with her thoughts even further.

She would have to play it perfectly, the role of a lifetime.

It was time for *il pranzo*, and she still hadn't found an opportunity or a way to sneak to Master's library. Warm-ups in the studio had been followed by a dress rehearsal onstage and a quick history lesson in their classroom. The girls were all ravenous as they raced down the hall.

"I'll be right there," Penny murmured to Maria. "I have to change out of these slippers. I feel a hole forming in the toe."

Maria fluttered her fingers in a wave good-bye as Penny veered off toward the dormitory. Once she was certain the other girls were gone, Penny snuck back and headed in the opposite direction toward the main wing.

She yanked on a strand of hair as she tiptoed onto the plush carpeting and into the foyer. A maidservant rushed by, a pile of linens stacked nearly to her nose. Big brown eyes peered over the top and she barely tipped her head to acknowledge Penny.

Past the sprawling stairs and down another short hallway, Penny arrived at the closed door to Master's library. She cupped her ear to the wooden panel but heard nothing. With a twist of the handle, she eased the door open and slipped inside.

She took a deep breath, the scent earthy with hints of tobacco and cedar, and stood with her back against the door as she surveyed the room. She hadn't really had a chance to take it in the day before; her nerves had been strung so taut from having been caught with Cricket.

Master's large desk was an island in the center of the floor, with plush chairs arranged like ships around it. The drapes were pulled open along the back wall to show off the expanse of lake beyond the clear glass windows. A narrow door on the right wall stood closed. Rich maple shelves lined the opposite wall. They were filled with gilded books and odd wooden sculptures. Underneath the shelves, a row of cabinets extended the length of the wall.

They looked as good a place to start as anywhere.

Penny pulled open the first cabinet to find an array of notebooks, carefully arranged and labeled with years on the front covers. She lifted a stack and flipped through them: 1861, 1863, 1865. They were dusty and of no interest to Penny. She would've been just a babe.

She dropped them back in the drawer and a loose piece of paper drifted from the pages to settle on the floor. Her eyes narrowed. The world *Lupo* was scrawled at the top right corner of the sheet. The center was filled with a sketch of some sort of body organ, bean-shaped, with notes all around it. The ink had been smeared in places, faded in others. But her eyes narrowed at some of the words.

. . . pain response . . . limited . . .
nodes . . . connect . . . and emotional knowledge . . .
disconnect . . . reroute signals

Nothing that spoke of getting past the wolves themselves. She shoved the paper back into the notebook and tried to shut the cabinet. It caught and she jiggled the handle until it slid into place.

Penny scooted farther down the length of the wall, glancing into each cupboard. She found more notebooks and even more books devoted to medicine and science. Pages were dog-eared, and slips of paper stuck out of the sides and tops of the books. Still nothing related to her or her *sorelle*.

She reached the last cabinet and squatted down to peer into the depths. The top shelf had collapsed at an angle; the heavy books sloped down to rest haphazardly at the edge.

Of course more books.

She slammed it shut and sat back on her heels. This was going nowhere, and she started to doubt Master would leave information out in the open for anyone to find.

The desk was the only other place to look. The surface was nearly spotless, the polished wood reflecting the sunlight streaming in from the window behind her. An inkwell and pen rested in one corner, a stack of envelopes in the other.

Two ornate drawer fronts sat on either side of the hard-backed chair pushed against the desk. Penny pulled on the brass handle of one, then the other.

They were both locked.

Good and bad. It meant something important lay within, but it also meant she'd have to find the key.

Her fingers reached underneath the desktop, feeling blindly for any sort of latch or other way to open the drawer.

Suddenly, voices trickled in from the outer hall.

"Let's talk in here."

Penny whirled around, trying to find a place to hide. She

certainly couldn't fit in the cupboards or under the desk. But the narrow door . . .

She reached the handle in two strides, twisted it, and hoped it wasn't locked. The panel flung open and she rushed inside, shutting it behind her. The only light in the small closet-size room was the slice that came in between the door and its frame. Penny inched backward until she bumped into a coat hanging from a hook on the wall. Several pairs of shoes were lined up neatly beside her. She tried not to touch anything and crouched down until she could sit on the cool wooden floor.

The voices were louder now; Master and his guest must've entered the room.

"Please have a seat. Can I offer you something to drink?"

"No, thank you." A woman's voice. Soft. Familiar. *Tatiana*.

Penny gasped. Her hands flew to cover her mouth, terrified they'd heard the sound.

But Master was already responding, "Why exactly did you come here, Tatiana?"

"I want to know what happened to Beppe."

"He's away on business, of course." The chair scraped against the ground and Penny could picture Master sitting tall, hands clasped in his lap.

"What kind of business?"

"How are you feeling? When was the last time you had a treatment?"

"What kind of business?" Her voice sounded clipped, the consonants hard, as if she spoke through clenched teeth.

"I'm curious," he said, and Penny imagined him leaning forward, his fingertips steepled in front of him, "since you're here. Have you heard anything about the disappearance of a certain ex-student of mine?"

"I know Primo searched my home," Tatiana seethed. "You may think you can do anything you want, but you've crossed a line, Cirillo." A pause and her voice returned to normal. "I have no idea where Rosaura has gone. That's not why I'm here. I want to know where Beppe is. I think you're holding him captive. And if you've harmed him—"

It was Master's turn to sound clipped. "I would be cautious with your implications."

"Where is he?"

"Go home and take care of yourself. You wouldn't want to cause any alarm, now, would you? Beppe did teach me how to administer your treatment, and I have all the equipment here. But if something were to happen to me, I do wonder who would be left to help you."

Penny cringed.

"What about this?" The sound of paper rustling. "I know some of these were elixirs and serums I created. Not all of them, I hope, as I can't imagine using any of them in such high dosages." The pages Penny had given her the day before. Tatiana must have compared them to her logs.

"Where did you get those? Those are private."

"That's not the point. What have you been doing to these girls, Cirillo?"

"You think you can show up here and blackmail me? Is that what this is?" The words were so very soft but laced with arsenic.

"No. But I think we both have something that the other one wants. You need my help as much as I need yours." Her voice sounded resigned.

"It's time you returned to your shop," Master said. Footsteps echoed across the room. "I'm sure I'll have news for you within the week."

"What about the gala? He would want to attend." Tatiana's voice sounded farther away, as if she'd stepped into the corridor.

"I'm afraid that's not going to be possible." He paused. *"Arrivederla."*

Penny waited, shifting to ease a cramp in her thigh. She could only hope Master had left as well, returning to whatever activity he'd been doing before Tatiana's arrival. The entire conversation left her unsettled. Beppe wasn't on a business trip, that much was clear.

The sliver of light remained steady, no shadows cutting off the ray of sun that shone through the gap in the door frame. She'd waited long enough. Her fingers had barely grasped the handle when she heard his voice.

"You can come out now."

$\mathcal{P}$enny winced and took a deep breath. She squared her shoulders and stepped out into the harsh glare of sunlight. She blinked away the brightness to find Master shaking his head at her. He crossed his arms over his starched white shirt. Fear pushed at her chest but she shoved it back down, taking a nod from Tatiana's strength in confronting Master mere moments before.

"What am I going to do with you?"

She knew it was rhetorical. She also knew she had only one chance to talk herself out of the precarious situation.

"I'm so very sorry. I was looking for you"—she cast her gaze downward—"and thought you might be working. When you weren't here, I figured I could wait. But . . ." She let her voice trail off and lifted her gaze to him again. "I heard you in the corridor, talking to someone else. I thought you might be angry to find me inside. So I hid. I know it was foolish and disrespectful, but I promise on my mother's grave that I didn't mean to eavesdrop."

At least that one bit was true. She certainly hadn't expected

Tatiana to show up at the estate. The rest of it, well, the lies were becoming more and more easy to spin. And the mother's grave was a nice touch, since it was his manipulation that had caused her to think her mother was dead all this time.

"How did you . . . ," she started, and he finished the question for her.

"Know you were in the closet?" He waited for her to nod. "I am very much in tune with my surroundings, Penelope. I could hear you rustling inside."

She should have known.

"As to why you were in my office to begin with, I don't know if I believe you." He cocked his head to the side and studied her.

Penny tried her best to stay still, to keep her breaths even. He couldn't know she no longer trusted him and was looking for answers. He couldn't know that her memories were returning. He'd lock her away like he had Rosaura, conduct tests, run experiments. "I promise I wanted to talk to you. I've been feeling out of sorts after twisting my ankle. I'm worried about the gala. I hoped you might have some advice." She rushed through the words, panic making her verbose, desperate to explain. She slowed down her stammering. "I'm sorry."

He paced to the door and held it open. "I'll walk you to your room."

"But my studies . . ." The entire afternoon stretched in front of her. He couldn't possibly intend to keep her in her chamber. Panic clawed at her chest.

"I'll have your schoolwork sent to you." Master rubbed at his temples and then motioned her toward him. He gripped her elbow tightly, as if to prevent her from bolting. Her body reacted as always, with a rush of heat and a craving to lean into him. She tried to tamp it down as they walked to the dormitory.

"Where were you?" Bianca's eyes narrowed as Penny rounded the corner into the corridor that led to their classrooms. "You missed the entire meal."

"Good afternoon, Bianca." Master stepped forward and her eyes widened. "Penelope will be absent from her afternoon studies. Will you please take precise notes and gather any study material that she might need to catch up?"

Bianca nodded. "Of course."

"Thank you. Now, if you'll excuse us."

Bianca realized she'd blocked their path and slipped to the side of the hall. "You get all the attention. It's not fair," she hissed in Penny's ear as she passed.

Penny shuffled farther ahead, not bothering to respond. Let Bianca think what she wanted. But even as the anger started to boil, a thought occurred to Penny and the frustration settled to a simmer. Bianca was more controlled than any of them. She was Master's perfect puppet. Perhaps her animosity and control weren't *really* her, as much as dancing wasn't really Penny. She was one of the oldest girls at the estate, one of the first pupils. It only made sense that she was the first one to respond to Master's needs, the first one to take charge. It was as if she was responsible for molding the girls, too.

A glimmer of empathy caused Penny to glance back over her shoulder. She promised herself that she would save Bianca.

She would save them all.

✦

You don't need to lock the door. Penny leaned against the door and slid down, the words barely a whisper that never left her mouth.

She couldn't fight Master or give him any further reasons to suspect her memories were shifting.

But when the lock had turned, a part of Penny's heart cracked, too. She fought against the dread that seemed desperate to fill her lungs and drown her.

She closed her eyes and rested her hands flat on the cool floor. Cricket would come looking for her. Bianca would bring her books. She wouldn't be alone or trapped in the room forever.

Penny stood and paced. She stopped in front of the small, clouded window and peered out over the field at the back of the manor. Three stilts circled in the air, equally spaced apart, their wings tipped at the exact same angles.

It was uncanny to watch. Mechanical and unnatural.

Penny spun away from the glass and collapsed on her bed. She pulled the lumpy pillow over her head, and then, only then, did she let herself cry.

She must've cried for hours. Cried for herself and the sense of loss she felt about her childhood, her memories. Cried for her family, if she had one, who had been missing her all this time. Cried for her *sorelle*, who most likely didn't have a clue what had been done to them . . . what was still being done to them. For her future, which might turn out to be horrible . . . Master could very well be sitting in his library, planning ways to remove her from the estate. Permanently.

Her eyes were swollen, her skin tight where the tears had dried on her cheeks, and her chest hurt from all the sobs. There was a light rap at the door, and she brushed her palms over her face.

She pushed herself up from the bed and stepped close to the wood frame. "Who is it?" She knew it wasn't Master. He had the key.

"It's me, Cricket. Are you all right? I ran into Maria, and she said you'd been dismissed for the afternoon. What's going on?"

"I'm locked in." She leaned her cheek against the door.

She could hear his sharp intake of breath. "I'll be back in a moment."

Loose strands of hair stuck to her cheek, and she pulled them away with trembling fingers. She brushed them back and braided her hair down the side. The room was nearly dark, the sky outside her window a somber shade of navy. She went to the dresser and lit her lamp.

A scratching sounded at the door.

"Cricket?"

"Yes." A *cling*, a *clink*, and some more scratching.

Finally, the door eased open. Cricket stepped inside and shut it behind him. He wore his apron and a worried half smile. He must've come as soon as Maria told him. Penny could read the concern in his expression as he took in her tearstained face.

He placed a plate, covered by a napkin, on her nightstand and stepped closer. "What happened?" He brought his hands slowly to her shoulders. She sighed and leaned into his chest. New tears began to form, but she dashed them away before they could fall.

"Master caught me in his private library."

His breath whistled as he inhaled through his teeth. "That's not good."

Penny snorted, the sound taking her by surprise. Her shoulders shook with uncontrollable laughter. She knew it was inappropriate, completely uncalled-for, and bizarre, but she couldn't seem to stop. "No. It's *not* good." She lifted her head to look at him.

His pale eyes watched her with something between amusement and worry. "What were you doing there?"

She fell back onto her bed, her legs dangling off the side so her feet could brush the floor. She patted the quilt and Cricket sat beside her. The mattress sank and his leg brushed hers.

"I was looking for correspondence from my family. Letters, notes, information about myself. Photos, my name . . ." She winced, wondering if Penelope was even her given name. "There has to be information about us girls, something, somewhere."

He picked at a thread on her quilt. "Did you find anything?"

Penny shook her head. "His desk was locked, but I doubt there could have been much in the drawers anyway. Certainly not enough information to cover twelve girls. Thirteen. Fourteen. She bolted upright. "Cricket, have you heard anything about the girl? Extra food being prepared and sent somewhere in the manor? I wonder if she's here or if there is another workshop on the estate grounds."

He shook his head. "I've asked around, but nobody knows. The chef seemed to think a new girl is scheduled to arrive shortly."

"I wish we knew where Beppe was. I wonder if he could save her before her thoughts are all scrambled and her memories erased."

Silence grew like a living thing between them. Penny tucked a leg beneath her.

Cricket stared at the floor. His voice was soft when he spoke again. "I'm worried about what Master will do to you."

"I know." Penny wrapped her arms across her chest, suddenly cold.

"I think you should leave. Tonight. You can hide out at Beppe's cabin if necessary, until we can figure out a way to get you past the boundary."

"Cricket, I can't. He can still control my mind at the workshop." She paused and glanced at the door, imagined the hallway and other chambers beyond. "And I don't know if I can just run out on the girls. They don't know to fight him. They don't know what's going on."

"But he could take you away, lock you up, tonight even. You can't help them then." He brushed his palm against the mostly faded bruise along his jaw.

"He won't. Not this close to the gala. I think . . ." She swallowed against the corset of fear crushing her lungs. "I think he would try to manipulate my thoughts here first. Push it further than he ever has." She nodded to herself. "Yes, he'd do that before trying to remove me from the estate."

Cricket dropped his head into his hands, raking his fingers through his hair repeatedly before looking at her. "Should I stay in your room tonight? To make sure you pull out of it?"

Penny wanted to tell him yes. She wanted to beg him to stay. But Master absolutely could not find Cricket in her chamber, and she didn't trust that he wouldn't stop by.

"I'll be fine."

Muffled voices drifted from down the hall.

"You're certain." Cricket rose and walked toward the door.

"I'm positive. We can't raise any further suspicion. I need to see what he does, what memories he tries to alter, so I know how to respond to him tomorrow."

He opened the door and slid through. "I have to lock this again, but I'll try to return later. I brought you a couple of pastries"—he nodded at the nightstand—"but I'll see about putting together a late supper."

"Thank you." Penny smiled at him.

"Good luck." He whispered the words before the door clicked shut and she heard the lock snap back into place.

It was louder than a gunshot.

CHAPTER 20

$\mathcal{P}$enny awoke to the sound of the bells pealing their wake-up call. Her eyes blinked open and squinted against the buttery sunlight streaming through her window. Leon curled into his tail at the end of the quilt, oblivious to the busy day ahead.

She reached for her memory album, but it wasn't on the nightstand as always. A glance around the room and she still didn't see it. Her eyebrows furrowed. She didn't have time to search; she needed to ready herself for rehearsal. She rose from bed and slipped into her chemise and skirt. With sweeping loops, she twisted her hair into a bun, wrapping it in a dark pink ribbon. She stopped in front of her small vanity, frowning at the circles under her eyes.

That wouldn't do. She was sure to run into Master this morning.

Dipping her hands into the basin, she splashed cool water onto her face and neck. She brushed her teeth with a brush and powder. Then she pinched her cheeks to bring a blush to the surface.

After wrapping the ribbons on her slippers up and over her

calves, she raced into the hall behind Maria. She threw her arms around her friend. "I can't believe the gala is almost here!"

Maria hugged her back. "You're in a chipper mood today. Are you excited for dinner this evening? I heard the prince arrived late last night."

"I wonder if we'll see him this morning. I heard he's dreamy." Ana brushed up behind her, her nimble fingers smoothing back a stray strand of Penny's hair.

Penny could recall seeing the prince at the previous year's gala, and Ana's assessment wasn't altogether false. However, nobody could hold a candle to Master.

They made their way quietly toward the dining room. Penny waited patiently for her turn to pour a small cup of coffee. She added a scant bit of sugar and cream, not too much, and sipped on the drink. Her stomach rumbled, but she ignored it. It was a mere pittance to pay for perfection.

A female servant in an apron slid in from the kitchen to replenish the sugar cubes. Penny stared at the door, feeling as if something was missing.

"Are you finally feeling better?" Bianca's voice was scathing, and Penny turned to find her glaring from across the room.

Penny glanced around before realizing the question was directed at her. "I . . . feel fine."

Bianca's teeth gritted together and she spun on a heel. Penny blinked at her back, confused. She leaned toward Ana. "Why did she ask me that?"

"You hurt your ankle and you've been feeling a bit under the weather," Ana murmured. "You missed all your classes yesterday. Dinner, too."

Penny tugged on a strand of hair and twirled it around her finger.

"Don't. You'll mess up your bun." Ana tucked it back into the ribbon. "Master likes us all neat and tidy."

"Of course. Everything for Master," Penny said. But she still pondered Ana's strange revelation as they walked toward the studio. Penny didn't recall missing classes yesterday; she didn't recall much of yesterday at all. Just a vague sense of routine and preparation for the gala.

With her chin lifted and her posture perfect, she greeted Madame and slid into place at the barre. Her entire body relaxed into the stretches, her limbs lengthening and warming up as they moved through their positions.

They ran through the performance, flawlessly, of course. Madame pulled her aside as the girls took a quick break and sipped from cups of water. "*Brava*, Penelope. I'm so glad to see you paying attention. You were impeccable."

Penny gave a small smile, even though she didn't quite understand. She always paid attention.

Madame clapped her hands and motioned the girls forward. "Let's move to the grand hall and run through a last rehearsal before *il pranza*." Penny fell into the back of the line as the girls made their winding way to the main section of the house. Suddenly, the girls fell silent and stood straighter. Penny could hear Master talking to someone, his baritone sending a shiver down her spine.

She rounded the corner to see his head tipped toward a dashing young man with dark lashes that framed even darker eyes. His nose was long and straight, his jawline strong and square. And the thick auburn waves of his hair looked soft enough to sink her fingers into. His palm rested on the ivory hilt of a walking cane.

Prince Jacobus.

Penny remembered the prince at last year's gala. He had a perpetual grin on his face. He was lighthearted, gracious, and complimentary, his lips firm but soft when he kissed the back of her hand. She'd seen him watching from afar, his gaze on her even when her *sorelle* took center stage.

It was the same gaze he gave her now as he and Master greeted Madame and each of the girls in turn. The prince graced them each with a smile as they passed, but he seemed very aware of Penny at the back of the line. She ducked her head, knowing somehow that Master would be angry with her if she acknowledged his attention. Master didn't like the prince; that much was obvious to everyone.

Penny kept her eyes on her slippers as she neared them. She was almost past when Master spoke.

"Penelope." It was a plea and a question and resignation all wrapped up in four syllables.

Her chin jerked up and her eyes met his.

He stared at her. "How are you . . ."

"I feel fabulous—"

The prince interjected. "You're looking especially lovely this morning. A healthy glow on your cheeks. All prepared for the midnight dance, I assume. I'm looking forward to it immensely. Even more so to dinner this evening. Perhaps we can find time for a quick waltz?" He smiled down at her.

Master's fingers wrapped around Penny's shoulder and pulled her tight against his side. He made a point to glance at the prince's cane. "I think you'd find it rather difficult."

The prince twisted the head of his cane so it spun in a circle on the polished floor. His jaw tensed, but he didn't respond to Master's provocations. "Well, I'll look for you at dinner. I'm sure we'll have much to talk about."

Penny ducked her head again and moved past the pair. Dinner. She wondered if Cricket would be there serving the guests.

Cricket?

The kitchen steward?

She raced into the ballroom. Madame sat at the piano, her fingers ready to play the opening notes. Penny nearly tripped onto the stage as yet another thought distracted her. She'd been with Cricket recently. Running through the woods to . . . somewhere. Or were they running *from* something? He'd been . . . protecting her.

It was like her brain had tied itself into a series of knots. Pulling on a strand only confused her more, led to more questions. She rubbed at her temples, wondering if she was dreaming. The entire morning had been odd.

The music began and Penny forced herself to focus on the easy rhythm of dance. She leapt, she spun, and all the while her mind twisted its own tale. After a series of *jetés*, she twirled off stage right. Catching her breath, she rested her forehead against the cool wall.

Think. Think. Think.

Everyone had been asking her how she felt.

She couldn't remember what had happened yesterday.

Yesterday.

She willed herself to remember.

Yesterday.

It came back in bits and spurts, like jelly filling the pockets of air inside a pastry roll. Memories of the past week bubbled to the surface. She was in danger. All the girls were in danger. Penny glanced down at her practice wear in dismay. She despised dance and the gala and . . . Master.

Penny fought back a groan as she recalled the dinner that

evening. She'd have to keep up the pretense for hours, especially after how docile she'd been that morning. He couldn't know that his manipulations had failed.

Cricket would not be happy.

Cricket.

Somehow he was the key in all this, even without his touch. Mere thoughts of him had brought her true memories to the surface.

But he'd promised to find her that morning, in case this very thing happened. He hadn't. She gnawed at her lip. So much could've happened during the evening hours when Master influenced her memories.

She had to find Cricket.

Penny heard the music swell, signaling her cue to enter stage right. She eased away from the wall. Her movements weren't nearly as light as before, her leaps fell short, and her *pirouette* felt wobbly. She could see frustration glint in Madame's eyes when she dared to glance over, but she couldn't help it. Her love of dance disappeared as soon as she realized the falsehood behind it.

But she'd trudge through, paint a smile on her lips, gush over the costumes, anything to keep them from suspecting the truth.

❧ ❧

The hours of pretending exhausted her more than the rehearsal itself. Penny covered a yawn that stretched her mouth in an exaggerated oval and rushed to join Maria and Ana as they left the studio. She hooked her arms through theirs and nodded along with their chatter, hoping Madame wouldn't drag her back into the room for some much-deserved reprimands.

They neared the dining hall and Penny straightened, hoping

to catch a glimpse of Cricket. The buffet was already lined with steaming soups, lemon-drenched vegetables, and puffed pastries, but Cricket was nowhere in sight.

Penny gathered a plate of food and set it on the table, intentionally pushing it too far and knocking over her glass of water.

"Sorry! I'll go grab some fresh napkins." Before anyone could speak she'd rushed to the doorway, through the small corridor, and into the kitchen.

The room was heavy with steam and smelled of oregano and basil. Penny slid along the outer walls, her back to the shelves piled high with spices, dried goods, and jars of pickled vegetables. She spotted the *pasticcere* and moved over to him. "Have you seen Cricket?" she whispered.

"What are you doing here?" His eyes widened and his floured hands trembled over the marble countertop.

"I haven't seen him all morning. Do you know where he is?" She tried to keep from ogling the piles of date scones stacked on platters off to the side.

He shook his head. "I haven't seen or heard from him."

Penny's chest tightened. *Where could he be? What has Master done to him?* She backed away. "Well, thanks anyway."

"Have a scone." He offered her the pastry as if it was a consolation prize.

"Thank you." Penny snatched the scone and took a bite as she hurried back toward the dining hall. She chewed and swallowed, hardly tasting any of it as fear for Cricket's whereabouts dulled her senses. He would've come searching for her, if he could. She knew that with all certainty.

Which meant that he couldn't.

The rest of the afternoon passed in a fog, Penny's mind chasing the various reasons Cricket might have been delayed. He could be in town running errands. He could've been taken to the asylum for disobeying Master. He could be suffering from food poisoning, unable to leave his bed. If only she had time to race to his room to check on him.

But time was not on her side.

❧ ❧

The girls were released from their French lessons early so they could dress for dinner.

"*Au revoir*, Madame," Penny called out as she walked toward the door. The wall surrounding it was painted with a whimsical landscape, so out of character with the rest of the stark classroom. Many of the rooms had these random murals featuring fantastical characters: dragons, fairies, and elves. Bizarre.

"*Au revoir, Penelope. Sois sage.*" She peered over her pince-nez at Penny. "*Et fais attention.*"

Penny frowned as she made her way down the hall. Why would Madame Desrochers tell her to behave herself and take care? She couldn't get into *that* much trouble at dinner. Or perhaps it was more than that.

Perhaps it was a warning.

But a warning from someone in Master's employ.

Strange. Penny chewed her lower lip. She wondered if it was an invitation to talk to Madame. But how could she possibly trust her?

The girls made their way back toward the dormitory, arms flailing and high-pitched words showcasing their excitement for the evening's festivities.

Penny eased closer. "I wonder if Cricket will be there. Has anyone seen him?" She tried to act nonchalant, hoping the girls might have spotted him.

Ana chimed in first. "Why would we see the kitchen steward? Does he normally serve us dinner?"

A dash of fear tripped down her spine. Ana hadn't blushed when she mentioned Cricket's name. She didn't even know what meals he worked. Master must be reprogramming her mind so she would forget her feelings for Cricket. She had to find Cricket. She had to find Beppe and a way for this madness to stop altogether. An entire day had passed and she was no closer to an answer.

Penny left the girls at their rooms with a meager smile and a wave of her fingers before she fled to her own chamber. She threw open the door and halted in dismay.

A gown lay on her bed, the skirt draped over the edge, where it puffed up and out with a multitude of layers of crinoline underneath. The waist was narrow, the bodice tight. It wasn't anything she'd have chosen for herself.

At least it wasn't pink.

Penny lifted the dress and held it against her waist as she

looked down. The jade-green satin shifted and settled like ripples in the lake. She knew without a doubt it would fit her like a glove, but she still didn't want to wear it. She let the dress fall from her fingers, watching as it settled into a pretty puddle at her feet.

She collapsed on the bed, the lumps in the mattress pressing into her shoulder blades. Penny didn't want to go to the dinner. It was a waste of time and nearly as bad as the gala, but in many ways even worse. She'd be expected to smile, to dote, to make small talk with everyone there. At the gala, the guests were free to dance and mingle with one another, and there would be other entertainment to distract the crowd. At tonight's dinner, the girls *were* the entertainment. And she'd have to pretend she knew nothing.

A rap at the door only caused more stress.

"Yes." She didn't even bother to raise her head from the coverlet.

"Signorina?" It was one of the maidservants.

"What?" The word was a sigh of exhaustion and frustration.

"I'm here to help you get ready. We have a bath prepared."

Penny nearly launched off the bed. *A bath.* Why didn't she say so in the first place? The girls usually took cold showers in a communal bathing space. A bath, in a separate room, away from prying eyes, was used only for special occasions.

Today must be one of them.

With a yank, Penny opened the door and nearly fell into the girl's arms. The maid narrowed her eyes at something in the room. Penny glanced over her shoulder to see the gown still on the floor, getting more wrinkled with each passing second. "Oh. Sorry." She ran to scoop it up and arranged it quickly on the bed, smoothing out the satin beneath her palms.

With a raised eyebrow and a shake of her head, the maid spun on her heel and padded away. Penny raced to catch up. The maid stopped outside the private bathing room and waved her inside. "I will be back in a few moments to wash your hair."

A large porcelain tub sat in the middle of the room, three marble tile steps leading up to the lip. Jasmine-scented steam curled off the water in fragile tendrils. Glass bottles, filled with oils and tiny beads and topped with cork stoppers, sat on a low shelf next to flower-shaped soaps and wooden brushes.

After slipping out of her day clothes, Penny made certain to fold them neatly in a pile and climbed into the tub. She sank into the water. The tension of the last few days eased a bit from her muscles, and she wondered if she could stay there through supper. Sure, her skin would be wrinkly as an overdried prune, but it was a small price to pay to avoid all the guests.

Of course the door slammed open at that very moment, a cold gust of air seeping in along with the equally frigid and surly maidservant. She obviously thought this task beneath her and took out all her frustration on Penny's scalp as she kneaded the soap into her hair and scraped it all out again with her nails.

This was followed by an oil rinse and an aggressive brushing, as if the girl was determined to remove every bit of curl from Penny's hair.

"I can do it!" Penny finally yelped after a particularly painful yank.

"Splendid." The maid dropped the brush into Penny's outstretched fingers and handed her a thick cotton robe. "I need to see to the next girl. If you'll please get back to your chamber now?"

"Fine," Penny muttered. So much for relaxing. She scooped

up her clothes and dashed back to her room. Her hair was smooth at least, after all the combing and tugging. She twisted it back into an intricate knot and threaded in the length of green ribbon that had been left along with the dress.

With a wrinkle of her nose, she reached for the gown and stepped into its mass of skirts. She pulled the front up over her chest and opened the door to peek into the hall.

"Maria? Ana? I need someone to button me up." She stepped into the corridor.

Maria popped out of the next room, her rose-colored dress a near replica of Penny's. "Turn around."

Penny offered Maria her back and sucked in a breath as the buttons were tightened.

"Goodness, what did you eat today?" Maria pulled the fabric tighter.

"The same as you all: practically nothing," Penny squeaked out, her lungs still full of air. "Signora even had to take my costume in. This gown must have started out extra tight."

She finally exhaled when the last button hooked through the hole and held fast. "I only hope the seams don't split on you at dinner." Maria patted her shoulders. "But the color is lovely. I'm certain Master will adore it."

Penny shrugged. She couldn't care less what Master thought. In fact, she'd prefer the opposite.

"Here, let me dot your neck with a bit of rose oil." Maria glided into her room. "It's Master's favorite."

"No, thank you," Penny called out, trying to mask the look of horror she knew must be creeping over her face. She didn't want Master smelling her skin. "The bath was already scented with lavender."

She flew back to her chamber, stepped into matching satin

slippers, and deemed herself ready. It wasn't yet time for them to make an appearance, but she wanted to look for Cricket. With her skirts lifted so she didn't trip over them, Penny hurried down the corridors to the kitchen. The sharp smell of garlic and onion wafted from a large pot filled with escarole soup. A slab of counter was laid out with fresh ravioli dough waiting to be filled with butternut squash and brown butter.

"Penny," Cricket hissed from where he was working over some vegetables near the sink. "What are you doing here?"

Her shoulders fell with relief. He was safe. She stepped back into the hall and he followed her until she paused in the darkness of the corridor. He stood in front of her, all warmth and sunshine and freckles and mussed hair. "What's going on?"

"I was worried about you!"

"I'm sorry. I only just returned from town. Primo woke me before dawn with an errand to run." He shook his head. "I think they wanted me away from the estate. I had to pick up spices from the market, but there was no merchant that fit the description they'd given me. Then the glass smith hadn't finished the order for new bulbs yet. So I ended up returning to the estate empty-handed. And there was no word on Beppe. I asked everywhere." His words were a rush as he finished, as if to assure her he wasn't making up excuses. "I hated being away. I was terrified Master manipulated your thoughts last night. I'm so thankful he didn't."

"Actually . . ." She frowned. "I awoke this morning with no memories of the past few days."

He stepped closer. "But you managed to free your thoughts."

She looked down at her dress and brushed at the fabric. She couldn't tell Cricket that it was thoughts of him that had pulled her out of the trance. "I don't know how, really. . . . Things didn't make sense, and everyone kept asking how I felt. I guess my mind pushed through the lies is all."

He grabbed her by the waist, lifted her, and spun around. Her pulse leapt, and she could feel his heart against hers as he lowered her slowly back to the ground. "That's fabulous news. We have to try to get past the wolves. Let's talk as soon as supper is over." He released her and stepped back. "I would say we should try to leave now, but we are both expected. In fact, I need to get changed to help serve the courses."

"You'll be there?" *Thank goodness.* The evening seemed far more palatable now.

"Of course. And thank you for checking on me, but it wasn't necessary. Only you would risk getting your gown splattered with sauces by sneaking into the kitchen."

She waved her hand in dismissal. "I couldn't care less about staining this thing. In fact, I'd prefer it. I'd certainly have an excuse to change into something a little less formal."

"And a little less revealing." His face flamed red before he even closed his mouth. "Not that you don't look stunning." He stumbled over the words.

"Thanks." Penny fought back a smile. "If only I could breathe."

"You should probably head to the main hall. The guests are due to arrive any minute." He reached his hands out, his fingers gripping her waist once more. The pressure was intoxicating, and she longed to step closer into his embrace. "I beg you to be careful. Don't do anything to upset Master. Don't let him contemplate, even for a second, that some of your memories have returned." He twisted her around. "Now go."

Penny lifted her skirts and made a meandering route through

the manor. Unfortunately, despite her best efforts to get lost along the way, she found herself soon enough in the main wing.

Primo eyed her warily from his post, and Penny ducked her head. He was most likely there to make sure she didn't sneak off in the middle of the event for a tincture from Beppe's home.

"Penelope." Primo stepped forward, his hands tucked behind his back. "You're the first of the girls to arrive. Why aren't you in your room waiting for the group to get ready for their entrance?"

Of course they were waiting.

Of course there was a grand entrance.

Of course Penny had failed to follow directions.

What else could go wrong?

❧ 1867 ❧

Cirillo tossed the latest letter from *l'ispettore* onto a pile of mail intended for Beppe. It was the exact same missive he'd received every week for two months. He could recite it by heart.

Dear Sir, I regret to inform you there has been no word of your sister. We will continue our search. —Signor Bruno

Cirillo didn't care. He was only placating Beppe and his obsessive need to find Sofia. Cirillo himself rather hoped she rotted in whatever hole she'd fallen into.

Beppe had not been happy when Cirillo approached him to rewire his sister's thoughts. But Cirillo had already concocted his argument, intent on coercing Beppe to help him. "We'll be careful," he'd said. "I promise. And think of all the good we can do. If we perfect this procedure, there are so many uses. We can help someone forget a traumatic memory, or even correct a criminal's behavior."

"But why Sofia?" Beppe's eyebrows, already prematurely white like the rest of his hair, knit together.

This was the question Cirillo had been waiting for. "Because we know her and can gauge the results. If we performed the alteration on a stranger, we wouldn't be able to detect any subtle differences."

Beppe reluctantly agreed to a small manipulation, and they'd moved forward with the experiment. Unfortunately, it hadn't gone quite as planned.

It was a science, this concept of mind modification. And, Sofia being the first subject, they may have suffered a few glitches. Instead of being more subdued, kind, and compassionate, Cirillo's sister became depressed. Her husband left. Beppe kept a constant watch on her and her seven-year-old son, to make sure she didn't harm him. And then she disappeared.

Cirillo had paid the inspector a hefty sum to find his sister and keep her quiet. The last thing he needed was Sofia out telling the world what happened behind their closed doors. But she hadn't left even a shred of a trace. And after a few weeks of searching, Cirillo stopped worrying. If she began to spread rumors, he'd say she was insane. If her behavior alone wasn't enough to justify his claim, he had enough money to purchase a physician's confirmation.

A knock on the door brought him back to the present. Primo stepped through. "Sir, *l'ispettore* is here to see you."

Signor Bruno entered with Beppe right behind.

"I've just had news." Signor cut right to the chase. "She was found in a river two towns over. Facedown and dressed all in black."

Cirillo shrugged. "Thank you. I'll see to burial arrangements."

Signor nodded. "And the boy?"

"I don't care."

"You're his only living family." Signor paused, as if waiting for Cirillo to grasp his intent.

"No." The word was definitive, spoken through clenched teeth. No way was Cirillo raising a child.

Beppe glared at him and stepped over, stopping when their noses were mere millimeters apart. "We have no choice. We killed her."

Cirillo sighed. "All right. He can stay at the estate. It's not like I won't find *some* use for him."

Beppe directed the inspector to the door and bid him good day. He turned back to Cirillo. "You wouldn't. He's an innocent in all of this. He's your blood."

"He's *her* blood." Cirillo settled back in his chair and stretched his stiff leg in front of him.

"Go ahead, then." Beppe threw his arms in the air. "We'll see if *my* experiment is a success."

"What experiment?" Cirillo narrowed his eyes.

"I knew your desire for revenge would lead us down an uncertain path. So I've been working on a countermeasure."

Cirillo launched out of the chair, and before Beppe could breathe, he had the letter opener against Beppe's throat. It was dull, but it would do the job.

"I'll let the transgression slide this time." Cirillo smoothed his lapel and dropped the opener on the desk. "I'll leave the boy alone. But I suggest you do not cross me again. You are indebted to me. Don't ever forget that."

Beppe looked at the floor and Cirillo smiled. He'd won.

He won every time.

❧ 1879 ❧

*E*ntrances are overrated," Penny said, covering up quickly and peeking past Primo. "I far prefer a grand exit. I'll be going in now."

She inched away from Primo and into the room, before he could send her back to her chamber. Let the other girls make a grand entrance. She would rather camouflage her way into the background.

As much as a frilly jade gown could camouflage, anyway.

The large space had been filled with several long tables set with gilded serving ware and embroidered cloth napkins. Red, yellow, and pink tulips rose from brass vases, their petals reaching toward the ormolu gasoliers hung on long chains from the high ceiling. The flames danced and reflected off the now-darkened windows, making the room appear to have doubled in size. Bronze incense burners wafted a delicate vanilla scent into the heavy air.

Penny moved toward the hearth on the opposite end of the room, hoping to hide in the shadows of the immense marble columns supporting an overly wide mantel, but before she even took two steps, someone blocked her path.

"Buonasera." Prince Jacobus kissed her cheek, his lips lingering. He grinned down at her, his smile infectious. "I can hardly believe it's been a year, darling. You are more beautiful this year than last, if it's even possible." He waved over a gentleman who had only just walked into the room. "Gideon, over here. You remember Signorina Penelope, yes?"

"Penny, please," Penny rushed in.

Gideon stepped closer, his broad shoulders stretching the seams of his jacket. He wore the royal crest on his sleeve, and Penny figured he was some sort of *attendente* to the prince. His watery blue eyes blinked slowly as he surveyed the room.

"Prince Jacobus!" An older woman, draped in silk with rings on every finger, came swooping in to kiss him on both cheeks. "How are you feeling, darling? It's so dreadful about your injury."

He smiled and flashed perfect white teeth, but Penny could feel his hand tense against her arm. She remembered reading about the accident in the slips of news they pored over. The prince had joined his men on the front lines of the Austrian border. Although they weren't at war, some sort of skirmish broke out and the prince was shot in the leg. An infection had caused further nerve damage and only recently had he been seen out in public again. It was hard to reconcile the written image of him cooped up in the palace infirmary with the healthy young man in front of her. His cane was the only indication of an injury.

"I'm feeling quite well, Signora. Thank you. Beppe took great care of me."

Penny's eyebrow arched, surprised at this. Beppe had never mentioned traveling to the palace. Not that he would've bragged about his distinguished patient—he never bragged about any of his work—but she would've thought he'd share details about his trip. Except, she realized, he kept many secrets from her. What was one more?

"I'd love to talk further," the prince continued, "but I only have a minute before Master Cirillo is bound to sweep in and take Penny here away from me." He stared the woman down until she got the hint and stepped away.

The prince edged them away from the entrance. "After spending time with Beppe, I feel as if I know so very much about you and the other students."

Penny's eyes widened in surprise and suspicion. "What did he say?"

He paused. "Alas, I can't remember all the specifics. I was in somewhat of a stupor much of the time. You can hardly imagine the work he had to do."

"And you still need a cane?" This surprised her. Beppe performed medical miracles.

And catastrophes, too.

The prince leaned in closer. "It still hurts on the rare occasion, and I want to make sure I'm in perfect form for dancing with you—"

"Prince Jacobus." Master suddenly stood next to Penny. His eyes were dark as coal.

The prince grinned. "Cirillo. Good evening. I was just chatting with Penny here—"

"Penelope." Master nearly seethed the word. "Her name is Penelope. And she belongs with the other girls as they finish preparations." He refused to even look at her.

"I'm sorry," Penny intervened, trying to appease him. The last thing she needed was to have his anger directed at her. "I didn't realize we were supposed to enter the room together. I came as soon as I'd dressed, for fear of being tardy."

"Yes, well, thank you for that, I suppose." He slid between the prince and Penny, forcing the prince to step away. Master eyed his cane warily, his jaw locked tight. He finally turned his gaze back to Penny. "Since you *are* here, I shall take the time to introduce you to our other guests."

Master grasped her fingers and tucked her arm in his. As he led her away, she cast an apologetic look over her shoulder at the prince. He smiled, his lips forming a crooked grin, and winked.

His mouth near her ear, Master whispered, "You look radiant. You'll do me proud this evening." He gripped her arm tight and ushered her over to an Admiral Picelli, where she learned of the most recent attack on the Austrian front, followed by a Conte di Mordano, who told a mournful tale of his third wife's recent passing. All while he eyed Penny's cleavage. Master almost knocked her over in his haste to move her from the count's prying gaze.

They'd traversed nearly the entire room when he finally deposited her with *l'ispettore*. Master had barely made the introduction, which was unnecessary because Penny had met the inspector on several occasions already, when he was signaled by Primo to the sprawling entrance doors.

"How are you faring, Penelope?" The inspector was thin as a reed and nearly a head taller than her, so his words rained down from above.

"Very well, thank you."

"Are you certain?" The words were low, and he paused to cough into a stained ivory handkerchief.

Penny stood silent for a moment, unsure how to respond. It

seemed as if the inspector was trying to delve further into the intrigue of the estate. But she wouldn't put it past Master to entice the inspector to ask the girls questions, to see how much they were willing to divulge.

"This is all in confidence." He stood at her side, talking low as they continued to face Master. "Whatever you say shall go no further than this bit of space surrounding us."

She opened her mouth, but nothing came out. The words froze in her throat as she thought of Rosaura's story. Primo would whisk her off to the asylum at the first sign of disobedience.

Instead, a different concern burst forth.

"There's one thing, sir. Have you seen my grandfather? Beppe. He left the estate suddenly, and I haven't heard from him. I fear something bad has happened."

The inspector shook his head. "No. He was supposed to come to give me another treatment yesterday." He knocked his fist against his chest and rattled up another cough.

Penny tensed. If the inspector was getting medical assistance from Beppe, it was nearly impossible for him to be disloyal to Master. It was good she hadn't said anything. He couldn't be trusted. The inspector continued, "I haven't heard from him or why there's been a delay, but I'll see what I can find out."

She forced her head to bob in a slight nod of thanks.

The inspector patted her arm. "It was nice to speak with you."

"You as well, Signore."

Master waved at her from the other side of the room. She begged the inspector's pardon and followed Master to the parlor to join her *sorelle*. They gathered in a line and then entered the hall again to a smatter of applause. Penny knew they presented a beautiful portrait, arranged in a colorful array of jewel tones and artfully braided hair. After a brief bit of pomp and spectacle, they scattered to the various tables. Penny and Bianca had been directed to chairs at near opposite ends of the front table, where she assumed Master would also be sitting.

"Is this seat taken?" The prince's lips were so close to Penny's ear, it tickled.

"I don't . . ." But before she could answer, he'd already slid into the empty chair at her side. He leaned his cane against the back of the chair and waved for Gideon to take the seat next to him. As Gideon lowered his large frame into the chair, the prince reached for a glass of wine. He nodded at the crystal goblet in front of Penny. "A toast. To me getting you on the dance floor, despite the supposed rules against it."

Penny glanced around the room for Master, certain he would swoop in and relegate the prince to a different location, but he was nowhere to be found. She wrapped her fingers around the thin stem and lifted the glass. A soft *clink* echoed as they brushed the rims together and Penny took a sip.

"Tell me more about Beppe," Penny said. "When did he arrive at the palace to treat you?"

"Not nearly soon enough. After the shooting, they took me to a hospital near the border. It was cramped, stuffy, and dirtier than a vagabond's foot. When the infection spread, I was moved home. Beppe met me there and immediately began to work his magic. Still, it was dreadfully boring. I was under strict isolation because he feared my immune system was too weak."

Gideon nodded at the end of each sentence, as if he was the punctuation to the prince's monologue.

Penny began to respond, to ask what happened next, when suddenly Master appeared, his shadow lengthening over the table. "Jacobus." Master gripped the back of his chair as if he meant to pull it out and dump the prince on the floor. His jaw clenched as he took in the rest of the room, all the seats taken. It seemed he had no choice but to leave the prince there or cause a scene. He leaned over, his voice so low that Penny barely caught the words. "Behave yourself."

The prince winked at Penny as Master turned and walked around to the head of the table. He remained standing and waited for the conversation to die down to hushed whispers. "I'd like to welcome you all again as we begin our festivities for the spring gala. After the meal, there will be a bit of music and dancing." He gestured toward the musicians who sat clustered in a corner, playing a soft tempo. "In the meantime, enjoy the food, wine, and the company of my students. My girls. I'm so very proud of them and their work. They are the life force behind this school." He took time to rest his gaze on each student. Penny fought not to squirm as his eyes settled on her. There was another round of applause and he finally sat in his seat, a high-backed chair with scrolling designs.

Everyone waited in silence as the servants entered in a flurry of black tails and silver platters. Penny sensed Cricket before she saw him, as if a thread connected them. Their eyes locked for a brief moment and then Cricket passed by. He stopped a few tables over and focused on presenting the *antipasto* to the guests there.

Jacobus leaned over and whispered in her ear.

"Why is Cirillo's nephew serving us dinner?"

$\mathcal{P}$enny froze. "His what?"

The staff continued to set the dishes—mushrooms, cheeses, cold salmon, and aubergines—throughout the tables and exited silently.

"His nephew. The tall one with the messy hair. The one you had eyes for. Surely you knew they were related?"

"Of course I knew." Except she hadn't known. Penny speared a block of cheese and nibbled on the edges. Master's nephew. It didn't make sense why Cricket wouldn't tell her, why he'd keep it a secret all this time. Penny wouldn't have cared much that he was related to Master, and he had to know that. They were two different people, and Cricket had proven himself to be the near opposite of his uncle.

Unless he thought she *would* care. That there was something else in her scattered memories that he worried she'd discover. But that didn't make sense. His touch brought forth the truth, leaving the false thoughts behind. If anything, she had all the more reason to trust him.

She felt a prickle at the back of her neck and glanced up to find Bianca's eyes narrowed in her direction. Penny turned away, trying to interject herself into the conversation the prince had started with the general sitting across the table from them.

She quickly was lost in their discussion of the art of warfare and could only nod her head with Gideon at regular intervals.

The meal was a series of courses and presentation. Soup was served for the *primo* course: a light broth of tomato and basil filled with winter squash, beans, and small pasta shaped into stars. After the bowls were whisked away, platters of salt cod, stuffed sausage, lobster, and lamb made up the *secondo*, followed by dishes of rosemary potatoes and asparagus and zucchini *crudi* for the *contorno*. Every time the door opened, Penny felt her pulse jump at the sight of Cricket. His eyes were even paler in contrast to the black attire, and the cut of the jacket showed off his broad shoulders. His hair was damp and slicked back, which added depth to his cheekbones and jawline. He passed by her table and she longed to touch his arm, if only briefly.

"Not hungry?" the prince asked.

She pushed flaky bits of fish around her plate.

It wasn't that Penny felt particularly full; it was more that her bodice strained with each inhale. She'd hardly have room for the *dolce*, and that was all she really cared about. She shook her head and nibbled on a bit of asparagus. "I'm nervous is all."

"You have nothing to be nervous about. You'll perform beautifully. I have no doubt." He grinned, his full lips pulling up on one side. Penny couldn't help but smile in response. She liked the prince, his self-assurance. It must be nice growing up with everything you ever wanted at your fingertips.

The meal finally concluded with immense trays of *zuppa*

inglese. Penny indulged and let the savory custard and lemon zest dissolve on her tongue. The musicians began to play a lively tune and the prince rose to his feet beside her, the cane grasped in his right hand. He bent at the waist and held out his left hand. "Would you honor me with this dance?"

Penny really did not want to. Not publicly. Not at all. She opened her mouth, hoping some excuse would tumble out, and as if by magic Master loomed over them. "I won't allow it." His voice dropped to a whisper. "He's an invalid."

The words were matter-of-fact, almost childlike, but Penny flinched all the same. "That's . . . that's not true." She twisted and rose from her chair. "We'll manage just fine." She grabbed the prince's hand and steered him into a wood-floored clearing near the musicians. His cane tapped a rhythm at his side. Penny's jaw clenched and her back teeth ground against one another. She couldn't believe Master's behavior.

"Don't worry about him. It's all jealousy." The prince slipped ahead and spun lightly so he faced her. "You should see the way he looks at you." His left hand circled around her back and brushed her side. "It's adoration at its best."

Penny doubted that. Master didn't adore her. He wanted to control her, wanted to control all the girls.

The musicians eased into a slow waltz and Penny let the prince lead her in a few turns. She could feel everyone's eyes on them, could only imagine from Bianca's snarl that she held the guests' attention, but she tried to tune them out. "Tell me more about the palace, about your time with Beppe."

The prince grinned, no doubt more than happy to continue talking about himself. He painted a vision of a grander version of the manor, more acreage, more splendors within the walls. "I'll admit that the recovery itself was rather dull. I spent most of my hours watching Beppe at work. It was fascinating, the tools and procedures he implemented. There was this one device—"

"I am cutting in." Master gripped Penny's elbow. A flood of chills coursed through her body. The prince sputtered out protests, but Master had already moved her toward the center of the floor. "You looked as if you needed saving."

Penny blinked at him, her thoughts whirling faster than her skirts. She had to play docile and doting even though it went against most of the instincts in her body. "Thank you."

Master led her with precision, his movements light and graceful. He pulled her in and away, spun her effortlessly, and danced with ease around the floor. Soon enough other couples joined them, her *sorelle* dancing with gentlemen of all ages.

The prince gripped her arm as the next dance started, continuing his conversation exactly where he'd left off. "It had this dial that could change the interval of electrical pulses sent to a nerve. But it wasn't connected. The machine was in another room. I still don't understand how he did it. But—"

Penny could sense Master before he cut in. The prince stepped just off to the side, waiting until his next chance. It was a game of possession and posturing, and she quickly grew tired of being the prize trophy.

"Beppe did tell me one thing," the prince resumed his story. "He always builds a fail-safe into his equipment. In case there is a malfunction, he has a way to stop it. Isn't that genius? I wish I had his foresight and medical knowledge. Not that I'd be able to put it to use. Medicine and politics don't often work together."

Master was at her side just as the band switched to a lively polka. Penny's feet dragged to a stop. "Master. I . . . my ankle. Is it all right if I sit down for a moment?"

He must've seen something in her face, in her eyes, because he ushered her back to the table. "Stay here. I don't want you to move."

Penny nodded. She had no plans to. As soon as Master turned back to the dance floor, whisking Bianca away from her consort, she.looked around for Cricket. The kitchen staff had tapered off when the music began, appearing only to freshen drinks or remove any last remaining dishes. Unfortunately, he was nowhere to be found.

The prince collapsed in the seat next to her and gulped the remaining wine in his glass. "Why the forlorn look? It doesn't suit you."

Penny forced a yawn. "I'm tired is all."

Master moved to the edge of the dance floor and spoke loudly over the din. "I want to thank everyone for coming. You are more than welcome to stay and enjoy the music, but I must escort the girls back to their chambers so they may rest. I look forward to showing them off two evenings hence."

The prince lifted Penny's hand and brushed his lips against her knuckles. "Sleep well."

She pushed back her chair and nearly smacked into Master. His green eyes flashed nearly the same color as her gown. "Come."

There was no arguing.

He held out his elbow as a chivalrous display and Penny threaded her arm through. The other girls huddled behind them, waving at the guests and tittering behind their hands. Only Bianca remained quiet. She stood on Master's other side and glared at Penny. They exited the hall and made their way as a group to the dormitory. Master bid good night to each girl individually at her room, never releasing Penny's arm. Bianca was the final girl. He told her to sleep well. She slammed the door without even a response. Master ignored the transgression and ushered Penny to her chamber.

The door closed, and he released her arm. It left her with a sudden lack of warmth and a very strong sense of disconcertion. She shouldn't miss the touch of this man who had done such despicable things, a man who forced people to serve under his control.

They stood facing each other, Penny's back to her bed. Gooseflesh dotted her arms as the cool draft in the room settled around her.

Master reached inside his jacket and removed something from a pocket within. He held his palm out. Inside rested a small oval painted portrait framed in delicate brass. It was a beautiful woman with porcelain skin and a soft smile that lifted her rose lips.

Penny looked quizzically at Master.

"It's your mother." He seemed to be watching her reaction, so she swallowed down a gasp. She wondered if the image was of her true mother or if it was merely another ploy, a falsehood of a memory. She couldn't know, but she truly hoped it was her mother, that it was something to go by if she could ever escape to search for her family.

"Thank you. I shall cherish it always."

"It's a peace offering." He took her wrist with his free hand and placed the portraiture in her palm. "You said this week has been difficult, and I'm sure you miss her."

She thanked him again and turned to lay the portrait on the stand next to her bed.

Master's hands were warm on her shoulders as he rotated her slowly back around. His eyes could have burned through stone, they shone so bright. His gaze shifted to her lips and then back to her eyes. He stepped in closer, his knee brushing her lower thigh, nudging her skirts. His lips neared hers and his eyes settled closed.

As if he was about to kiss her.

Penny sucked in a breath and pulled back. Her hands splayed wide to push against his chest, her fingers pressing against the thin length of cord that stretched beneath his shirt.

She knew it was the wrong thing to do, by the way his nostrils flared and his eyes turned several shades darker.

He straightened his lapel and stood tall. "I'm sorry. This was a mistake."

"No." Penny tried to make eye contact, tried to calm him down. "I didn't mean to stop you." She twisted her hands. "It was so sudden. And . . . and I don't feel worthy."

"We both know that's not true." The words were sad, resigned. But then anger masked his features. "Perhaps if you weren't so attracted to the kitchen help, we wouldn't have this problem." She couldn't help but flinch. He stepped away. "It's time for you to rest."

His fingers reached out to grip her chin so tightly the skin bruised against her teeth. "There's no need to be upset. Once the gala is over, I'll convince you that you belong to me. And only me."

She'd made a huge error, an insurmountable mistake. She

should've let him kiss her, convinced him that she cared for him. Instead, he was angry with her, and Cricket, and who knew what he'd do when he returned to his quarters. Tamper with her memories, that much was obvious.

Master released her chin and she apologized again. He held up his hand to cut her off. "Please let it be. I thought tonight would be different. I was wrong. It wasn't the first time, but it will certainly be the last."

Penny swallowed hard.

"Sleep well, Penelope." He spun on his heel and shut the door behind him. At least he didn't lock it.

She stood in stunned silence, staring at the dark wood panel. She couldn't let Master destroy the truths that she'd learned. Not tonight. Not after the gala. Not anytime.

She no longer had a choice. She couldn't wait for Beppe. She had to end this herself.

Penny performed a feat worthy of an acrobat in order to dismantle the corseted bodice and slide out of the gown. It lay discarded on the floor as she slipped into her bedclothes. She turned down her lamp and snuck out of the room.

She wound through the manor toward Cricket's chamber, but found herself stopping at the entrance to the hall where she'd found the door leading to nowhere. There had to be something there, beyond that brick wall.

Penny tugged on a strand of loose hair before she ran the rest of the way to the servants' wing.

The door was open before she even reached it, as if he knew. Cricket waited inside, sitting on the edge of his mattress with his hands buried in his hair. He stood as soon as she walked in. "Is everything all right?"

"Why didn't you tell me you were Master's nephew?" It

wasn't what she'd come there to say, but she had to know the truth.

One of Cricket's eyebrows rose toward the low ceiling. "I thought you knew. Everyone knows."

She frowned. "But I didn't. I don't. And I can't fathom why Master would remove that knowledge from my memories."

"I'm not sure." Cricket shrugged. "He probably wanted to destroy as many thoughts of me as possible." His lips pursed and he brushed his knuckles over his jaw. "You know I wouldn't lie to you, or keep it from you on purpose." His eyes caught hers. "I don't consider him any sort of relative of mine. I have no loyalty to him, Penny. I promise you that. He never even acknowledges me as his family."

"I know," Penny said. She exhaled a breath she hadn't realized she'd been holding. She did know. And she did trust him, but she still couldn't tell him about the near kiss with Master. "I need your help. The evening ended rather horribly. Master walked me to my room and seemed to want . . . a different reaction. He said that after the gala he'd convince me that I *belonged* to him."

"That doesn't sound very promising."

Penny would've laughed if the situation weren't so dire. "No. Not exactly."

"Do you think he'll do anything tonight?"

"Yes." She wrapped her arms across her chest. "I really do."

"What should we do? Do you think you can sneak past the wolves?" Cricket reached out his palms and barely brushed the arm of her sleeves. The gesture was in such stark contrast to Master gripping her arm earlier. She felt safe with Cricket.

Safe enough to admit she was seeing other things.

"There's something I want to try first." She told him about

the walled doorway in the corridor nearby. "I have this memory of stairs and a tunnel beneath the manor. If there's something down there that will help us, some sort of information, I think we should go. Now, before he tries to manipulate my thoughts."

He nodded without pause. "Lead the way."

Together they crept through the silent hallway. When they turned into the dark corridor, Penny slowed her pace. The air was icy, causing her to shiver beneath her thin nightshirt. Only one lamp was lit, at the entrance to the hall, and it cast the opposite wall in shadow. They kept to the dark side of the passage and scooted along its edge until Penny pointed out the door. Her pulse steadied only slightly. At least it was still here, with its ornate carving and dull brass handle. She took a deep breath and pulled it open.

The brick wall barred any entrance.

"Do you see it?" she whispered.

Cricket reached out his arm and Penny watched it disappear through the solid gray stone. "See what?"

Her nose wrinkled as she braced her palms on the bricks and pushed against the wall. It didn't budge. She turned around and leaned her back against it, putting all her weight against the stones. Cricket grabbed her arm. "You'll fall!"

"No. I won't." She banged her fist against the stone. "It's solid rock."

"Watch." Cricket brushed past her and his foot pushed through the wall as if it were silk. Another step and his entire body had disappeared.

"Cricket," Penny whispered. It was disconcerting to see him vanish like that. She had no idea what was on the other side.

He stuck his head out, like he was peering at her from

between closed curtains. "There's a light at the end of the stair-well. Shall I see what's down there?"

Penny sighed, defeated. "I guess."

He retracted his head and Penny slumped down against the opposite wall. She hated for Cricket to place himself in danger over some vision she may or may not have had.

She shut her eyes, placed her palms flat on the frigid floor at her sides, and willed herself to remember what was beyond the bricks. The thoughts slowly appeared, bits and pieces of memories. A pitch-black corridor that she descended, barefoot, her toes brushing the edge of each step before she lowered herself again. The air smelled sterile, chemical even. At the bottom the flooring changed to something smooth, like marble or metal. A harsh glow emanated from tiny bulb-shaped lights strung along in a fierce, straight line down the length of the hall-way, a hallway that stretched forever, reflecting off the pale gray floor and walls.

Without realizing it, Penny had pushed herself to standing and walked toward the brick wall.

She could picture a row of steel doors, perfectly spaced on either side of the corridor. She passed the first ones, not caring what lay behind. Her only focus, her mind seemingly free of any other thoughts, was to enter the fifth door on the left.

Penny stumbled forward, her arms windmilling to stop her sudden pitch down the stairs as her eyes flew open. Steep steps descended away from her. She dared a glance behind her.

The bricks were gone.

Penny sprinted to the bottom. "Cricket!" She loudly whis-pered his name.

The corridor was exactly as she'd remembered, the strange

bulbs casting a steady stream of light down its length. The first door she approached was sealed shut. She peered closer, forehead furrowed as she looked for a handle. The only spot marring the pale gray exterior was a narrow, raised bubble on the right-hand side at about chest level. It was circular in shape, nearly a centimeter in diameter, and had a small hole in the center.

The door across the hallway, and those farther along, looked exactly the same. She'd passed several before she noticed an open room ahead. A blue tinge of light filtered into the hall, and a slight scuffling noise came from within.

She tiptoed forward. "Cricket?"

He appeared in the door frame, a huge grin deepening his dimple. "You made it!" He ushered her inside. "How did you push through?"

"I'm not certain. I sort of visualized it and then found myself on the other side." Her voice trailed off, her focus on the oddities of the room. The ceiling seemed to be constructed of a large, single tile, pulsing with a pale blue light. It cast a sheen on everything and turned her white chemise a glowing shade of azure. The room itself was barren of furniture and decoration. Running lengthwise on both sides were cabinets of floor-to-ceiling drawers. It appeared Cricket had started at the opposite end, as several of the compartments sat propped open.

"Have you found anything?" Penny asked.

"I've definitely found *things*, but not much that would help us." He lifted a glass jar by its lid so Penny could see more clearly.

She flinched, nausea rolling in her stomach. Translucent green liquid, almost glowing in the strange light of the room, filled the jar to the top. A small bird floated within, its beady eyes staring ahead and its wings slick and oily.

"There's more." He put the jar back and reached for something else, but Penny stopped him.

"I don't need to see anything else." Trying to stay away from Cricket's discoveries, she scooted to the cabinets closest to the door. Each drawer front was etched with a number. She reached for 2. It slid open with barely a whisper and Penny glanced inside. No animals or glowing jars, thank goodness. Instead, it was filled with a hodgepodge of nonsensical items. A gold link bracelet. Three silk handkerchiefs severely creased and folded into small squares. An empty perfume bottle. A leather-bound book rested against the front of the drawer, and Penny lifted it to see more clearly. She flipped open the cover and nearly dropped it.

BIANCA, SPRING 1876

The next page listed personal belongings, which seemed to be the very items Penny had spotted in the drawer. She couldn't bear to read on, dropped the journal, and slammed the compartment shut.

Penny pulled out the third drawer.

MARIA, FALL 1876

Maria had arrived at the estate shortly before Penny had.

Her trembling fingers paused at the handle of the fourth drawer. With a deep breath, she slid it open. She barely registered the quill pen or the puff of fabric that might have been a shirt or a blanket. She reached for the journal and opened the cover to the front page. A loose piece of paper was tucked there.

Suddenly, Penny heard a noise.

She turned toward Cricket at the same moment he spun to face her. Their wide eyes flitted toward the open doorway. They heard it again.

Footsteps.

Someone was walking down the hall, but from the opposite direction. Muttered unintelligible words echoed toward them. The voice sounded distinctly like Master.

Cricket rushed forward and flipped a small lever on the wall. The room darkened instantly. He inched the door closed until only a sliver of light from the hallway remained visible.

Penny stood, the journal clutched to her chest as her pulse thudded against it, as the footsteps moved closer.

They were doomed, perhaps even dead, if discovered. There was no excuse for being found in the basement at night, or during the day for that matter. Master would know she'd passed his brick wall boundary. And after everything that had transpired the past two days, his anger would be absolute. She'd be locked up forever. Her eyes squeezed shut as she waited for the inevitable.

But the steps, hasty and heavy, passed them by without pause. They abruptly stopped, the sound replaced with a metallic scraping and then a soft *whoosh*.

Silence descended.

Cricket and Penny waited, unmoving, in the darkness. "We need to run," Cricket finally whispered.

"We need to shut the drawers." They couldn't leave evidence of their snooping.

"I don't want to turn the light on again."

"Maybe open the door a little farther." Penny tucked the journal flat in the drawer and eased it shut.

Cricket had closed the cupboards around him and together

they moved toward the exit. Penny peeked her head out. They had to go back the way they'd come, for neither knew where the other exit lay.

All the doors were sealed, although a sliver of pale light, a violet hue, seemed to pulse from one of the last doors on the right-hand side. "I think he's inside," Penny whispered back to Cricket.

He stood on tiptoe and looked out over her head. "Let's leave before he comes back out again."

Penny knew it was their best option, their only option really, but it didn't stop her heart from scampering and her pulse from beating like a drum in her ears as she raced down the hall on the balls of her feet. They began to ascend the steps and she nearly tripped, fearful that the bricks would be back in place when they reached the top. She dared a glance and fell forward, hardly noticing as her palms scraped the hard edge of the stair.

The opening was blocked.

But then Cricket was there, above her, turning the handle of the door and pushing it open so she could see the corridor beyond. "Hurry!" he urged, reaching his hand out to pull her up.

She clambered up the few remaining stairs and skittered into the hall. Cricket shut the door behind her and they hurried back to his chamber. They stood in the middle of the room, panting as the fear and anxiety dissipated only slightly.

"We should leave tonight. You got past the wall; surely you can make it past the wolves." Cricket turned toward his wardrobe as if ready to change into traveling clothes.

"No." She put out her arm to block him. "I need to see what else is down in the cellar. We'll go back to the room before dawn, after Master has gone to bed. And then we will leave."

She hated lying to him. Cricket, who had been her steadfast

companion since the beginning. The words were acid on her tongue.

He opened his mouth as if to argue, but she jumped in. "I know it's better to leave under cover of darkness, but I still have a horrific fear of passing the wolves. Daylight will be better."

She stepped closer and buried her head in his chest, unable to make eye contact for fear he would see the dishonesty there. He wrapped his arms around her and held her close.

"Okay."

Penny inhaled his cinnamon scent and took comfort from the steady pulse of his heart.

"You should probably stay here for the night." His heartbeat tripped against her cheek. "I mean, if you are comfortable. It's only that . . . I fear what Master will do to your thoughts."

She nodded. "Thank you. I'd feel much safer with you."

He released her to grab his quilt from the bed and wrap it around her shoulders. Then they sprawled on the floor, side by side, stretched out so the lengths of their arms and legs, covered in nightclothes, brushed against one another. The slightest touch, but electric all the same. Penny tried to relax as she counted Cricket's breaths and waited for them to fall into a heavy rhythm. When she was certain he was asleep, she slipped from under the blanket and left the room.

C—

If you find this, it means I made it past the estate border safely and have yet to return. I'm sorry I didn't wake you, but I need you to watch over the others. I will be fine. If M discovers my absence and it's not safe to return, please send word to the far blue.

—P

The words were vague, but Penny hoped they carried enough clues for Cricket to decipher her intent and go to Tatiana with any news. After folding the paper in half two times, she tucked it under her pillow such that only a corner was visible. She left another note on her bedspread, addressed to nobody in particular, saying she'd woken early and gone for a walk to ease her headache.

Penny reached into her pocket and pulled out the loose piece of paper again. She had pocketed it before they'd left the cellar, having already resolved to leave the estate that very evening and travel. Her pulse thundered as she read the address again.

Via del Rinnovamento, 34, Marconze

Marconze was a village outside of Ravinni. It had to be her family's home. Why else would it be in her drawer? She gripped the paper to her chest, took a deep breath, and allowed hope to bloom just a little.

She threw open her wardrobe and dug through the chemises, skirts, and gowns, none of which seemed appropriate for traveling through the night. Her hope was to make it past the wolves and return to the estate before midmorning, when a search party was sure to be dispatched to find her.

She caught a glimpse of canvas on the floor of the armoire and pulled out a bag, the same bag she'd tossed there the night of her first attempted escape. It seemed only fitting to don the heavy riding skirt and blouse now.

Leon twined between her feet while she laced her boots. He meowed as if to ask her what she was doing awake in the middle of the night, instead of cuddling up next to him on the mattress. She scooped him up to her cheek for a quick nuzzle and then dropped him near the note on her bedspread. He gave her a last curious look, curled into himself, and closed his eyes.

Penny went to turn down the lamp when her eye caught the miniature portrait Master had given her earlier. She stuffed it in her pocket and made her way through the manor toward the servants' exit.

She tried to tune out thoughts of Cricket, but it didn't work. He would be angry and disappointed she'd left him behind. But this was a journey of discovery she needed to make on her own. Proof that she was her own person and not some pawn in Master's schemes.

She had brought herself out of the memory change that morning.

She had pushed past the phantom wall.

She was ready to do this.

Every nerve in her body seemed to crackle with energy as she followed the moonlit path to the stable and felt her way through the darkened building to the tack room. Several minutes passed as Penny saddled the horse and adjusted the stirrups and harness. She rested her forehead against the stark white blaze along the animal's nose. "Please, let us make it to Marconze and back safely . . . and quickly."

It was as close as she could get to a prayer.

※ ※

The manor was out of sight when Penny eased the horse into a gallop. She leaned forward, her chest tight against the pommel. Frigid air seeped down her collar and in through the gap between her gloves and sleeve. At least the wind helped keep her awake.

That and the adrenaline coursing through her veins.

And the fear of a wolf appearing to tear holes in her chest.

They were still several hundred yards from the estate's borders when Penny closed her eyes and tried to mimic what had happened earlier. She took deep breaths, pushing away all thoughts and fears of the wolves, and tried to recall a time she'd left the border.

Wisps of another scene surfaced. A sun-drenched spring day. The fields were in bloom all around her, blue pimpernel and wood sorrel and red poppies, so bright they painted an impressionist design on the landscape.

I ride beside Bianca, but she's pulling ahead. It's a race, even though she refuses to declare it. It's always a race with us. The horse inches forward at my urging and I grip the reins tighter. Master is due back today and we've decided to greet him from his return to Rome. I draw even with Bianca, and then ahead. She shouts her frustration as I turn onto the main thoroughfare. I ride several more yards before I see it: his carriage. But who is the new girl waving out the window?

Penny's eyes flew open and she willed away the burst of envy that flooded through her, a remnant of the vision. The girl in the carriage, with the carefree smile on her face. It was Ana.

The horse kept its steady clip and Penny glanced around, the strange jealousy replaced with wonder and excitement. For, even though she'd hoped it would happen, and didn't dare consider the consequences, a small part of her had thought she wouldn't make it past the boundaries.

But she had. She'd escaped. Her mind had pushed past the phantom images again.

With a slight pull on the reins, she turned onto the highway that led to Ravinni. In the midst of her relief and thoughts of the remainder of her journey, Penny failed to notice the lone wolf patrolling the tree line to her left. It kept pace with her for several yards before scampering into the forest and out of sight.

❧ ❧

Less than an hour later she began to see evidence of the town. Houses were built closer together and the fields beyond were a grid of olive trees and vineyards and maize. Several roads combined into one main thoroughfare and Penny funneled into the city. Even at this late hour, lamps blazed and people meandered. She briefly gazed with longing at the kaleidoscope of storefronts. Wooden signs with calligraphy lettering invited her to enter into an ironmonger, a blacksmith, a textile shop. An entire life outside the estate.

A few blocks later, a pulsing beat of music and laughter spilled from the next street over. By the time she hit the intersection, she couldn't even cross to the other side. Revelers were a tangled knot as people tried to maneuver in and around one another. Her horse neighed softly and Penny slid off the saddle. She walked toward the edge of the street, out of the way.

Just as she looped the reins over a post, a series of bells gonged. It must've been a signal, for lights instantly flickered everywhere. Bits of flame danced as candles were lit behind curtained windows and in the hands of the foot passengers. Crystal lamps blinked in one carriage. Glowing paper lanterns flickered in all shades of pastel as they dangled from balconies.

"Excuse me." Penny stopped a man who strolled by wearing a woven metal candelabra on his head. "What is this?"

"It's the *moccoletti*. I think the tradition started at the Carnival in Rome. The goal is to keep your own candle lit, while extinguishing others. Watch."

And watch she did. People rushed by, dodging and dashing, ducking and darting. Boys climbed up carriages; girls scampered off with high-pitched giggles trailing after. Revelers went to elaborate lengths to keep their flames from being extinguished. Two boys rushed by with tall poles, each balancing a candle on top.

Penny was enthralled and longed to participate, to dance with abandon and laugh with friends. She'd missed so much at the estate: a chance at a normal life. True relationships and the ability to explore her own interests. Anger at Master surged through her body. He'd kept her from all this—

"How dare you." The words were a rumble behind her. She

snapped around to find an older man holding a young boy by the back of his neck. The boy stared up at the accuser, unblinking, while his hand slipped something into the pocket of his trousers.

"Give me back my coins," the man seethed.

Penny inched closer. The boy didn't look like a miscreant, with his styled hair, white shirt, and clean boots. Dark brown eyes flicked to her briefly as he pulled his fingers from his pocket, empty this time.

"Sir." She didn't know why she interrupted. What was she thinking, exposing herself like this? She only needed to ask for directions, get on to Marconze. But the boy, he looked defenseless, and she was so sick of people being treated unkindly.

"This doesn't involve you." The man squeezed harder and the boy's eyes widened.

"You're crushing his neck!" She angled herself in between them. "Please. Don't hurt him." The man looked her over and dropped his gloved hand to his side.

"This boy is a pickpocket."

Penny squatted until she was at eye level with the boy. He looked perhaps twelve or thirteen years old but seemed small for his size. "Is it true? Did you steal something?"

"No. I'm not a thief." He stuck his hands in his pockets and pulled them inside out. There was nothing there except a dusty-looking, half-eaten sugarplum.

Penny had seen the boy with something in his hand. Could it have been only the sweet? Either way, she felt relief and glanced up at the man. "You could turn him in to *l'ispettore*, but I think you'd come away feeling foolish."

The man glowered down at both of them.

Penny rose. "I'm sure it's all a misunderstanding. Now, if you could be of some assistance, perhaps? I am wondering the best route to Marconze from here." She tucked her hands behind her back and motioned for the boy to escape. He edged away into the shadows.

With animated gestures, the man described the route. "Continue down this road and out of town. Follow it for approximately fifty kilometers, and make a right at the crossroads. You can't miss it."

Penny thanked him and he tipped his hat to her before disappearing into the crowd. All around, people still chased one another, attempting to snuff out candle flames. A street performer had propped a table in the middle of the avenue and shuffled his cards. He flipped over the top of the deck and the crowd hushed.

Penny stepped back over to the mare and gripped the reins. The nonpickpocket appeared at her side.

"I owe you a debt of gratitude." He certainly didn't speak like a criminal.

She waved him off. "You'd best be going before he returns."

"How might I repay you?"

"There's nothing to repay."

"That's not true and you know it. Now please name your price. I hate owing people."

Penny gazed over at the magician. "You don't owe me. I was doing you a favor. Besides, if you had money to repay me, you wouldn't be lifting it from others."

"It doesn't have to be monetary. I told you, I'm not a thief. But I know this city inside and out. I know its secrets. Perhaps there's some information you need."

Penny frowned. "What is your name?"

"Alidoro."

"Well, Alidoro, I do need some information." Her voice dropped to a whisper to match his. "I'm looking for a man. Beppe."

"The physician?"

"Yes. I fear . . . I fear he may have fallen into some sort of trouble." Something caught her eye from across the plaza. A glimpse of a jacket winding around a group of children dancing in a circle.

It couldn't be Master. Could it?

It was of no matter; she needed to be going now. She un-looped the reins and looked at Alidoro one last time. "If you find anything, no matter how insignificant, please send word to the Azul Apothecary Shoppe. Now go."

The last words were a hiss.

CHAPTER
27

The road flowed like a river under the horse's feet and the landscape slipped past, dull as a smudge. Penny's mind was as numb as her fingers.

She steered the mare along the route until she finally reached Marconze. Closer to the sea, the wind picked up, carrying with it the heavy smell of salt water. Her braid felt thick with moisture. Dark clouds stained the sky as she urged the horse down the narrow streets. The town was much smaller than Ravinni, and less resplendent. No carnival atmosphere, and the shops had all closed. Penny wished she could have stayed in Ravinni, but it wouldn't have been safe. Master could have discovered her missing from the estate and already have a search team gathered to look for her.

He wouldn't find her here, she hoped.

Penny yawned and her eyelids drooped. She knew she had to find a spot to rest. For both her and the horse. Even if just an hour or two until the sun crept over the horizon. Her mind was scattered, and she certainly didn't want to look like a lunatic, banging on someone's door in the middle of the night.

She led the horse along various empty streets until they

finally stumbled upon a small marketplace. A maze of empty stalls greeted her. She slid down from her saddle and led the horse down a side aisle, searching for the best shelter to ward off the wind. The clouds had opened, letting first a sprinkle of mist fall through, and now a sleeting stream. Finally, she stopped under a tall overhang and tied the horse up loosely. She removed the saddle and wiped down the mare's back and flank as best she could.

A heavy canvas wall at the back of the stall kept out a bit of the cold and protected them from much of the wind. A table sat in the middle of the floor space. She tipped it on its side and scooted it back to create a shelter from two angles.

Penny lay down on the hard ground, pulled the jacket over her head, and curled her knees against her chest. Despite the unrelenting dirt and the whistle of wind around her, she managed to doze off, her cheek resting on her palm.

※ ※

"Rocco, I need help moving this table back. Dratted hooligans messing with my stuff at night," a woman's voice muttered above Penny, waking her from a dreamless sleep.

It was nearing dawn and the marketplace was draped in shades of gray as Penny opened her eyes and pushed herself into a sitting position.

The woman shrieked. "Who are you? Stay back." She whipped a knife out of her pocket.

Penny threw her hands up in defense and stood. "I'm sorry. I had nowhere to stay, so I slept here. I didn't touch anything . . . well, except the table, but I'll help you move it back."

The woman lowered her knife. "All right, then. Help me and be on your way. You don't look like no hooligan anyway." She motioned toward the horse. "And I'm assuming that there is your animal?"

Penny nodded and shooed the mare away from where she ducked her nose under a piece of fabric covering a woven basket.

A lanky young man appeared from around the back of the stall. He bent to grab the other end of the table. Locks of light brown hair fell in his eyes, and he shook his head to clear them.

"Ah, Rocco, about time," the woman said. "Let's bring in the wares and arrange the items for *colazione*."

"Who's she?" he asked, tipping his head toward Penny.

"I was leaving." Penny shuffled the table with him until it was near the front of the stall.

Once it was in place, Penny walked over to the horse. She raked her fingers through the animal's matted coat before rearranging the saddle. Rocco moved around her to grab his basket. He upended the container. Fruits and nuts tumbled onto the table and he began to sort them. Penny's stomach grumbled at the sight of the persimmons, and when he lifted the towel off fresh minitarts, she nearly swooned. His eyebrow lifted and he snorted. "Here. Have one."

Penny mumbled a thank-you through a mouthful of food as she tore into the pastry. The flaky crust dissolved on her tongue, leaving the taste of warm persimmon laced with nutmeg. She couldn't eat it fast enough.

"For your horse." He tossed her an apple.

She held it out and the mare took the fruit between her huge teeth. Sunlight broke through the clouds and warmed Penny's face. Morning had officially arrived. It was time to go.

"Another favor." She turned back to Rocco. "Could you possibly direct me to Via del Rinnovamento?"

"It's toward the edge of town." He pointed behind her.

"Follow that avenue and look for Via Viaggiare. Make a left and you can't miss it."

"Perfect. Many thanks again. For the food and the directions." She walked backward, bumping her hip into the table. Rocco and his mother stared at her, their heads tilted to the side as if they couldn't quite figure out what she was up to.

With a quick wave of her fingers, Penny gathered up the horse's reins and made her way out of the stall and the maze of a market.

Her back and shoulders ached from sleeping on the ground, and her legs were sore from riding. Her muscles strained as she pulled herself into the saddle and urged the horse into a walk down the avenue. Rocco's directions were easy enough to follow, but it still took Penny half an hour to get there. Her nerves were near shattered as she stood in front of the house, her heart hammering at her chest like a bird desperate to be set free from its cage.

Fear warred with excitement in a battle that couldn't be won. Her family might live here, in this small wooden cottage nestled among a grove of towering trees that kept it cocooned from the world. Her mother might be inside, cooking breakfast, her dark curls pinned on top of her head and an apron tied around her narrow waist. Her father would be working, perhaps pausing every now and again to wonder if his daughter was okay. And she might have little siblings—scurrying to finish their morning chores before going to school.

Or maybe, just maybe, this house had nothing to do with her at all.

Penny tied the horse near the end of the drive and tripped up the path. Her feet refused to move in sync, like she was some sort of marionette being dragged along the dirt. Her throat felt swollen and she feared the words would clog there when she attempted to speak. But hopefully that wouldn't matter. Hopefully someone, her mother perhaps, would open the door, recognize Penny as her lost little girl, and embrace her tightly, without any words needing to be shared.

It was this thought that kept her moving forward until she arrived at the faded saffron-colored door. Penny took a deep breath, tried to swallow past the knot, and rapped her knuckles on the wood.

The door swung open and a woman stood in the frame. Her dark hair was pulled tight into a long braid. She looked exhausted, like she hadn't slept in days. Sagging eyelids fell over her cerulean eyes. Shoulders slumped, as if at any second she might tumble to the floor.

"May I help you?"

No recognition. Not from the woman, nor from Penny.

Penny's chest constricted with the vital need to belong. To someone. Anyone. She desperately wanted this woman to be her mother. Her gaze took in the woman from head to toe, waiting for something to nudge her thoughts. A scar or beauty mark or some telltale line or curve that held a memory.

It was all for naught.

"I . . . I . . . nothing," Penny choked out. "This was a mistake. I should go." With each passing second, she knew.

This wasn't her family.

This wasn't her house.

CHAPTER 28

The woman inhaled a sharp gasp, her eyes dropping to Penny's wrist. "You're one of them. You can help me." She fell to her knees, much to Penny's horror and dismay. "I'm sorry I let her go. I didn't know what else to do. But we want her to come home. We'll do anything."

Penny stood, still as a statue, her eyes wide. Whatever she'd been expecting, it wasn't this.

The woman's face crumpled. "You can't help me, can you?" She launched to her feet and shoved the door closed. "Go away. I have nothing else to give."

Penny wedged her foot against the frame, biting back a yelp as the woman crushed the heavy wood into her boot. "Please. Wait." Penny braced herself against the door. "I don't understand, but I may be able to help."

Perhaps this was her destiny, the reason for her coming all this way and facing Master's wrath when she returned. Because this woman knew about the girls and the school and it was obvious someone there was important to her.

The woman's face appeared in the gap, her skin pinched and her eyes narrowed. "I will give you two minutes to explain

yourself. But that's it. I want only an explanation. I won't ac-
cept any more enticements and I'm done playing games."

Penny held up her hands. "I promise." Even though she had
no clue what the woman was talking about. Penny had no *enticements* to give. She had nothing at all but her dusty clothes and
the horse at the edge of the property. And the mare wasn't even
hers to hand over.

The woman waved her inside. "We can't let all the heat out."

The room was sparse, a red-and-yellow-striped woven rug
lending the only color to the muted brown tones of the furniture. Flames flickered in the fireplace and Penny couldn't help
but be drawn closer to the heat after being outside all night. She
stood for a moment, her hands outstretched toward the warmth.
The marking on Penny's wrist peeked out past the hem of her
sleeve, and she stared at the pointed, starlike symbol, wondering why all the girls had them, wondering what it meant . . .
whether she was branded, tampered with.

Human even.

Penny suddenly itched to run from the room, run as far as
she could away from all of this madness. She knew this woman
wasn't her mother, so why did she stay? There was nothing for
her here. Her family would have to wait. Penny needed to find
Beppe and learn how to stop Master's manipulations once and
for all. And then she would free the girls. Whether they wanted
to be freed or not.

She spun on her heel, ready to leave, and stopped short. The
woman blocked her path. "Are you all right?"

"I . . ." Tears scalded the back of Penny's eyes, and she
couldn't talk past the pressure building in her chest.

"What's the matter?" The woman stepped forward. "Is it
horrible there? Did you run away?" Her jaw tightened. "Come.

Sit. I'll get us tea." She bustled around the small kitchen area, preparing a kettle and steeping the leaves. "I fear we haven't been properly introduced. My name is Glis."

"Penny." She eased onto the edge of the sofa and thanked Glis for the steaming cup.

"So, why are you here? Do you know Nella? Is there any way we can bring her back home?"

Penny shook her head. "I don't know anyone by that name."

Glis strode toward a table near the door. She grabbed a portrait tintype and carried it back to Penny.

Penny glanced at the silvered image and tilted it to the light. "Is that—"

"Nella. He sent it to us. It's the only thing we have to remember her by."

Penny leaned over the portrait, her pulse thundering so loud she feared Glis must hear it. She did recognize the girl. Nella was the comatose figure Penny had found on the table in Beppe's workshop. The girl who had disappeared.

She forced her voice to remain steady. "Oh yes. She's new."

Glis's eyes widened. "How is she doing? Does she miss us?"

Penny paused a brief moment, debating if she should tell Glis the truth. But the woman had already started pacing, the words flowing as if she was desperate to explain herself, to tell her side of the story.

"Nella isn't our real daughter, not by birth. Although I think of her as one of my own." She rushed the words. "She was an orphan when we took her in a couple of years ago. Master Cirillo has been her benefactor all this time. And then one day, three months ago perhaps, he showed up at our door. He wanted her to join his school." She took a shaky sip of tea. "Why would he want Nella? She's only a child."

Penny shook her head. She didn't know. She didn't *want* to know. "So you let her go?"

"We had no choice. He threatened to force us to pay back all the money he'd provided. It would have destroyed us. We have other children to care for." Her face paled and her eyes sought Penny's, as if asking her to understand, to confirm she'd done the right thing. "He promised her a lavish life resplendent with servants and dancing and balls. She seemed excited. It was more than we could ever give her. Is she happy? Please tell me she's happy. It's the only way I can forgive myself."

Penny leaned in. "Glis, I need you to listen to me."

Glis settled on the sofa, the teacup shaking in her grasp. Penny gently extracted the cup and set it on the side table. She clasped Glis's bony hands in her own.

"She's in trouble."

Tears filled Glis's eyes. "I knew it. I've known all this time."

Penny's chest squeezed tight. She could only hope someone, somewhere, felt the same about her. But for now, she had to focus on what she did know. Nella was in danger and she had a family that cared for her. Penny needed to free her and return her to her home. Return all of the girls home.

"What has he done to her?" Glis asked.

Penny paused and gathered her thoughts. "The girls are in danger—Nella, me, all of us. It will sound bizarre, what I'm about to tell you, but I promise it's the truth." Glis's grip tightened and Penny continued. "Master has found a way to tamper with our thoughts. He can change our memories—erase them or replace them with ones of his own design."

"I don't understand." Glis shifted and her skirts rustled.

"For instance, I don't remember anything before I arrived at the estate."

"Nothing?"

"Not one true memory. I have a photo album in my room, filled with pictures that are supposed to be my mother, but they're false. I don't recognize her."

Glis frowned. "Nella won't remember us?"

"I don't know. But I can promise you I will do my very best to return her to you."

"You're going back there?" Glis looked startled.

"Of course."

"But I thought . . . I figured you'd run away."

"No. I came here hoping you were my family." Penny couldn't stop her own tears from pooling.

"Oh, *mia bambina*." Glis gathered Penny into a hug, tucking Penny's head against her shoulder. "You are surely missed by your loved ones, but if you can't find them, you will always have a place here. If you return Nella to me, I will be ever grateful. You're so very strong to return to the school."

Penny wiped at her nose. "Thank you," she whispered, and pulled away. "I have to go."

"Is there anything I can do to help?" Glis asked.

"Yes." Penny stood. "Be here for Nella when she returns. She will need you."

"Of course." Glis walked Penny to the doorway and gave her another embrace. After releasing Penny, Glis paused as if considering something. She hurried over to the sideboard and rummaged in a drawer. A moment later she pressed something hard into Penny's palm. Penny glanced down to see she held the hilt of a small dagger.

"Oh. I can't take this." Penny tried to give it back.

"I insist. You need some sort of protection. I'd feel better if you had it." Glis stepped back. "Godspeed, Penny, and I hope to see you soon."

The door shut quietly behind Penny. She slipped the dagger into her boot, raced down the steps toward the tree-lined street, and worked quickly to untie the mare. As her fingers pulled at the knot, Penny's head began to throb.

Not now.

She was in the middle of a road, with nobody to help her. She'd been so stupid to come, such a fool to leave Cricket behind.

Oh please, not now.

The pain took over and intelligible thought took flight.

CHAPTER 29

❡ beg you one last time to reconsider."

Cirillo clenched and unclenched his fingers in an attempt to keep from swinging his fist at Beppe. He took a final look at the small bedroom. It was perfect, down to the pink skirts gracing the wardrobe. His staff had done an amazing job, and the first girl was due to arrive tomorrow.

He brushed past Beppe and down the hall. It was cool in this wing—damp, too, but he figured the girls wouldn't much care. They were mostly poor, desperate little things. He would be their savior, raising them up, giving them a chance to be something. Someone. They would be the most intricate beings, with grace and beauty and an ability to move like no others.

"They aren't animals. They're not dolls." Beppe's footsteps echoed as he caught up. "They're human. You can't experiment on them."

Cirillo spun on his feet, stopping so abruptly that Beppe nearly slammed into his chest. He jabbed a finger toward Beppe. "Stop. Stop with your lamenting and whining. I will not let you ruin this for me. You can hide out in your little cabin in the woods and pretend nothing is going on here at the estate. But when I need you, you will come running."

"I don't know that I can do that." Beppe ran his fingers through the curly mop on his head. "I fear you're losing your humanity, and I can't follow you down that dark and twisted path."

Cirillo leaned forward, inhaling the musty air of the hallway. "Oh, you will be my companion on this journey. Or your consort will suffer for your stubbornness."

Beppe sucked in a sharp breath and stumbled backward.

Cirillo chuckled. "What, did you think I didn't know?" His palm flattened against his chest, above his heart. "I'm hurt. I'm hurt you didn't trust me enough to tell me, but I'm also hurt that you didn't think I was smart enough to figure it out." He dropped his hand to his side. "I have eyes and ears everywhere, Beppe. I know all about the girl you've been courting this past year. I know she's ill and needed a lung replacement. You used the equipment paid for from my inheritance to do just that. I know she needs medicine every week so she doesn't reject the artificial organ. And that it has turned her hair an unnatural shade of blue."

Beppe's shoulders rounded in a slump and his lips turned down.

"I know she will need another surgery soon. I've seen the second lung you're creating. It looks so fragile, suspended in the laboratory. I'd hate to see something happen to it."

Beppe jerked upright. "You wouldn't."

"I would, Beppe. I most certainly would. And what of the boy?" Cirillo's shoulders tensed even thinking of his nephew. "You seem to be rather fond of him. Perhaps something will happen to him, too. Something a little less subtle. A hunting accident, perhaps, since I can't use my equipment to manipulate him. You ruined that opportunity for me with your little intervention. I will never forgive you for that."

"What do you want from me?" The words were a whisper that caressed the stone walls.

"Your commitment. You're a brilliant scientist." Cirillo grabbed Beppe's shoulder. "I'm doing this for you. You can push your boundaries, further your research. I know you're not comfortable. But think of the name you'll create for yourself."

Beppe shrugged off his hand and shoved past him.

"I fear my name will only be used in vain, Cirillo. And yours, too."

Cirillo shrugged. His friend would come around.

He always did.

❦ 1879 ❦

Penny wrapped her arms around her bent legs and tucked her head against her knees. The pain spread throughout her forehead, a thousand needles worming into her brain and subconscious. She dug fingernails into her thighs, fighting to stay coherent. With eyes shut tight, Penny concentrated on keeping her breaths even. Then she fought back against the pain. Nudged the needles back a millimeter. And in their place was something new.

Memories.

It was as if she flipped a picture book so fast the images moved—only they were in her head. Penny could see each true thought behind her closed eyes, only to have it ripped away. Dinner, talking with the prince, dancing. And then, with a pain sharper than the slice of a knife, the picture was gone. A new image took its place, of Penny dancing with Master. Sitting at his side at the table. She radiated adoration.

A true memory replaced with a lie.

Nausea curdled in her stomach at the distortions, like her vision was moving but her body stayed still.

As each image changed and Penny forgot the original one,

she felt her anger dissolve and her desire to go to the estate, to home, rise into the empty space. She missed the grounds and calming lake. She missed the girls and their unwavering friendship. She missed the beauty of dance, the art of her sewing, and the ease at which her life unfolded. Warmth spread through her veins, cradling her and urging her to her feet. Penny felt nothing but love toward everyone back home, even Master.

Especially Master.

A smile pulled at her mouth and she lifted her fingers to brush the loose hair from her face. Her eyes lingered on the marking on her wrist.

"No." The word tore from her mouth in a wail. Horror and pain and anguish and fear. A memory clawed its way to the surface. Beppe leaning over her, a thick white jacket draping his shoulders and a thin metal strip clasped between his fingers. With his other hand, he touched a spot right behind her ear.

It was the same spot where Nella's skin had been sewn together.

With a shuddering breath, Penny reached up with her hand and began to dig. Fingernails scratching at the surface, she fought to break through the skin. But it wasn't enough. With precision focus, she forced herself to remember exactly where Beppe had implanted the device. She worried it might kill her, detaching it from her mind, but she couldn't take it anymore. The implant was foreign, used to control her.

It had to go.

With unconscious thought, she reached into her boot and removed the dagger Glis had handed her only minutes before. Gripping it tightly in one hand, she lifted her hair with the other. She stretched her neck to the side and forced the skin taut before piercing it with the knife. Penny breathed through the fiery pain and almost immediately felt the blade hit something hard. With shallow breaths, she sliced a small line along its length. She dropped the dagger into her skirt and tore at the metal device with her fingers. Clasping the edges, she managed one more gulp of air before she yanked. Hard.

The pain was horrific, burning, acidic. Fiery pulses through her brain. Unwelcome tears streamed over her cheeks and she shoved the corner of the small square metal strip, now free from her head, into the center of her palm, trying to stay alert.

With a gasp and startling clarity, the torture ended, and Penny remembered everything.

Everything.

She grabbed the edge of her skirt and pulled it toward the side of her head, shoving the fabric against her skin to staunch the blood that dripped from the wound. Her eyelids fluttered closed. She raced along her thoughts as far back as she could, to the beginning, to waking in Beppe's home two years ago.

As if a door had been thrown open wide, scenes brightened in her mind.

⁂

She opened her eyes and took in the room around her. Yellow walls and a window that overlooked a forest. It was her room in Beppe's cottage. He stood over her, eyes anxious but excited. "How do you feel?"

"Fine, thank you." Penny pushed into a sitting position. "Who are you?"

He smiled, a quick half sort of grin, and sat beside her. "I'm Beppe. Your doctor. Welcome back to the world, Penelope." And then he leaned in, eager to ask questions.

Beppe had seemed so involved, so interested, so intrigued.

He *couldn't* have known what was in store for them, what Master really intended.

Her memories jumped forward and she saw herself in the same room, lying curled on the hard mattress. Her fingers pressed hard into her temples. "I'm so sorry." Beppe held a cold compress to her head. "You're not taking very well to this. Are you sure you don't like ballet?"

She didn't . . . she didn't . . . and then one day she did.

It was like a whole different Penny, one who seemed foreign. Like a twin growing up in a different city. Two lives zipped together again.

Her thoughts raced along, past glimpses of life at the estate, her *sorelle*, their classes, and . . . of course, Master. She tried to skip over those, fighting not to remember any of the agony from inside the walls of his quarters. Instead, she focused on the hall outside. Because every time she left his room—in pain and altered and broken—Cricket stood waiting to escort her away.

He'd wrap his arm around her shoulder and lead Penny through the halls, asking if she was okay, if she was hungry, if she needed anything. And always, just before he'd leave her at the entrance to the girls' hall, he'd bid her *Ciao, mia farfallina*.

And she would smile. Because she knew.

He had been the one to give her that nickname, *my little butterfly*. Many years before the estate.

Penny gasped. Cricket was the boy in the memory of chasing butterflies in the field. They'd known each other all along, been friends as children. She could picture his blond curls, his lanky legs forever outpacing her. The bright smile that always lit up his eyes and the freckles that multiplied each summer.

Master had blocked it out. All of it.

But why?

Penny fought to remember, searching for a reason. And there it was. One day last year. She slid out of Master's room, eyes glassy and body trembling from the attempts at distorting her thoughts. Cricket launched himself at his uncle, rage burning in his eyes, but Master stopped him. He grabbed Cricket's wrists in his hands. "Don't do it, boy. These girls aren't worth getting kicked out of the estate and losing any chance at an inheritance. They will never love you. She"—he inclined his head toward Penny—"will never love you the way you love her." He let go, shoving at Cricket so he stumbled backward. "I'll see to that."

"How dare you?" Penny seemed to snap out of her trace. She rushed forward, her fingers curling into fists as she pummeled Master's chest. He didn't own her.

And yet . . . I guess he did.

Master had stood there, a smirk on his face as if a kitten scratched at his leg.

"I could love him," Penny shouted. "More than I could ever love you."

His expression morphed. His eyes darkened to near onyx and his teeth ground together. "You. Ungrateful. Little . . . I give you everything and this is how you repay me? Perhaps you need more improvements."

Master grabbed her by her hair, loose and tangled around her shoulders from the treatment, and dragged her back into the recesses of his parlor.

Penny had no cohesive memories of the following days other than a lot of pain and the pulsing throb of wires attached to her head and neck.

And after that, Cricket never met her in Master's wing. He was relegated to the kitchen, where she saw him at mealtimes, if she was lucky. And by then, her thoughts had been conditioned to ignore him, to view him as a mere lowly member of the staff.

Oh, Cricket.

He'd tried to help Penny escape, stood by her side as she was forced to return, and assisted her at every step. He'd waited for her to regain her memories as she continually cowered from him and cringed from his touch. He'd never pushed her to remember.

Because memories of him meant memories of everything.

And in return for his infinite kindness and patience, Penny had abandoned him.

Another wave of nausea swept over her and she tipped her head. She took deep breaths, fighting to gain control.

Penny wanted to leave then, to find him, to apologize for everything. But she couldn't go just yet. She had to stay a few minutes more. She had to absorb all the truths in her memory, every last one, for fear that they would disappear. She had no idea what her mind was doing, healing itself or slowly shutting down.

So Penny pushed back in time. *There has to be more.* She had to have a history before the estate. Just a glimpse of her family, of her life, of anything.

***

She stood on top of a small hill, looking down at the still-smoldering remains of her family's farmhouse. The tears had long since dried, leaving a tight trail down her cheeks. Her sister's small hand was clasped in her own.

If only Penny had stayed. If only she hadn't been selfish . . . She loved her mother dearly, but she'd felt so trapped. Day in, day out, at the farm. Mother always needed help, now that

Father had passed away. Taking care of her sister. Taking care of the animals. Penny understood the responsibility bestowed upon her, but it still wore her down.

All she'd wanted was to go to town. For one day. One afternoon. See the festivities. Buy a bag of sweets and suck on them until her fingers were sticky. Dare to try on a costume and pretend she could afford to purchase it.

"Penny, you can't go," Mother had said, her voice holding a strength that belied her frailty. "The cows need to be milked, the chickens fed."

But Penny had gathered up her skirts, raced to the stable, and saddled the old pony, Cavallo. She lifted her sister behind her, and they were off.

She never even said good-bye.

And now. This. A fire had swept through their home in the few hours she was gone. Her mother had been trapped inside, too weak to run from the flames. Penny knew she could have saved her, helped usher her outside. If only she'd been there. It was that knowing that killed her, wrung her dry from the inside out.

If only she'd stayed.

If only she'd said good-bye.

If only . . .

But now her mother was gone. The woman who sang while doing the chores, who taught Penny to sew and praised her first misshapen quilt, who never once complained as the illness ravaged her organs and settled in her lungs.

The woman who loved Penny and her sister more than anything.

Penny started trembling, her eyes desperate to leak tears that had already dried.

Someone stepped beside her, his shadow longer than hers in the tall grass. A thick jacket was placed upon her shoulders.

"Come with me, Penelope." His voice was low and smooth, the words dipped in honey. "You'll be happy at the school."

Penny had been refusing him for weeks now. But he stuck around, insisting. She bumped into him at the oddest places, and it had happened again today in town. He'd offered to escort her back to the farm. It was his hands that braced her and stopped her from racing down the drive toward the burning building. He'd worked with the neighbors to put out the fire and stayed after they took her mother's body to the nearby church to hold until burial.

She didn't know what to do. The land would be sold to pay the debtors. How would she tend to her sister? She had nothing.

Master Cirillo pulled out his crisp handkerchief and wiped at her face. "I will plan the funeral. I will make sure your sister is well cared for. But only if you leave with me today."

Numb, inside and out and every cell in between, Penny nodded.

She'd go.

For where else did she have to turn?

❧ ⸱ ☙

Mother? I have a mother? A family. A history.

A mother who had died. She was the same woman pictured in the portraiture in her pocket. Master had given her the truth for once. Tears coursed down her cheeks. Fresh ones, not the phantom ones of her memory. A mixture of sadness and joy. Because while her mother had died, she also had a sister who lived. But who was this girl and how could she find her? Penny closed her eyes for a moment, willing herself to return to the memory, to look down at the girl gripping her fingers tight on the hillside.

She screamed.

Her knuckles dug into her mouth to stifle the sound, to keep her body from splintering for good.

Her sister . . . her sister was Nella.

Beautiful, sweet, shy, patient, calm Nella.

The house in front of her now was Nella's adopted home. And her sister was a prisoner at the estate.

She had to go.

Mud clung to the back of her skirt as she stood, one hand still pressing the cloth against the side of her head. She barely glanced at the small strip of metal, with its strange etchings and blackened edges, before she shoved it deep in her pocket. Part of her wanted to throw it into a gutter, but another part acknowledged that it might be useful someday.

Her body felt coiled tight, ready to split and release all the pain and grief building inside her body. If someone brushed up against her, she would explode.

But she didn't have time for this.

She had to get back to the estate.

She had to warn Cricket.

She had to free Nella.

Before Master did any further damage to anyone.

$\mathcal{P}$enny had untied the mare and was nearing to mount her when Glis appeared like a vision. "Is everything all right? I noticed from the window you hadn't left yet. . . ." She gasped as her eyes took in Penny's gaping wound. "*Mia bambina!* Let me get you something for that."

Seconds later, she appeared with a damp cloth and began to wipe the blood away. Her touch was delicate, but Penny still winced as she brushed over the gash.

"Why did you do this?" Glis whispered.

Penny held out the metal strip. "This is how he controlled us. I had a vision."

Glis inhaled through clenched teeth when she saw the strange appliance in Penny's palm. "I understand. Still, you should've had a doctor remove it." She used a dropper to drip colloidal silver on a gauze square and then placed it behind Penny's ear. "Hold this."

She went back into the house and returned with a simple pastel bonnet. After resting it on Penny's head, she strategically wove the ribbon past the gauze and under Penny's chin. "That should hold, but you need to have it looked at soon."

"I will." Penny gathered up the reins.

"Promise me." Glis stood, hands on her hips.

"I promise. And thank you again for your help." Penny managed a small smile in spite of the pain. She clambered up into the saddle, and with a wave behind her, she headed back toward Ravinni.

⚜ ⚜

"I won't be but a moment," she argued with the stable boy after he asked for five *lire* to board the mare. After riding for over an hour, she'd led the horse to the livery stable next to the stagecoach station. "Surely Master can cover the tab when he is in town next?"

She glanced around, wondering if her decision to stop in Ravinni had been a good idea. But she'd told Cricket to send word to Tatiana if she was in danger. The least Penny could do was follow her own directions. If only the boy would let her stable the horse for a brief time.

"You'll havta pay before I can give yer horse back ta ya." He shrugged as if he didn't care whether she left the animal with him or not.

"Fine." She handed over the reins and hurried off before the boy could change his mind. Tatiana was sure to lend her some coins. Once she found the apothecary shop.

Penny stepped into the postal shop, certain they knew all the local businesses.

"Of course. Nobody can forget Tatiana and the blue strands." The desk clerk pointed to his own balding head of hair. "She's two streets over, make a left. You can't miss it."

Penny forced herself not to sprint down the road and around the corner. The building was easy enough to spot, tucked at the end of the street and bathed in a stream of sunlight.

AZUL APOTHECARY

Penny hastened up the steps and pushed open the door.

A bell rang a sweet chime as she walked into the front room. Wooden shelves and counters displayed a dizzying array of potions and medicines, many glowing in unnatural hues. Yellows, blues, greens, and pinks. All twinkling and swirling as if they were alive.

"Hello and welcome." Tatiana peeked out from a doorway hung with jeweled fringe. "Penny!" She rushed forward and engulfed her in an embrace. Penny winced and pulled back. "Oh dear." Tatiana's gaze skipped to the bonnet and the bandage that poked out, surely stained red. "I'll prepare a salve and a fresh dressing for you."

"I don't have time," Penny said. "Has Cricket sent word? I need to get back to the estate, but I left him a message, that if I was in danger to contact you. So if he hasn't, I'll be going. I need to return."

She knew she was rambling, but the pain from her wound and the shock of her memories didn't make for very coherent conversation.

"Go wait in the back room." Tatiana began pulling down jars and tinctures.

Penny pushed through the fringe and stumbled into a drawing room of sorts. A long table, spread with assorted platters of food and drink, stretched along the side wall. Plush sofas, dotted with colorful pillows, sat near a crackling hearth.

And staring down at the flames, with his back to her, stood Cricket.

"Cricket!"

He turned around, his wary expression turning to surprise when he saw her.

Penny raced forward and threw her arms around his neck, rising on tiptoes to bury her nose in the soft skin near his collarbone. Cinnamon and honey as always. She could feel him tense underneath her embrace, as if he was waiting for her to come to her senses and pull away. "I'm sorry," Penny whispered. "I'm so very sorry."

His hands settled on her back and pulled her closer. His chin rested on her hair. "Aren't you afraid? Of the memories?"

"No. I remember everything." Penny pulled back only slightly so she could look into his pale eyes. She wondered how she could ever have doubted him.

"Everything. Are you certain?" He blinked and swallowed hard. "You've been through some horrible things."

"I know." Penny still stared at him. "But I know you always tried to protect me. From the beginning. Even when we were children."

Cricket pulled one hand from her back and ran it across his jaw. "I felt so helpless and weak. You were in a fog, and it kept getting worse as the months passed. Then last week, suddenly, you were the most alert I've seen you in months. I knew it was your only chance. But he kept altering your memories. Every time you reverted back, I worried I'd lost you for good."

"There's nothing to worry about now."

"And you're okay?"

"I will be." She slid her arms to his waist and rested her cheek against his chest. Her voice dropped to a whisper. "I'm definitely okay with my memories of you. I only wish I'd never lost them in the first place."

They stood still as statues, gripping each other tightly, as if at any second they might be wrenched apart.

The fringe rustled and Cricket took a reluctant step back. Tatiana approached, her hands laden with a bowl and clean linens.

Cricket narrowed his gaze at Penny, only then really noticing the wound mostly covered by the bonnet strings. His eyes widened in concern. "Did someone attack you?"

"No," Penny said. Her fingers brushed against her skirt pocket. "I did it to myself"—she pulled the metal from her pocket—"to remove this."

Tatiana flinched at the sight of the device. She motioned Penny to the sofa and had her lie down. As Penny settled in the deep cushion, Tatiana handed her a smooth ivory ball. "Grip it tight. This will hurt." She unlaced the bonnet and pulled at the strings, now scabbing and sticky with dried blood. Penny bit down hard on her lower lip as the dressing ripped from her skin. Tatiana gently probed the area around the wound. "I'm going to have to make a few sutures."

Penny rolled the cool, smooth ball around her palm while Tatiana gathered more supplies and threaded a needle. She applied an ointment to the skin that made it tingle and go slightly numb, but Penny still felt the piercing each time it shoved through her skin. Cricket knelt at her side and held her other hand while she squeezed the ball tight. Tatiana finally finished and applied a salve. She left it uncovered, saying it would need air. "It will itch, but it should heal just fine."

Penny thanked her and pushed herself into a sitting position. Cricket rose and moved to sit across from her. Penny finally asked the question she'd dreaded since realizing he was at the shop. "So, I'm guessing Master discovered my absence."

He nodded. "This morning. He threw the entire manor into a frenzy, searching for you. I was barely able to escape before he could interrogate me. I fear it's not safe for you to return."

"I have to go back." Penny stared at him. "To save the girls. To save my sister."

"Your sister?" Cricket looked at her as if perhaps she'd lost a bit of her mind when she'd removed the metal implant.

"Yes. Nella. The girl in Beppe's workshop."

He stiffened and reached for her hand again. Her fingers tightened against his.

"Are you positive?" he asked. "I didn't recognize her. But then I haven't seen her for years. . . ." His voice trailed off.

Penny nodded. "I'm positive. I remember her clearly. And I met with the woman who took her in before Master removed her to the estate." Penny explained how she'd found the address in the journal, and her overnight trip. "Master lied to me. Even back then. He lied to us both. He promised to care for Nella if I went with him." She squeezed his hand tighter and her voice rose. "I know we were in danger before, but the risk is even higher now. He could harm any of the girls as retribution for my actions. I couldn't live with myself if anything happened to Nella." Her voice cracked, and she swallowed hard. "I have to save them. I have to." She knew she was repeating herself, but she had to make him understand. Her body hummed with the desire to leave immediately for the estate, but she needed a plan first. She couldn't act on impulse.

The shop bell jingled and Penny froze.

Tatiana gathered up the bowl and dirty bandages, and swept through the curtain with a "Hello, how may I help you?"

She returned a moment later, a young boy right behind her.

"Alidoro!" Penny's shoulders fell with relief. She motioned the youth over and he collapsed beside her on the sofa. "You can't possibly have news of Beppe this quickly." It was hard to believe she'd made the request only the night before, and yet the timing couldn't have been more perfect. Beppe would know where Nella was being held and could help free the girls.

Alidoro shrugged. "It wasn't difficult at all, seeing as how I know the right people to ask such questions."

"And are these 'right' people trustworthy?" Penny asked.

"Of course."

Tatiana tipped her head, blue hair draping at an angle over her cheek. "Do you know where he's gone?"

Alidoro glanced at her and then back to Penny. "He's at the asylum on the edge of town. Locked in a room on the second floor. Reports say he's fallen ill."

Tatiana sucked in a sharp breath.

"We must free him," Penny said, but even as she blurted the words, her chest tightened. She was torn. The girls needed her. Nella needed her. But so did Beppe. And he held answers that could help the girls at the estate. "Today. Now. We'll go to the asylum and have him removed."

"It won't be that simple," Alidoro chimed in before he turned to Tatiana. "May I have a pastry, please? I've been running around all morning trying to answer the young lady's questions. I hate to leave a debt unpaid."

Cricket snorted and Tatiana waved the boy over to the *cannoncini* on a platter at the edge of the table.

"He's right, you know." Cricket slid into the spot Alidoro had just vacated. "We can't appear at the asylum and request that they turn Beppe over to us."

"Not to mention Cirillo owns the entire staff." Tatiana rubbed at her forehead.

Alidoro stuffed the treat in his mouth, his cheeks bulging. "Well, I best be leaving. I believe we're even now?" He looked at Penny, who nodded. "I can see myself out." He twisted through the curtain and a moment later the shop bell chimed.

Silence descended over the room.

"How can we get in?" Penny slumped. Time was not on their side. The gala was the very next day, and Penny feared what Master might do to Nella in her absence.

"Rosaura might have an idea."

Penny's spine straightened. "She's still here?"

"Upstairs." Tatiana glanced at a narrow doorway at the back of the room.

"Why didn't you say so?" Penny bounded toward the opening.

Tatiana stepped in front of her. "Penny, wait." She paused. "Rosaura is not exactly as you remember."

CHAPTER
32

"Penny?"

They'd followed Tatiana up through a slender, spiral staircase into a tiny hallway and chamber.

Near the window, wrapped in at least two quilts, a girl sat holding a steaming mug. Upon seeing Penny, she stood, the material pooling heavy at her feet.

She whispered Penny's name again, her eyes wide and bulging with tears.

Penny only stared, unable to reconcile the bright and beautiful ballet prodigy Rosaura had been with this waif of a person standing in front of her. Dark hair hung in thin strands to her waist. The sallow skin that stretched across her cheekbones looked paper thin, and the bare wrists protruding from her sleeves were knobby bones.

But Penny knew those eyes. A dark purplish blue, as rare in color as her own aquamarine ones.

"Master's not with you, is he?" Rosaura asked. Her voice was a hoarse whisper and her eyes flitted to the hall. Her chest heaved as Tatiana rushed over and tucked the quilts around her shoulders.

"Of course not, dear," Tatiana said. "I wouldn't allow him to find you again."

Rosaura sank into the chair again, pulled the quilts tighter, and tapped her fingernails against the mug. Penny followed the movement, watching Rosaura dance *Giselle* with her fingers. They'd performed it at the previous year's gala, mere weeks after Rosaura had been whisked away. "I'm glad you escaped," she croaked to Penny.

"Rosaura," Tatiana said. "We need your help. Beppe has been locked away at the asylum."

The quilts shook with Rosaura's tremors. "I can't go back there." The words were raw, as if dragged over sharp glass.

"We're not asking you to." Tatiana crouched down, forcing Rosaura to meet her gaze. "We only need you to tell us how to get inside. Can you remember anything about the building, anything that could help us free him?"

Rosaura shook her head repeatedly, manically, as if the motion could force the thoughts and memories from her brain. "I don't care. After all the things he did to me? I don't care. He deserves to be there. They both do."

"Please." Tatiana carefully placed her palms against Rosaura's cheeks. "He helped free you, Rosaura. He wants to help free all the girls. Is there nothing you can tell us?"

Penny reached for Cricket's hand and squeezed his fingers. She could've ended up like this. Any of the girls could wind up as tormented as Rosaura. The thought filled her with horror.

With fingers leaping and dancing *entrechats* along her forearm, Rosaura spoke in raspy eruptions of thought. "There's a hallway to the right of the entrance—leads to another corridor—a flight of stairs—upstairs ward under lock and key—restraints . . ." She stopped speaking and shook her head.

Tatiana shushed her. "That's enough for now. Thank you for helping. I'll be back in a short moment with more tea."

She motioned for Cricket and Penny to follow her down the stairs. "I have some herbs that will calm her down."

"Is she always like that?" Penny's chest tightened and she rubbed at her arms, unnerved at Rosaura's transformation. The lively and optimistic young dancer was now a terrified shell.

And it could just as easily have been Penny.

"She's getting better. Her voice might be permanently strained, though. I fear it's from screaming."

Penny's entire body tensed, and she was unable to shake the image as she followed Tatiana into the shop. Tatiana moved from cabinet to cabinet, pulling down jars filled with dried leaves. "I should probably stay here with her," Tatiana said as she ground the herbs with a pestle and poured them from a mortar into a teacup.

Cricket dashed his knuckles against his jaw. "I think it would be better if both of you stay behind." He looked pointedly at Penny. "I can go to the asylum and work to free Beppe."

"Not on your life. I'm going with you." Penny buttoned her coat, as if to prove a point.

Tatiana gave her a long glance. "The asylum has a small hospital attached. You might gain entrance if you say you need them to look at your wound. They shouldn't recognize you, and it's obvious they'll do anything for an extra *lira* or two."

Cricket clenched his jaw as if he thought the idea a horrible one.

"Perfect." Penny nodded at Tatiana.

Tatiana reached into a drawer and tossed Penny a pair of long gloves. "Keep these on so they don't see your mark. Stay safe, the both of you. And bring Beppe straight here."

The door shut with a soft *click* behind them. Cricket gave Penny his elbow and she tucked her arm through. The pair wound through the streets, avoiding the crowded marketplace and the main thoroughfares, where, even though it was only late morning, revelers had already collected to celebrate the eve of the spring equinox and gala.

Cricket pulled her closer as they finally left the businesses behind. They turned a corner and there it was. A barren street stretched in front of them, leading to a gate and then the asylum at the top of a hill. The grass had been left to grow haphazardly, and patches of it clumped dry and wilted on the side of the road. A wrought-iron fence stretched across the horizon. Beyond the arched gate, the dusty dirt road led to a large stone building that bowed in the middle under its own crushing weight.

They stood at the threshold of the drive. Penny took a deep breath and urged Cricket forward. After shutting the gate behind them, they walked quickly up the path and approached the gray concrete steps, where cracks and weeds threatened to turn the stone a sickly shade of green. Cricket took them two at a time and shoved open the main door, holding it for Penny.

A young woman, her skin as pale as the white dress and apron she wore, greeted them from behind a small counter. Penny showed her the stitches on her neck. "It stings. I fear there's an infection."

"I will have a physician examine it." With a quick jot in a journal, she led them into a short, whitewashed hallway and turned through the first open doorway. The room was empty, save for two chairs and a table of sorts. A dirt-crusted window overlooked the front drive. The woman told them it would be only a few minutes and returned to the reception area.

As soon as she'd left, Penny nudged open the door and they

scooted into the empty hall. Penny turned in the opposite direction from the foyer and Cricket followed close behind her. At the end of the corridor, she pushed on the handle and raced through the doorway, only to stumble to a halt on the other side.

It was as if she'd walked into another dimension. The corridor extended in front of her, but this one was gloom and shadows where the front room was bright and crisp. Dim light flickered from lanterns held by wrought-iron hooks at random intervals along the wall. The floor was uneven and covered in mottled splotches. Dark red and brown stained the chipped tile.

"Go," Cricket urged. They ran down the hall and past closed doors. Low moans of pain curled from the rooms, twisting like smoke around Penny and almost choking her. A shriek erupted from somewhere ahead, and she cupped her hands over her ears to block out the sound.

Cricket pushed her forward with brief nudges to her lower back. "Rosaura mentioned stairs. Be on the lookout."

A door flew open and a man stepped out. Red dotted his white lab coat, and he gripped a tray of sharp instruments in both hands. He stopped when he saw them rushing toward him. "What are you two doing? You're not allowed back here."

Penny slowed, not wanting to confront anyone with an array of knives within reach. Cricket stepped to her side.

"We're looking for an exit," Cricket said. "Is there one on this side of the building?" He remained calm, eyes locked on the physician.

"No. You need to go back the way you came." His jaw tightened. "Now."

"We can't do that." Cricket snagged Penny's sleeve and yanked her forward. She hugged the wall as they hurried past the doctor and raced ahead. He shouted at them to stop and called for his nurse.

Penny turned a corner and came face-to-face with a graying brick wall. Two doors were closed on either side of the hallway. Cricket pulled open the one on the right. It was a closet holding shelves piled high with linens and what looked like medieval torture devices.

Penny lunged for the handle on the opposite wall. "Stairs." Narrow steps led to a landing before turning and disappearing.

"Let's go." He motioned for her to lead the way. With a deep breath, she plunged into the stairwell. Dust glittered in the slice of sunlight peeking in through a crack in the outer wall. Penny raced through it and up the stairs. At the top, she eased open yet another door. Her nostrils flared and she fought back the urge to gag all the air back out of her lungs. The stench was horrific, sour, and foul, a mix of body odor and mold and . . . she didn't want to know.

The sounds weren't much different from those on the floor below—moans, yells, faint rattling—but it *felt* different up here. It felt like death. Or waiting for death. And the rooms seemed more like cells, what with the small, barred cutouts located at eye level on each door.

Pinching her nose against the putrid smell, Penny rushed down the corridor, ignoring the sudden rush of emaciated humans running to their glassless windows and peering out.

"Help me," someone croaked.

"Please, I need water."

"Get me out of here."

Penny walked faster, breaking into a sprint.

"Open the door."

"Open the door."

And then it began. Soon everyone began yelling in chorus, rattling at the bars. "Open the door. Open the door. Open the door."

A door at the opposite end of the hallway flew open. Fearing it was the unhinged doctor and his staff, Penny pushed Cricket back the way they'd just come. They nearly tripped over themselves in their haste to retreat.

Until she heard a hoarse voice. "Penny?"

Her head whipped toward the sound. It was Beppe, his face mashed against the rusted bars.

She reached for the handle and they flew inside.

Beppe opened his mouth and croaked, "Don't let—" but it was too late.

The *click* of the self-locking latch echoed like a gunshot through the small space.

They were trapped.

Cricket ran his hands over the blank slate of a door, looking for some sort of latch or way to exit the room. No handle, no lever, no keyhole.

Penny couldn't take her eyes off Beppe. His face looked as if he'd been mauled by one of the wolves at the estate. Deep scratches lined one cheek. His curling white hair was matted with what looked like mud. And yet he still cracked a smile for her. "I knew you both would figure it out." Then he shook his head. "But why did you come? There's no way out. I've tried everything. You shouldn't have risked it for me."

A scuffle of footsteps in the hallway had them all scrambling away from the door. The mad doctor stood outside, eyes slitted at them through the bars. "I might have known that's what you two delinquents were doing here. Still"—he leaned closer—"I'm sure Cirillo will pay a pretty penny for your safe return."

"We haven't done anything," Cricket said. "Set us free."

"Breaking and entering? That's something. I think I'll wait and see what the manor lord says."

Penny stepped forward. "If it's only breaking and entering you're accusing us of, then you should get *l'ispettore* and turn us over to him." It would be safer at his bureau, where she could explain all that had happened.

But the doctor only sneered. "Alas, the inspector won't give me any coins. You serve me better as wards of the hospital."

"Please!" Penny shouted as he turned and stomped back down the hall. She pounded her fists on the door, all too aware that she now mirrored the other residents of the asylum. "Please," she whispered, sinking to her knees on the cold concrete floor. Her shoulders shook with tremors as silent sobs threatened to escape. The three of them were trapped. Master would find her here and destroy her memories for good.

Cricket paced the small chamber. His eyes scanned the walls as if somehow an answer would appear, scrawled in pale ink.

Beppe sat on the edge of the mattress. "If there was a way out, I'd have found it already." He took a deep breath as if talking had winded him. "It's not like I haven't had hours to search. I wish you had both stayed in safety. Cirillo would have released me eventually."

Penny stood again, ready to scream and pound on the door, do something, anything, but a scratching noise stopped her before she even started. Her eyes widened and her pulse thundered. It was nearly impossible that word could've been sent to Master already.

The handle turned slowly, quietly, and the door inched open.

But instead of Master or Primo, or even the doctor or his staff, young Alidoro stood on the other side.

"Hurry," he whispered, swiping his hair back off his forehead. "Master's men are only minutes behind me."

Beppe glanced at Penny and she nodded. They could trust him.

Barefoot, Beppe padded behind them. He clutched his graying, stained dressing gown around his thin body.

Alidoro held a finger to his lips as he looked down the hallway, and then beckoned them to follow. Penny tiptoed behind him, almost tripping in her haste to escape the room before anyone caught them. Her breath had stalled, and she didn't exhale until they turned the corner and fled down a narrow set of stairs.

They emerged into a darkened hall, lit only by a couple of poorly spaced glass bulbs that seemed to fizzle and spurt with strange electric impulses. "Do you know where you're going?" Penny whispered.

"This is the way I snuck in." Alidoro hurried forward. "There's an exit ahead that opens on the side of the building."

The rotten scent of sulfur made Penny cough and cover her nose. Behind her, Cricket urged Beppe onward.

A burst of sunlight blinded her as Alidoro threw open a door. Penny gulped the fresh air. Cricket stumbled out, Beppe's arm wrapped around his shoulder as if he needed the support.

"This way." Alidoro pointed around the back of the building, where an alley stretched off to the right.

"A . . . minute . . . please," Beppe gasped out. His skin had turned shades paler, and a sheen of sweat coated his forehead.

Alidoro anxiously shifted from foot to foot.

"Did you follow us to the asylum?" Penny asked.

He nodded. "I wanted to make sure you made it out safe. And when you didn't come back outside, I snuck in."

"Thank you," Penny said. "Now it's me who owes you."

He shrugged. "We need to go. Now."

As if they needed more motivation, they heard a shout from

around the outer corner of the building. A gruff voice. "Check the perimeter."

Alidoro's eyes widened, and he took off at a sprint in the opposite direction. Penny scurried to Cricket and draped Beppe's other arm over her shoulder. Together they dragged him away from the building.

"Leave me," Beppe wheezed. "You have much more to lose. Cirillo needs me."

Penny ignored him, not believing him for a second. They tripped their way into the alley, which was really more of a dirt path overgrown with weeds trampled down in two even rows by wagon wheels.

The deep voice yelled out again, closer this time. "Over here. I see them."

Adrenaline kicked in and Penny dashed forward, pulling on Beppe. She couldn't let them be captured. Not now. Not when she was so close to getting answers and finding out from Beppe how she could free her sister and the other girls from Master's control.

The alley ended at a side street that led down a steep hill and into town. She caught sight of Alidoro motioning them forward from a few buildings away. Beppe groaned and Penny's grip on him slipped. A bloody tinge had soaked through his sleeve. She feared the depth of his wounds, hidden as they were beneath his clothes.

"We have to find a place to hide," Penny murmured to Cricket.

She could hear footsteps begin to pound behind them.

"This way." Alidoro disappeared.

Penny squeezed into the tight space between buildings. It wasn't wide enough for the three of them, so she moved ahead while Cricket pulled Beppe along behind. She slipped in a muddy sludge, her palm scraping on the wall as she caught herself from falling. A few yards later, they burst onto another street. A glance to her left and she spotted Alidoro turning another corner. Even with Beppe slowing them down, they somehow kept several yards ahead of Master's men.

After several more narrow streets, twists and turns, and backtracking, they arrived in the labyrinth of the marketplace. Alidoro wound his way through the booths, quick to duck in and out of sight.

"We have to stop," Cricket panted. "Beppe is fading."

Penny glanced around, eyes wide, trying to find a place to hide. Her vision skated across the crowded booths, the tables laden with dried meat and fresh vegetables and royal-colored silks. And tarts. Very familiar tarts.

She motioned Cricket forward and into the tent. "Rocco?"

The vendor's son turned around, a smile lifting his lips. "It's the girl and her horse. With no horse." He peered behind her. "And new friends."

"I have an immense favor to ask. My grandfather is hurt. My friends are going for help, but I need someplace to wait with him."

"An adventure." His smile grew broader. "Alidoro! My friend. Are you with these good folks?" Alidoro stepped into the tent and the two hugged like they hadn't seen each other in ages. "Come in, come in. Why didn't you say so?"

Cricket kept an eye on the nearby aisles, looking to see if Master's men were nearby. Rocco led Penny and Beppe to the back of the tent. He shifted aside some boxes and baskets to clear a space on the ground, hidden from view by a large table that displayed the fruit and tarts. Beppe collapsed onto the packed dirt, his eyes sinking shut.

Penny called Cricket over. "Go to the apothecary. See if Tatiana has some sort of stretcher. We need to get Beppe to her as soon as possible."

"I can't leave you." His eyes were pale and wide.

"You must. Take Alidoro. He knows the most obscure route, one that won't get you caught. Together you can return with something to transport Beppe." She rested her hand on his forearm. "Please, Cricket, you have to go."

Cricket nodded. "We'll return shortly."

The boys slipped out the back, between panels of linen that acted as a wall. Rocco greeted a customer near the front and Penny settled cross-legged near Beppe. She smoothed back damp strands of hair that stuck to his forehead. His breaths were labored and rattling, as if liquid had settled in his lungs. Penny didn't dare move him or check his wounds, for fear she'd only make them worse.

"Get down," Rocco hissed. He started whistling to himself and rearranged the persimmons on the table. Penny flattened herself on the floor. Through a thin gap between the table and the floor she could see dusty black boots walking past.

"Care to sample a tart?" Rocco's voice boomed. The boots slowed their pace. "They're freshly baked, just this morning. I picked the fruit myself."

"No, thank you. Have you seen anyone running through the market recently?"

"Can't say that I have. Are you certain you don't want to try a pastry? My mother is the best *pasticcere* in the area." He kept up a steady stream of one-sided conversation until the boots clomped off at a quick pace.

A minute passed and then Rocco whispered again. "They're gone."

Penny pushed herself off the ground. "What are you doing in Ravinni?"

"Isn't it obvious? Two markets, twice the sales. I get Mother set up and then come here to run this stall. The bigger question is, what are *you* doing in Ravinni?" He shoved hair out of his eyes and raised an eyebrow in her direction.

"It's a long story, and one you're better off knowing nothing about. But thank you for letting us wait here."

He glanced down at Beppe's prostrate form. "No need to thank me. I just hope Alidoro and your friend make haste in returning."

Penny sighed. "Me, too."

Me, too.

Nearly half an hour had passed before Cricket returned. Alone and empty-handed.

"Where's Alidoro?" Penny asked. She tried to stretch her cramped legs.

"Two aisles over. Tatiana lent us a cart. It's small, meant only to hold her supplies when she visits a client. Hopefully we can arrange him comfortably." He bent down and hoisted Beppe into his arms.

"Thank you," Penny said to Rocco as she pushed aside the linen panels. "We're forever in your debt."

He waved them away with another grin. "Good luck."

Penny followed on Cricket's heels as they hurried through the lanes and out onto the edge of the marketplace. He gently laid Beppe into the cart, where his feet dangled over the side. It was a petite wooden thing with long handles and a single axle with two wheels. Cricket tucked folded blankets beneath Beppe's head and positioned himself between the handles. He pushed them down so the cart straightened and set off to follow Alidoro's lead.

They were a somber group, feet tripping, eyes scanning every alley and street for Master's men, but they were nowhere

in sight. Relief settled over Penny as the apothecary shop came
into view. They'd made it. Cricket pulled the cart into an alley
at the back of the building, where Tatiana waited on the porch,
wringing her hands in her apron.

"Oh, Beppe."

Cricket lifted Beppe and carried him up the steep steps and
through a narrow door. Tatiana ushered them into a small room
off the living quarters, an office of sorts. She'd pushed the desk
to the side, and in its place sat a low cot with a white sheet draped
over it. Beppe's hand flopped to the side as Cricket lowered him
onto the narrow mattress.

Tatiana set the three of them to work, boiling cloths, steeping bandages in bright-colored tinctures, and grinding herbs.
Beppe's wounds were extensive. His back was welted with several lashes, and a deep cut on his shoulder looked an angry red
with infection. Penny flinched and tears stung the back of her
eyes. Master had allowed this, had perhaps even requested it.
It seemed his torture knew no bounds.

"I don't think they've fed him," Tatiana muttered. She asked
Penny to rummage through the kitchen cabinets in search of
honey. "And when you're finished, can you go to the shop and
bring a teaspoon of valerian oil? It will help thin the syrup and
aid him in continued sleep."

"But I need to talk to him," Penny said, her voice rising
against her will. "The gala is tomorrow. I need answers so I can
free the girls."

"Penny." Tatiana was calm but firm. "His head wounds are
considerable. He is malnourished. I need him to remain asleep
so he can heal. Now. Please. Get me the valerian."

Penny stormed into the shop and took her frustration out
on slamming the jars onto the countertop. A dark shape outside

the front window caught her eye. She shielded her eyes and squinted into the brightness.

A gasp froze in her throat. She dropped the teaspoon and ran into the back room. "Primo. He's here."

The group scurried into frantic motion, running in what seemed like circles, bumping into one another.

"I'll distract him," Tatiana said. "You need to get Beppe upstairs and barricade yourselves in Rosaura's room. He *cannot* find her here. He can't find any of you here." Her fingers twined together. "I'll have to think of something."

She smoothed back her hair and swept into the shop.

Penny positioned herself at Beppe's feet while Cricket moved to grab his shoulders. On a whispered count of three, they lifted him and shuffled across the room.

It was only when they were halfway up the stairs and Beppe's knee smacked the wall that Penny realized Alidoro had disappeared. She didn't blame him for sneaking off, and she silently wished him godspeed, even though they could've used his help.

She was out of breath by the time they dragged Beppe into Rosaura's room. Rosaura rose from her chair, her fingers fluttering at her mouth. Cricket maneuvered Beppe's head onto the small bed in the corner, and Penny twisted his feet so they draped off the end.

"What about the mess downstairs?" Penny whispered. "If Primo sees it, he's going to know we were here."

"It's too risky." Cricket nudged the door shut. "We can't go down."

"Primo?" Rosaura croaked. Her skin paled to a sickly shade of gray and her eyes darted to the window as if she was contemplating diving out of it.

Penny sank at Rosaura's feet and grasped her hand. "Everything will be fine. Tatiana is sending him away." She tried to think of something to say, something that might distract Rosaura while they waited, but all she could come up with were questions about her time away from the estate. And really, that wasn't going to help defuse her obvious tension.

Instead, Penny just held Rosaura's hand and let Rosaura grip her fingers tight. She sank back onto the seat.

Seconds later they heard Primo's voice, loud and angry. "Enough. I will take a tour of the premises, with or without your permission. It's obvious someone has been here recently."

"I continue to tend to clients, Primo." Tatiana sounded calm. "A woman came last night with labor pains. I set up the cot in case the baby was on its way. Would you like me to describe the process in detail?"

Penny could imagine Primo's grimace.

"No." His voice drew closer. "What's upstairs?"

"My room and the guest room, as you well know from the last time you ransacked it. I haven't had much time to clean, but I'm happy to show you around. I was able to crochet some new lace throws last week, if you'd like to see them."

Her obvious dissuasive tactics didn't seem to work.

"I need to examine those rooms."

Penny froze. There was nowhere to hide, not with four of them already crowding the space. Their only choice was to fight back. She stood and walked toward the door. "Is there any way we can brace it?" she whispered to Cricket. "Perhaps he'll think the handle is broken? Or he'll move on to the other room and we can sneak out?"

Loud, clomping footsteps echoed up the narrow staircase and headed straight to their door. Rosaura seemed to shrink, the only movement her fingers still dancing.

Cricket's gaze darted around, but nothing was heavy enough to hold Primo out. Cricket stood next to Penny, his shoulder brushing hers, and dug his heels into the floor as they put all their weight against the door.

The handle turned slowly. Penny closed her eyes, hoping that together they could keep the door from opening.

A shout echoed from downstairs. "The horses!"

The handle was released. "What?"

"The horses have been set free!"

A stream of curse words erupted, followed by a clattering of footsteps. A door slammed and silence fell. Penny and Cricket stayed still, their chests rising and falling in sync as they breathed. Finally, Tatiana spoke from the hallway. "You can come out now."

Penny threw open the door and nearly collapsed in the cool air of the corridor. The small chamber had turned stifling with the four of them inside. "Where is he?"

"Oh, he'll be busy for a while." Penny peered past Tatiana to see Alidoro standing on the top step. A grin stretched nearly ear to ear.

"I thought you'd left us," Penny said.

Alidoro feigned shock. "Who, me? I never shy from the chance to bring upper society a notch toward normal."

"Who does he think he is? Robin Hood?" Cricket muttered from the doorway.

Penny swatted him in the side and turned back to Alidoro. "You've proven yourself quite resourceful. What did you do now?"

"A better question might be, what didn't I do?" He ticked them off on his fingers. "I freed the horses, but not before giving them a healthy dose of bloodroot to ensure they're quite sick and will need care before they're useful. I also added the herb to the drinking water, in the hopes that the men are otherwise indisposed."

Tatiana's hands rested on her hips, and she shook her head. "I should punish you for stealing items from my supply. But in this case, consider yourself warned."

"And thanked!" Alidoro smiled again and arched an eyebrow. When nobody responded, he sighed and backed down the stairs. "I'll be eating a snack if you need me."

Tatiana turned to Penny and Cricket. "We need to make a plan."

"Yes." Penny nodded. "Yes, we do."

Tatiana followed Alidoro, and Penny made to go downstairs after her. She felt a hand on her waist and stopped. Cricket pulled her back down the hall, into the quiet darkness between the rooms. He folded her against his chest and held her tight, a cocoon of safety she didn't realize she needed until her shoulders relaxed and a soft sigh escaped her lips. He brushed his lips against the top of her head and a shiver raced down her spine.

"You two coming?" Tatiana called from below.

Penny took one last inhale of Cricket's cinnamon scent, and they walked down the spiral steps together.

***

"Are you sure you can get us a carriage?" Cricket asked Alidoro.

He snorted. "Of course I can. It won't be easy, considering they're all reserved for tomorrow evening, but with enough coins, or favors, anything can be purchased."

They sat in a circle near the fireplace, Tatiana on a chair, Penny and Cricket on the floor with her legs draped over his, and Alidoro sprawled out on the sofa.

Tatiana had initially refused to entertain their plan to re-turn to the estate, but Penny had made it clear there was no alternative. "I have to free Nella and the girls. It's not up for discussion."

The debate then moved to how they would do it.

They decided their best chance to sneak in was during the gala. The manor would be swarming with guests dressed in costume. It provided the perfect cover and offered enough of a distraction that they might have a chance of not getting caught. If only they had costumes and a method of transportation. Tatiana promised to find them something to wear. Alidoro prom-ised a carriage.

"We can get there." Cricket released Penny's knee and shoved his fingers through his thick hair. "Now we need tomorrow eve-ning to arrive without incident."

Penny leaned into him. "Is it too long to wait? Primo could return at any minute. I'm sure he knows we were behind the release of his horses."

"Don't worry about that." Alidoro crossed his hands behind his head and closed his eyes. "I have people in key spots around town. If Primo crosses their path, they'll distract him. He won't have enough time to return here until after the gala is over."

"Thank you so much. I don't know how you do it," Penny said.

Tatiana rose and gathered her coat and gloves. "I'd best go purchase costumes for the both of you. Will you keep an eye on Rosaura and Beppe while I'm gone?"

"Of course," Penny said.

Alidoro yawned and pushed himself up to stand. "I should head out, too." He grabbed another pastry and followed Tatiana into the front room.

Penny climbed the narrow steps and peeked in on Rosaura. She rocked in the chair and hummed to herself, her fingers busy knitting a butter-colored yarn into some sort of pattern. A few paces down the corridor, Beppe muttered unintelligible words. They'd moved him into Tatiana's chamber before convening downstairs, and Tatiana had given him the valerian-laced honey and a tincture to help with the pain. It must've worn off some.

His head thrashed from side to side. Penny sat on the edge of the mattress and rested the back of her hand against his forehead. His skin blazed. She reached for a ceramic bowl and cloth Tatiana had left on the nightstand. She dabbed the material into the pale blue water, folded it neatly in thirds, and draped it across Beppe's forehead.

His mutterings subsided to something only slightly more intelligible. "*Smascherate la fata.* Penny. Must tell. *Smascherate la fata.* Important."

Smascherate la fata?

Unmask the fairy.

Frustration weighed heavy on her shoulders. It made no sense. *He* made no sense. She wanted to shake him awake and ask for help in freeing the girls. But Tatiana said he wouldn't wake until his body was ready. He needed rest. And really, she did, too. Penny tucked the bowl back and slid to the floor. Her head leaned against the mattress and she slipped her fingers into Beppe's hand. She squeezed once and his ramblings eased.

Within seconds, she had dozed off.

CHAPTER
35

Penny rubbed the sleep from her eyes. Twilight must have fallen, as the room was lit only by a trio of candles flickering in the corner. Her body ached and she felt only a little rested from the nap. It would take her days to catch up on all the missed sleep. Her mind already whirled with all that might happen in the next twenty-four hours. She would risk a lot, her life really, by going back to the manor. But she had no choice. She couldn't leave Nella in Master's clutches.

She rose to her feet and checked on Beppe. His fever had broken and his breath rose and fell with a steady rhythm. Now if only he would wake and give her answers.

Barefoot, Penny padded downstairs to find Rosaura poring over packages and fabric spread across a long table. Cricket stood near the kitchen, as far from the costume decisions as possible.

"Glad you could join us, *dormiglione*." He smiled, but it didn't quite light up his eyes. He looked nearly as exhausted as she felt.

"You could've woken me."

"No, you needed rest."

She shuffled over to stand next to him. Their fingers wove together as if it was their natural state. Penny couldn't imagine a time when she hadn't wanted to touch him. It was all she could do not to throw her arms around him and bury her face in his neck. "Did they find anything suitable?"

"Tatiana brought back masks and fabric. There weren't any costumes that would fit you, so Rosaura offered to stitch something together."

"I can do it." Penny took a step forward, but Cricket pulled her back. "What?" She looked at him. "I actually like to sew. The only thing at the estate I would've chosen for myself."

"I know"—he lowered his voice—"but it might help Rosaura if you let her take on this project."

Penny glanced over again, noticing for the first time the change in Rosaura's demeanor. She looked more like herself, focused, her shoulders thrown back and her fingers lightly skimming the bolts of material. Her steps were graceful and lithe. Gone was the slouching girl who twitched at the smallest sound and movement.

At least for now. Penny could give her this.

"I've got it!" Rosaura's words were a rasp, but the inflection was obvious all the same. She lifted an elaborate peacock eye mask with both hands. Bright green and blue feathers spread to the sides. A beak, traced in golden thread and delicate beadwork, dipped out along the nose and curled under at a pointed tip. She laid it aside and began digging through the material to pull out an iridescent shade of turquoise-blue satin and yards of tulle.

"Looks like you're going to be a bird," Cricket whispered in Penny's ear. His breath tickled her skin and sent warmth racing through her entire body.

"It could be worse. She could've gone with a mule," Penny joked, but really she didn't care what she wore. She just wanted to get to the estate and find her sister. "Did they find anything for you?"

Cricket pointed at the armchair, where a black cloak, shirt, and pants were draped over the back. The majority of men went in the same black ensemble, complete with a black mask that would cover their eyes for an hour before they dumped the disguise unceremoniously. There were always the few who came in full costume, resplendent in rich leather and animal prints, but it was definitely not the norm.

Rosaura measured Penny from all angles, gathered the fabric, and slipped upstairs to her room. "It will be ready by morning."

"Thank you," Penny called after her. She rubbed at her forehead as a dull headache crept in. A wave of panic swept over her until she remembered Master couldn't control her thoughts anymore. This was just a normal pain.

She sank onto the edge of the sofa and closed her eyes.

Tatiana came over from the kitchen carrying a tray laden with plates of *antipasto*. She set it on the table near Penny and sat cross-legged in the armchair. "You all need to eat."

Penny squinted at the food and shook her head. Fear and frustration formed a ball just behind her sternum, stretching tendrils up into her throat and down into her stomach. She couldn't eat anything.

Tatiana sighed. "Try to keep your strength up." Cricket reached over and grabbed a slice of prosciutto. "I realize you must return to the estate, but I'd feel better if I knew you had a plan for when you arrived there."

Penny straightened. "We'll split up. Cricket, you gather everyone's journals from the cellar. I'll find Nella and then the girls. Once we are outside, we can procure some of the waiting carriages. We should also destroy any equipment we find; Master cannot do this again." The pain in her forehead intensified. The words sounded so easy, but . . . "This isn't going to work, is it?"

"We'll make it work." Cricket's voice soothed her nerves. "You've already proven that you can escape the estate. You just need to show the girls how."

"I wish I could talk to Beppe." She looked at Tatiana. "Is there *any* chance he'll wake before we leave?"

"I'll go check on him. And I need to rest. Will you both be fine down here tonight?"

"Of course," Penny said. "I slept on the dirt in a marketplace last night. Anywhere indoors is a great improvement."

Together, Penny and Cricket cleared the dishes and washed them in the small sink. Their bodies were magnets for each other, a constant stream of limbs brushing and tangling, fingers and shoulders, and at one point they just stopped moving altogether. Cricket put down the plate he'd been holding. His eyes darkened several shades and Penny fell into their depths. She nearly tripped forward against his chest. He caught her wrists with his hands and lifted them slowly behind his neck. His fingers spread against hers, pushing them into his skin, before he pulled his hands away to grip her waist and pull her closer. His lips parted only barely; his gaze never left hers. And then he ducked his head and kissed her.

Warmth and light and magic and feeling. She was pure sensation, weightless, her body only grounded to the earth where she touched him. His tongue nudged at hers and time stopped. Their kisses followed the path of their journey together. The safety and comfort of childhood followed by the chaos and reckless abandon of their time at the estate. Their mouths crashed together, and Penny gripped his neck tighter. She couldn't get enough of him, of his cinnamon scent, the soft pressure of his lips, the sweet taste of his mouth.

He was the one to finally pull away, his mouth trailing gentle kisses to her ear and up her hairline to her forehead. His chin rested against her head and their breathing slowly returned to normal.

The fire had nearly burned out in the hearth when they made their way over to the living room to rest. Penny curled on the sofa and pulled a quilt up to her neck. Cricket lay on the floor beside her, his hand resting on the cushion so his fingers threaded through hers. Her mind battled between wanting to replay the kisses and worrying about the upcoming day. Sleep made the decision for her.

· · ·

"I wanna go with you." Alidoro stood in front of Penny, his mouth full of fruit as he spoke. "I'm serious."

"Chew your food," Penny said with a sigh. It was the third time he'd mentioned wanting to travel to the gala with them. "You've done enough, Alidoro. I can't bring you to the estate. It's too dangerous. I need you here, to keep an eye on everyone."

The morning had passed in a frenetic pace of reviewing plans, worrying about Nella, listening for the bell at the shop entrance in fear Primo and his men would burst through, worrying over the girls, and going over plans again. The occasional shy glance at Cricket was the only thing to nudge back the mounting anxiety and stress smothering Penny.

"Alidoro," Rosaura called from upstairs. She'd been working on the costume all morning, waving Penny away whenever she peered in to see it. "Penny needs a pair of slippers. Black satin with ribbons, preferably."

"Finally, something to do." He shoved more grapes in his mouth and raced out the door.

Tatiana waved Penny over to where she sat, a book sprawled open in front of her. Lists of ingredients and dosages, pictures of herbs, and descriptions of benefits all lined the pages. "Can you go into the shop and gather me the jars for comfrey, calendula, bergamot, and persimmon? I'm going to try a new dark salve for Beppe. Perhaps that will wake him."

Penny pushed through the curtain and into a world of color and scents. The afternoon sunlight glinted off different-size glass jars and bottles filled with dried herbs and bright liquids. She traced her finger along a shelf of labeled herbs, trying to determine Tatiana's method for organization. It certainly wasn't by color or alphabetical. She spotted the jar for bergamot on the second shelf. The dark dried peels let off a citrus scent when she opened the lid and inhaled.

One ingredient down, three to go.

She was bent over behind the counter, searching for persimmon, when the tinkle of the bell sounded. Fear rooted her to the spot. It probably wasn't smart of her to be in the shop. Anyone could enter. She peeked over the counter lip to spot a young woman, probably her age, standing there.

"Can I help you?" Penny straightened and exhaled in relief.

"I'm looking for juniper oil?" She seemed confused and wrung her gloved hands. "I think that's what she asked for. Something about a stomachache. I don't know."

Juniper oil. Penny turned to the display of bottles, eyes narrowed at the tiny writing on the sides.

"Are you the new help?" the girl asked. "Tatiana mentioned hiring someone."

"No." Penny stood on tiptoe and reached for one of the vials on the top shelf. "I'm here visiting." She grabbed the bottle and set it on the countertop. "Do you know how much you need?"

The girl stared at Penny's wrist, exposed where the sleeve had pulled back. "You're one of them." Her brown eyes widened like a doe's. Penny yanked down the fabric and started to shake her head. This wasn't supposed to happen. The girl could expose her, expose Rosaura and Beppe. "What's it like? Is it amazing? I'm sure it's amazing."

Fringe rustled and Tatiana stepped into the shop. "I thought I heard voices. Carmela, how are you? Is your mother feeling worse?"

Carmela nodded. "Her stomach again. She asked for juniper drops."

Tatiana grabbed an empty vial and used a pipette to extract some of the oil and transfer it to the new glass. Meanwhile, Carmela stood gawking at Penny, seemingly waiting for answers. "Why are you here? Isn't the gala tonight?"

Tatiana jumped in. "I asked Penny to take some herbs back to the estate."

"Oh." Carmela looked rightly confused. Under no circumstances would Penny have been sent to town that day.

Tatiana sealed the vial and placed it in a small fabric bag. She tied it with a ribbon and handed it to the girl. "I'm sure your mother could use that sooner rather than later."

Suddenly, a commotion erupted outside. Shouts and clamoring, and the door flew open. Penny ducked behind the counter as a group of men came in, carrying a small body between them. Carmela shrieked and scooted to the side to give them room.

"Tatiana, this boy belong to you? He asked us to bring him here."

Penny continued to crouch down but peered around the edge of the counter. She could see an arm dangling to the side, blood staining a white shirt.

Black slippers dangled from the fingers.

Cirillo leaned against the stone building at the edge of the marketplace, the brim of his hat pulled low across his brow as he stood. Watching her.

For once he didn't mind the stench of the town, the sweltering cloud cover, the people daring to brush against his starched clothing as they swept past him into the marketplace. He was tuned in to her, every move she made.

He'd been following her for a while now, collecting information like coins in his pocket, and he couldn't wait to take her home, back to the estate, where he would begin to mold her.

Teresa, his sister's childhood friend, had fled with her daughters shortly after Sofia's death. She rightly assumed she'd be somewhere next on Cirillo's list of people to control. After all her taunting and torments during his childhood, it was the least he could do. But she'd moved to a town in the middle of the country, bought a farm, and hid in the mundaneness of a peasant life. It had taken years for the inspector to track her down. Cirillo could at least admit she'd covered her tracks well.

As fate would have it, her husband had died and she'd become ill herself. Cirillo hadn't had to do anything to exact his revenge. Although he hadn't quite planned on his attraction to her daughter.

The first time he met Penelope, he was immediately entranced. She'd been riding her horse at breakneck speed down a deserted stretch of road, almost barreling into his carriage. Then she'd had the audacity to blame him for the near accident.

She was the older of two children, burdened with the task of taking care of both the property and her younger sister, but somehow she still managed to be a spitfire, full of energy and quick to anger, with a robust love of life and ferocious loyalty. He couldn't stop watching her. He couldn't help but feel alive just being around her, even now, as she flitted from stall to stall. She purchased a bag of sweets and slipped one into her mouth. Her cheeks sucked in at the tart flavor, and she grinned. She handed her sister the rest and grabbed her hand as they weaved farther into the crowded market.

Cirillo stepped away from the wall and followed, keeping distance between them.

Penelope's fingers danced over pieces of jewelry, twisted gold tiaras and flashing bits of fake stones. If only she would take him up on his offer, come back to the estate with him. Once her transformation was complete, he'd shower her in precious jewels and the finest trinkets his money could buy.

But she kept refusing, telling him she couldn't possibly leave her family. She'd stare at him, her eyes boring into his as if daring him to argue.

He felt a desperate need to break her.

They stopped at another booth. Penelope held a gown in front of her, twirling around so the fabric flared and dipped in the heavy air. "This would look beautiful on you, Nella." Penelope was always thinking of her sister.

He needed to cut their bond, get Penelope to his estate, but time was running out. Beppe had already sent him two messages, asking him why he'd been delayed in Paese dei Balocchi. He had but one chance left to convince her to return with him on the journey home.

With a last glance at the sisters, Cirillo snuck back out of the market. He felt bad about it, but really, Penelope would only have herself to blame.

CHAPTER 37

❧ 1879 ❧

Penny dug her nails into her palms and bit back a gasp.

Alidoro.

She needed to get him help. Penny crawled toward the curtain and into the back rooms.

"Cricket," she whispered loudly. She rose to her feet and sprinted up the stairs. "Cricket!"

"It's almost done," Rosaura said when Penny burst into the small guest room. "Give me a few more minutes."

"Cricket, I need you. Downstairs." Her chest heaved. "Alidoro's been hurt."

Rosaura rose, but Penny motioned for her to sit. "Stay here. We can't be seen."

Cricket took the stairs two at a time with Penny close behind. She held back, her pulse pounding, while he raced into the shop. Penny could hear the men talking over one another.

"They was arguing about something. A horse, I think—"

"No, the kid stole something. From the one all in black—"

"No, he yelled he wasn't no thief. Anyway, the one pulled out a gun and everyone scattered. He said to give it back—"

"See, I told you he took something—"

"Hush now and let me talk. The kid said he best be going and he ran. Just up and started running. The one all in black started chasing him and the other one started shooting. The kid jumped over a cart, but one of the bullets hit him. In the arm, I think—"

"In the shoulder."

"He started fading fast, but told someone in the crowd to bring him here. To you."

Tatiana finally spoke. "Thank you for your help. Cricket, can you get them both some coins from the register?"

The men told her no, it wasn't necessary. "I'm glad we were there. He's only a boy."

The bell jangled as they exited and Penny flew into the shop. Carmela was still a statue at the edge of the room. Her face had gone white.

"Carmela, get back home to your mother. I'll check in on you both tomorrow."

She was gone without another word. Alidoro lay on the floor, his skin paler than Carmela's, if that was even possible. Penny grabbed the slippers and tossed them behind the counter.

"I need you two to help carry him to the office. Carefully, please." Tatiana moved to his shoulders while Cricket and Penny positioned themselves to lift him. "Keep him as steady as possible until I can get a closer look at the wound."

They placed Alidoro on the cot that Beppe had vacated less than twenty-four hours before.

Tatiana made quick work of cutting away the bloodstained shirt. Penny sucked in a breath and turned her head. Alidoro was lucky the bullet had only grazed him, but a large chunk of skin was flayed open across the inside of his bicep. If the gun had been aimed only a little to the left, it would have struck him in the chest.

"More stitches." Tatiana shook her head. "By the time I'm through with all of you, I will have exhausted my thread." She directed Penny to finish gathering the ingredients from earlier. "I'll need to make a double batch of the salve."

Penny raced back to the shop. She quickly mopped up the bloodstain in the foyer and the droplets that trailed into the other room. Then she gathered the slippers in one hand, the ingredients in the other, and made her way back to Tatiana.

It was midafternoon before Tatiana finished dressing the wound. Alidoro was starting to come out of his stupor, and Tatiana waved Penny and Cricket out of the room. "Let him rest. I'm hoping the salve will draw away some of the pain. And you two need to start getting ready. Thank you for all your time and help."

Penny made her way up to the guest room while Cricket readied to change downstairs. As she undressed, she quickly filled Rosaura in on what had happened to Alidoro.

"That's horrible. Do you think it was Primo? Is he all right?"

"It had to be Primo. Who else would shoot a child?" And she was practically going to hand herself over to him and Master. Penny shuddered and threw her shoulders back. "Let's do this." The costume lay in an unstructured mound on the floor. Penny stepped into the center of the crinoline and tulle, and pulled the costume up to her waist. She slid her arms into tight sleeves that flared out at the ends like bells. Rosaura stepped up behind her to lace a ribbon down her lower back to tighten the bodice. At her hips, the skirt flared out in overlapping scalloped layers of satin and tulle. The back line was a U shape, leaving much of her skin exposed. Penny wished it were a high-necked costume that would keep her completely disguised, but that wouldn't quite fit the peacock theme.

"Have a look." Rosaura scooted Penny toward the corner, where a full-length mirror rested at an angle.

"It's beautiful."

Rosaura sat Penny in an uncomfortable chair and quickly wove her curls into tight braids. She then braided those together and arranged a feathered headpiece that dipped low enough to hide the stitches behind her ear.

Penny reached for the mask, but Rosaura snagged it away. "Sit down," she rasped. "We need to hide your features." She dug through a pile of tubes and powders on the nightstand and then began to blot Penny's face with what felt like wet paint. Brushes and pencils and a bit of gloss to her lips and Rosaura stepped away.

Penny opened her eyes and watched them widen at her own reflection in the mirror. She looked so different, her eyes brighter and her face even more hollow from the blue and green cosmetics that swirled from her eyes to her cheeks to her jaw. She leaned in and gave Rosaura a quick hug. "Thank you, for everything." She eased off the mattress and grabbed the slippers from where she'd tucked them when she first came upstairs. Guilt settled around her as she thought of Alidoro lying on the cot.

"It's not your fault." Rosaura seemed to read her mind. "You didn't carry the gun. You didn't shoot him."

Penny knew that, but she swore she'd exact her revenge on Primo and Master all the same.

"Please be careful." Rosaura handed her the mask.

"I will. We'll be back soon. With all of the girls. I promise." Penny stepped into the hall and went downstairs.

"Cricket? Do you need any help with—Oh." Penny's mouth rounded as the room came into view and she spotted him.

He was stunning, with an edge she'd never quite seen in him. The black shirt and pants were cut close, showing off his lean muscles and broad shoulders. His hair was slicked back, the darkness adding a contrast to his skin that toned down the freckles Penny had come to adore. Even the short hair growth on his jawline made him look more mature and dashing, drawing her eyes straight to his lips.

The silence closed in on them. Nerves fluttered throughout her body as she descended the last couple of steps. Penny couldn't stop looking at him. Her eyes drifted from his hair to his eyes to his lips to his chest, skipping like a stone across the smooth surface of a lake. She lifted her hand and splayed her fingers, resting them just above his heart. His pulse leapt beneath the pressure of her touch. Cricket reached out and gripped her waist, pulling her closer. Their breaths came faster, and she tipped her head back to look at him. His voice was barely a whisper. "I fear Rosaura is going to be unhappy with me."

Penny opened her mouth to ask him why, but before she could get the word out, he'd cupped his palm against her cheek, his fingers stretching to the soft skin at the base of her neck, and leaned in to press his lips against hers.

Cricket's touch was petal soft at first. She leaned into him, pressing her mouth against his, desperate to inhale the air from his lungs, the spicy scent of his skin. Her hand slid up his back to his neck, and her fingers gripped the back of his hair to pull him closer. Her lips parted against his and the kiss deepened into something more urgent. As if they might never see each other again.

Because they might not.

Penny pulled away, willing her pulse to slow. She could still feel his lips on hers, his hand on her back. A phantom memory she hoped would never disappear.

"The carriage is here," Tatiana called from the front room.

Cricket gathered his mask and cloak and held out his arm for Penny.

"One second." She raced back upstairs, hoping against hope that Beppe had finally awakened. She knelt at his side and brushed at his forehead. There was no reaction other than the mumbled words.

"Smascherate la fata."

That phrase again.

She stared at the metal implant where she'd left it on the nightstand the evening before. It looked so thin and sharp, menacing and mechanical.

"Penny, we have to go," Cricket called from downstairs.

She wished she could wait, that she had more time. Beppe's information could be the key to their success. But she couldn't stay. Nella needed help. The girls needed help. Penny couldn't ignore that. It was time to get back and free them.

Time to go back to the belly of the whale.

CHAPTER 38

Darkness had fallen when they left the back entrance and stepped down into the alley. The driver stood beside an open carriage door. Cricket held out his hand and Penny gripped his fingers. She dipped her head to climb inside and sat on the bench as Cricket settled beside her. The interior was sparse but ornate. Dark burgundy velvet covered the bench seat, and the cherry-wood panels were carved with a looping design. Cricket tapped the roof to signal the driver, and the horses lurched forward.

It was a quiet ride, a reflective one, even though they were alone and rushing toward what could be their last moments together. It seemed every time Penny opened her mouth to say something, the words felt thick and impossible on her tongue, and she swallowed them back. She couldn't talk about what might happen, or promise everything would be okay.

And she refused to say good-bye, so she said nothing at all.

Instead, they sat on the hard bench, their fingers linked together, as the sky outside the window finished shadowing its canvas.

At one point Penny caught pale yellow eyes peering out at them from the depths of the budding foliage. She blinked and they were gone, but she couldn't stop the memories of the wolves from surfacing, and she wondered why they'd still be visible with the metal device removed from her head.

Perhaps they were real after all.

"We're almost to Beppe's cabin." Cricket finally spoke. His words were simple, but his voice carried a tightness that hinted at the stress humming in both their bodies. Penny shifted closer to him and took a shaky breath.

The carriage skirted around the edge of the forest, following it until finally the estate burst into view. The lights and colors were electric, flooding from the house and lawn to reflect a mirror image on the surface of the lake. It was blinding, rendering the scene as bright as day. The coachman slowed the carriage to a stop at the end of a queue of late arrivals moving up the driveway to the turnabout.

"You can let us off here." Cricket opened the quarter light so the coachman could hear.

"Don't you want to make an entrance?" he called.

"No, thank you." An entrance was the last thing they wanted.

The coachman urged the horses out of line, toward the side of the drive. He opened the door with a squeak of the hinges and they stepped out. Cricket handed him a small bag of coins. "If you could be so kind as to wait out along the main road, we would appreciate it. I don't believe we'll be attending all the functions tonight."

With a nod and a sweeping bow, the coachman bid them a good evening and Cricket led Penny toward the manor. They stuck to the far edge of the driveway, slipping from shadow to shadow. Penny kept running through the plan in her mind. It was the only way to fight back the panic that threatened to paralyze her, frozen on the cobblestones. *Find Nella. Free the girls. Escape. I can do this.*

They adjusted their masks and slowed as they neared the lead carriage. A footman jumped from the rumble seat and opened the gilded door. Two giggling women, clad in fairy queen costumes, stepped onto a length of plum-colored carpet leading to the front entrance. Their escorts climbed out of the carriage behind them. At the portico, they were met by one of the guardsmen and welcomed inside.

Cricket and Penny followed close behind the two couples as they made their way through the sprawling entranceway. The wide veranda was lined with columns that seemed lit from below, the white marble intricately carved with vines and grapes. Warmth radiated from the ground beneath her feet, as if the floor were heated.

Cricket pulled her forward into the vestibule. Servants hovered everywhere, taking heavy furs and overcoats from those who'd brought them and directing guests to the dining room for the buffet, to the ballroom for the upcoming performance, or to the drawing room for relaxing by the warmth of the hearth.

They slid along the outskirts of the foyer and squeezed around the guests, who mingled and greeted one another. Penny slowed as they neared the corner. Nerves fluttered in her stomach, and her pulse raced. "It's time."

She didn't want to let him go, didn't want to split apart, but there was too much to be done.

Cricket gripped Penny tight and leaned in to whisper in her ear. "Be safe. If anything happens, run. Head straight for the stagecoach, and I'll catch up with you as soon as I can."

Penny nodded. The din of the crowd and the violinist play-ing in the corner dimmed to near silence as he brushed her cheek with his lips. Time halted while she reveled in that brief touch.

She watched as he stepped back, memorizing the way his hair curled at the nape of his neck, the light dusting of freckles along his cheeks, the concern in his pale eyes, and then they went their separate ways.

Walking into the next room, Penny was struck by how many people actually attended the gala. As performers, the girls were confined to their quarters before taking the stage, and then they remained in the ballroom after they had danced. They weren't allowed to wander the manor.

As a guest, or rather an uninvited participant, Penny felt claustrophobic as the crowds continued to thicken. The parlor and drawing rooms were packed full of tittering birds and chat-tering flowers, costumes of the fantastical and flighty. And of course the dark shadows of men.

Penny stopped in each room, eyeing the costumed figures to see if she recognized anyone. There was little chance Master would have Nella out in the crowd tonight, but she couldn't risk passing her sister by. Opposing emotions turned her stomach into a knotted mess. She felt relief at not spotting Master or Primo mingling with the guests, but also frustration at not find-ing Nella.

The ballroom doors were flung open, chandeliers sparkling high above the expanse of polished wood floor. Bouquets of flowers lined the curtained edge of the stage, and guests had begun to arrange themselves in clusters to socialize and get ready to watch the performance.

Penny hated this room, where Master showed off his most lavish and prized possessions. Everyone would crowd in, anxious for the puppeteer to show off his dolls, excited for the performance, and hopeful that they might later dance with one of the girls. She felt disgust toward Master as well as the guests who perpetuated the insanity, even if they had no idea exactly how he coerced them to do his bidding.

She fled, turning back toward the dormitory hall. The corridors were dark and drafty on this side of the estate, probably to keep the guests at bay. Out of sight of the crowd, she paused and took a deep breath for clarity. Then she made her way toward what she assumed was Nella's room. She doubted her sister was inside, but perhaps there would be some indication as to where she was in fact staying.

Penny paced toward the door, which was cracked open. A low rumble of words erupted. "Of all the tasks to be doing tonight."

She recognized Primo's voice and stopped, unsure of where to go. If she retreated, he could exit the room and follow her through the manor. Instead she raced past, hugged the uneven stone wall, and turned the corner. She waited to see if Primo would go back to the main hall or come farther into the dormitory. The seconds ticked by slowly, and she pushed her back flush against the rough wall. Finally, his footsteps echoed in the hall, the sound dimming as he walked in the opposite direction.

She pushed away from the stones, but something on the costume snagged. The fabric made a tearing sound at the same time as she felt cool air against her hip. *No!* The seam had caught, the threads unraveling to leave a gaping hole.

Penny's teeth gritted in frustration. She couldn't walk through the manor holding her gown closed, or leave it gaping to show her undergarments. Between that and her visible stitches, she would surely draw unwanted attention.

So she did the only thing she could think of.

She dashed to her room. Everything was the exact same as she'd left it, her quilt pulled to the pillow, her sleeping clothes draped over the bedpost, her photo album still open on the bed to a random page. With her fingernail, Penny traced the picture of the girl and her mother, wondering who they were. Shutting the leather-bound book, Penny turned to the armoire and froze. A costume hung there. Her pink-and-green dying-tulip tutu.

Her pulse skipped. Master expected her to perform. He'd held out hope that she would return, and had even laid out her costume. *How dare he?* What made him think she'd come crawling back, begging to be a part of his charade?

And yet it seemed she was doing exactly that.

She reached behind, clasped the length of ribbon at her waist, and pulled. The bodice loosened. She pulled the satin off her shoulders and pushed the sleeves down off her wrists. Free of its constraints, she stepped out of the crinoline and pushed down the rest of the peacock skirt, leaving it on the floor in a heap.

Penny slid the costume off the armoire and dressed quickly. She dared a glimpse in the mirror; her nose wrinkled at her reflection. The feathered mask had to go. So did the eye makeup. She dipped a cloth in the water basin and scrubbed off most of the blue paint.

She pulled loose a bit of the braid to hide her stitches, but it was all she could do. There was nowhere to hide. Penny looked like herself now. And that meant she had to act like one of the *sorelle*.

After donning her slippers, she raced back down the hall.

She halted at Nella's door and peeked in. Pale pink silk hung from a canopy bed. Porcelain dolls lined an entire shelf, all staring glazed-eyed in her direction. The armoire was opened to display shades of pastel dresses, all hung in a neat row. They were small, certainly smaller than hers.

Penny slammed the door shut. Nella was definitely here, ensconced at the estate. A wave of anger coursed through her veins. She had to find her sister. But first she had to warn the girls, convince them to leave before they were trapped in a dance when the clock struck midnight.

She raced through the empty halls and stood outside the thick double doors to the dance studio. She threw them open and stepped in, her chest heaving.

"You're not allowed in here. . . ." Bianca's high-pitched whine was cut short as she realized Penny wasn't some bumbling guest lost in the maze of corridors. She gained her voice and attempted to pull her thoughts together. "You—you—traitor." She launched herself at Penny, fingers hooked as if to claw the skin from Penny's face.

"Stop." Madame Triolo stomped in mere seconds behind Penny. "Leave her alone; she's already a mess."

Bianca's nostrils flared as she stepped away.

Madame acknowledged Penny with a tip of her head. "So nice of you to have returned. I'm glad you came to your senses. Now our ensemble will be complete." Before Penny could open her mouth to correct her, to tell her she had no plans to perform, Madame waved everyone forward. "Let me have one last look at you."

The girls arranged themselves silently in a straight line. Not knowing what else to do, Penny joined them. Madame strutted from one end to the other, straightening costumes, tucking back loose hair, and tilting chins upward. She got to Penny, her face crinkling in dismay. "What is with this blue kohl under your eyes? And why is your hair in a braid? And stitches on your neck." Her narrow lips pulled down. "I don't have time to fix this, but we will have a discussion first thing in the morning. There are punishments for stepping out of line, Penelope."

Madame reached to brush a strand of hair from her face, and it was then that Penny saw it. The same marking on Madame's wrist. Penny's eyes widened and she grabbed Madame's hand. She couldn't stop herself. "You have it, too? But you danced for the king. Why would you allow him to leave a mark on you? Do you know?"

Madame's eyes slitted and she yanked her hand away. "Watch yourself, Penelope. Infractions are not taken lightly here at the estate. Master gave me a career I never dreamed possible. He turned me into the best dancer in all of Italy." She leaned in close, her words a hiss. "But he never needed to control me. I gave myself to him willingly."

She shoved Penelope back into line. The rest of the girls stood still as statues, wide-eyed. Somewhere a gong chimed. Madame clapped her hands together and motioned toward the door. "It's time. Single file, please. And keep your heads high. Do me proud."

It's time? How was it possible? She felt like she'd just gotten to the estate. Fear clawed at her chest and Penny bit her lip hard, forcing herself to focus and put together a new plan. When she reached the door, she'd make a run toward the main wing. She'd look for Nella while the girls performed and the entire estate had their attention focused in the ballroom. Then afterward she would return and convince her *sorelle* they had to leave. It was the only way. If she made a commotion now, she'd never find her sister.

The last in line, Penny rushed past Madame and into the corridor. But before she could flee, Madame had already gripped her shoulder, pushing Penny straight toward the ballroom. She was strong for such a little thing.

Penny stumbled forward. She couldn't do this. She refused to dance. She'd surely be ripped from the stage by Master or Primo and dragged off to the asylum. This had to be on her terms. She wiggled and yanked away from Madame, but her grip shifted to Penny's wrist and she continued to shove her forward.

The side door to the stage had been propped open, and Madame ushered them in. She slammed the door, the noise barely heard over the din of the crowd, and stood in front of it, arms crossed over her chest, daring Penny to try to run. The other girls took their places silently on the wooden floor. Penny stumbled into her spot, dead center, her body reflexively taking first position. The orchestra must have cued the audience, because the roar of voices dimmed to silence.

Bianca rose *en pointe*, her arms in fifth position, and the curtain lifted.

A sea of faces stared back at them, each one a perceived enemy. Penny almost shrank back, curled into herself in a ball on the floor. Instead, her feet tiptoed sideways, her arms lifted to their proper positions, her fingers stretched. Her body did what her mind could not.

It danced.

Penny spotted him, nestled in a pocket near the back of the room. The chandelier above cast a sheen over his dark, wavy hair and the black satin of his dinner jacket. He hadn't bothered to wear a costume. Or a mask.

Master.

And in front of him, tucked right against his chest, stood a girl.

Nella.

She appeared unhurt, but something was off. Penny spun, her *pirouettes* perfect and precise. With each rotation, she took in further details.

Nella's eyes were unfocused, dull, and unseeing.

Dark red smudges lined the side of her neck.

Her arm was bent at the elbow and tucked behind her back.

When Penny finally tore her eyes from Nella to glance at Master, she realized he'd been staring at her, his jaw clenched tight, his lips pressed together into a thin line, his gaze unwavering.

Nella's head dropped forward, as if her neck was too weak to support it. Her skin was pale and as thin as paper. Penny's stomach clenched. Something was wrong with her sister. She looked like a mere shell of herself.

Penny had to save her.

She let herself sink further into the routine, forced her shoulders to relax, and then she nodded at Master. A slight dip in his direction. An acknowledgment. An invitation of sorts.

He blinked, eyes narrowing. Penny glanced down at the floor, trying desperately to look remorseful without showing any of the terror lying right below the surface of this charade.

It was a very dangerous game she played, but Penny needed him to release Nella. Needed him to let Penny take her place. She had to convince him she'd made a mistake, that she should never have left the estate. She would ask him to take her back and play into his desire to control her.

It was time to give him one more chance.

With one last round of *pirouettes* and *jetés* across the stage, the ballet ended and the girls took their bows, to thunderous applause.

Master had already begun to shove his way through the mass of people, Nella tucked under his arm. The other girls flitted offstage toward the side door, hands waving high above their heads as the adoring crowd threw flowers at their feet. In past years, Penny would follow them back to the dance studio. The girls would giggle and change into their masquerade costumes for the evening. Then they would make another entrance into the ballroom.

Not tonight.

Tonight, Penny walked toward the front of the stage, as if drawn by a magnet toward Master's advancing steps. The orchestra began to play a rousing waltz, and the noise of the crowd rose with each passing second. Penny crouched as he neared, fighting every instinct to sprint after her *sorelle.*

She watched him, strength and hatred building side by side, brick by brick, to lift her shoulders and meet his gaze. He stopped, mere inches away. His hands gripped Nella's waist as she stumbled forward, her head flopping like a rag doll.

"I'd like to talk with you, alone," Penny said. She needed to get out of this room, convince him to release Nella. "Please, Master?"

He lowered his mouth until it was next to her ear. "Don't believe you won't be punished for your disobedience. We shall talk in a bit. But first, let's dance." He waved Primo over and shoved Nella at his steward. Primo lifted her into his arms and Master shooed them away. "Get her plugged in."

Penny stiffened as horror lodged in her sternum. Master turned his full attention back to her. His fingers ran down her bare arms, gripped her waist with both hands, and lowered her from the raised stage to the ballroom floor. Her feet were steady, but he didn't let go.

Penny gazed after Primo, who swept through the crowd without much notice. Anger filled the crevices in Penny's heart, which had splintered at seeing Nella this way. Master wouldn't get away with this. Primo wouldn't, either. Not with shooting innocent children and helping Master take girls captive.

Master guided her to the middle of the dance floor, the guests clearing the way in front of them. His presence was hard to ignore, large and turbulent, filling the entire ballroom, even the spaces between the balusters on the spectator balcony above. He led Penny in a slow waltz. Her fingers rested on his shoulder and she forced her muscles to relax. Penny knew the entire crowd would be watching and Master would retaliate if they failed to put on a good show.

It was an easy enough rhythm, the waltz. But time was wasting. Penny couldn't get to Nella while stuck in the ballroom. She raised her chin and stared unflinching into the bottomless depths of his eyes. "I was wrong." She could feel him stiffen beneath the jacket.

"About what?"

"About everything. I was wrong to doubt you, to leave the estate." She willed her lips to tremble. "It was horrible, the outside world. I thought it would be filled with wonder, but it was frightening. The people, the noise, the chaos."

Their movements slowed to a near standstill. His gaze roamed her face, as if trying to gauge the truth of her words, finally landing on the wound behind her ear. Her words continued in a hurried flood.

"I removed it. I'm so sorry." She tilted her head in an attempt to hide the stitches. "I hoped it would help clear my thoughts and make me less afraid, but all it did was make me want to come back here, back home, that much more."

She needed to make him believe. It was her only chance of escaping his grasp, her only chance to get to her sister. "Master, can you please fix it? Implant a new one?" Penny hated saying the words, and the anger, buried just under the surface of her fraying nerves, bubbled up in the form of scalding tears that slid down her cheeks.

Master faltered.

"We can do it now, and then the rest of the night I'll be at your side." She tugged at his hand, willing him toward the ballroom doors. If he took her to where he kept the equipment, she might find Nella there. And then she could end this once and for all.

She'd barely nudged him an inch when a commotion erupted at the entrance. The music stopped and everyone turned. Her *sorelle* appeared, dressed in skin-baring costumes, jewels dotting their hair and decorating their wrists and ankles.

Penny frowned. More wasted time. Master would want to stay and watch over them. But he gripped her elbow and pulled her the opposite way across the room. He slipped behind a series of painted screens in the corner and shoved open a hidden door. It led to a corridor she'd never been in, with thick carpeting and dark red walls. After a couple of twists and turns, she recognized the door to his quarters.

The sitting room was empty, save for the lounge chair and cabinet laden with equipment and tools. Penny slowed her forward movement and stopped in the doorway. Master released Penny's elbow and turned to face her. He unbuttoned his top button and rolled up his sleeves, uncharacteristic movements that set Penny on edge. "Let's get started."

"Here?" Penny couldn't stop her voice from rising, her eyes from darting toward the shelves. This wasn't what she'd intended; she couldn't actually let him place the device back into her head, attach it to her brain, take control of her . . . again.

"Yes, here. Where else do you think?" His eyes narrowed and his fingers played with the thin length of cord at his neck.

"I don't know. I only thought it might be a more sterile process." Surely it couldn't be done in the drawing room. "What if you get blood on the carpet?"

He exhaled. "What are you really doing here, Penelope?"

"I told you. I returned to the estate to be with you."

"Don't." The word was crisp, sharp. "I want the truth, please."

She couldn't tell him the truth. Not until she knew what he would do with it. "I didn't mean to disobey you."

He paced away. "You try my patience."

She blocked his movement. "I don't know what you want me to say."

He towered over her, his head bent so he could meet her eyes. "I could say the same." His agitation was clear, and Penny knew she had very little time before he snapped. Nella wasn't in Master's quarters, that much was obvious. But Penny needed to discover where Primo had taken her.

"That girl who was with you during the performance"— Penny paused—"is she a new student?"

Master's eyes narrowed and she tried to keep her face impassive. He couldn't know why she asked.

"Yes. She was brought to the manor during your little jaunt to the city."

"And she's . . . staying in the dormitory?"

"Of course." His head tilted to the side. His fingers slid along the length of cord at his neck. A bit of copper glinted at the end before it fell back beneath his shirt.

"She's younger than the rest of us. I wonder where she came from."

She could see the flash in his eyes the moment everything changed.

"You know, don't you?" He raised an eyebrow. "I wasn't sure what exactly happened when you removed the implant, whether your memories returned in full or were damaged forever, leaving you in a sort of stasis of current thought. We've yet to experiment on any of it. But now I can test a multitude of things. Thank you, Penelope, for giving me this opportunity." His hand reached toward her, but his finger caught on the cord and it yanked free from his shirt. At the bottom hung a copper pendant. It was shaped like Penny's tattoo, a narrow six-pronged starburst, but the tips were odd, marred with notches.

Notches that would fit perfectly in a circular keyhole.

Master lunged for Penny as she crashed forward into him. Her fingers gripped the pendant and she pulled hard, feeling the release as the cord snapped and the lengths of string trailed down over her knuckles.

She sprinted toward the door, yanked on the handle, and spilled into the hallway.

"Penelope!" His shout echoed down the corridor. She turned to the right, back the way they'd just come. They'd passed a series of closed doors on the way to his room. Nella might be behind one of them. Or down in the cellar, locked by this key in a desolate cell.

He yelled her name again, closer this time, as she pushed open the first heavy wood-panel door. It was a frigid, empty room with a single bed in the middle.

She moved on, but the next room was just as barren.

Why does he have all these?

The third room flew open, and she nearly fell into empty space. Stairs led down at a steep angle and the darkness was so thick and heavy it felt alive.

Without a second thought, she began to descend.

CHAPTER
40

Penny's palm scraped along the uneven wall, the bricks her only guide as she slipped farther into the stairwell. At the bottom, her hand braced in front of her against another door. Her fingers swept across the surface, but there was nothing to grab, just a small raised knot where a handle might be.

She lifted the cord and nudged one of the ends of the key into the hole in the center of the knot. After twisting it each way, she removed the key and tried another tip. This time the lock clicked and the door swung open on silent hinges.

"Penelope." The echo oozed from the darkness behind her, spurring her to race into the cellar corridor. She recognized it immediately as the same hall she'd been in mere days before. The same row of lights cast an eerie glow on the hallway.

"Penny?" It was a different shout this time. "Penny?" Muffled pounding sounded from behind one of the doors.

"Cricket?" She heard her name again and skittered to a stop in front of a steel door, her fingers already working to shove the key into the inlaid hole. Three attempts this time, and the door swung open.

It was the room of cabinets. Papers and files and random bits of objects lined the entire floor. Cricket stood in the middle of the chamber, his hair even more on end than normal, as if he'd been pulling at it. He gripped loose pages and a shallow wooden box in his hands. "Come, let's get out of here."

"What happened?" Penny asked as they crashed into the hallway again.

"Primo locked me inside. I was going through the files and by the time I heard him it was too late. What about you? Have you found your sister? Are the girls free?"

Penny shook her head, feeling even more like a failure. They'd been here for hours and she'd done nothing but dance.

"You changed." Cricket took in her costume.

"It's a long story." Penny stood in the hallway, fingers tripping along the prongs of the key as she rotated it in her palm and puzzled over which room Nella might be in. At the far end of the corridor, a violet light pulsed beneath the gap in the door, its rhythm like a heartbeat.

"What do you think you're doing?" Master's words echoed from the other end of the corridor. Her head whipped around. How had he gotten in? She still had the key. The entrance must not have shut behind her. A bare bulb of light flickered above, casting half of his face in shadow. He stood still for a moment, hands clenched into fists at his sides.

Cricket shoved the papers into the box and dropped it on the ground at his feet. He turned toward Master, arms spread, filling up Penny's vision of the hall as if he could wipe Master from her thoughts.

Penny dashed away, toward the violet light and the only room Nella might be held captive in. She jammed the key into the hole, twisting and turning and yanking it out again. She tried again with each of the tips.

Nothing happened.

A wail of frustration built in her chest and she forced the key in farther, twisting and jiggling it until finally she heard the faint *click* of the lock slipping.

"Cricket!" She yanked on the handle and raced into the violet light of a laboratory. Steel-plated machines hummed in the corners, pumping and hiccuping and bleating like lambs. In the center of the room sat a sterile, uncomfortable-looking metal cot. Nella lay on her back, the pale pink dress she'd been wearing earlier now wrinkled, the skirts tumbling off the sides. A single wire protruded from the side of her head, draping down nearly to the floor and then up again, where it disappeared into a small, foreign device resting on a wide counter lining the opposite wall. Penny's nose twitched at a tangy scent that filled the air, and she coughed as it scalded her throat with each inhale.

She heard a low groan outside the hall and seconds later Master was there, breathing down her neck. "Pe-nel-o-pe." The word stretched, holding much more than a warning. It was a full sentence, telling her to leave the room and forget all she'd seen.

The problem was, Penny had no intention of doing any of that.

"Cricket? Are you okay?" she shouted, trying to look past Master and get a glimpse into the hall. Her focus swung back. "If you so much as hurt him—"

She could feel the slight shift in the air as Master went to lunge for her. Her head ducked out of his grasp and she scampered around the table to the other side. Master's arms fell and he leered at her from across the cot. His teeth ground together and his jaw locked tight. He took a deep breath as if to calm himself. His eyes blinked once, long and hard, and seemed paler when they opened. "What are you doing?"

There was no going back now, so she finally opted for the truth.

"Destroying you."

He snapped. His eyes flashed, and he roared, crouching as if he'd jump over the bed and strangle her. Penny reached for the wire hooked into the machine behind her. She gripped it tight, ready to pull.

"Let go, Penelope."

"*You* let go." She screamed the words at him. "Let go of me, of my sister, of all the girls. Stop this insanity."

"You know I can't do that." He shook his head, resigned, and took a step to the side, like he planned to move around the cot toward her. She dropped the wire and scurried back, determined to keep some distance between them. He stretched out a hand, still in denial and asking her to join him. "You really don't want to do this. Not after everything I've done for you."

"What have you possibly done for me? Tampered with my mind? Removed all free will from my brain?" She couldn't believe his audacity. "You can't just control people. I don't know how you get away with it. How everyone goes along with you. The townspeople. The inspector. But this time you've gone too far. You may think you're giving me a grand future, a life full of dance and pretty things, but it's not enough. Not when I have zero choice over what the future is, no say in what I like or feel or even remember."

"A grand future?" He spit the words back at her. "I gave you *a* future. What did you think would happen when your mother died? You and your sister would've been orphans, wards of the government. Separated even."

"You *did* separate us." Penny glared at him. He wanted her

to thank him. It was absurd. There was no way she'd express appreciation for what he'd done to her.

He shrugged. "What was I to do with a young girl? The foster home suited her for a while." He paused. "It was you I wanted anyway, Penelope. I gave you everything you could possibly need, and I made good on my promise to take care of your sister. She is perfectly safe here."

"No, she isn't, you . . . you beast!" Rage coursed through Penny's veins. She balled her hands into fists, ready to attack him. Suddenly, a shadow lengthened across the room and Cricket's voice echoed from the open doorway.

"Stand back, Penny. I'll take care of this."

Her head pivoted toward the door. A gasp sucked all the air into her lungs. Cricket stood in the open door, murder in his eyes, a gash marring his forehead, and a dueling pistol held in both hands—aimed at Master's chest.

"Get back." He motioned Master away from Penny.

Penny's gaze darted from side to side, focusing first on Cricket and then on his uncle. She wondered where Cricket had found the weapon, probably somewhere in the room of cabinets. Not that it mattered. It would serve its purpose. Taking advantage of the distraction, Penny inched toward the table and tried to figure out the best way to free her sister from the contraption.

Master shook his head slowly, almost in mock dismay. "I always wondered if I'd regret letting you return to the estate, nephew. I should have fed you to the wolves when I learned that I couldn't manipulate you. It's Beppe's fault. All that guilt he had over your mother."

"What do you mean?" Cricket asked. The gun dipped a little and he reached to steady it with his other hand.

"Your mother. When I tampered with her mind, it didn't

work as we'd hoped." Master shrugged. "The process still needed some tweaking."

Penny drew a sharp breath through her teeth. "Cricket, don't listen to him. He's just trying to distract you."

"Cricket." Master leaned closer. "Listen to me. I speak the truth. Your beloved Penelope is confused. How could she not be? After all I've done to make her forget about you. To forget *all* of her memories."

"I trust her," Cricket seethed. "I don't know how you've managed to get away with this over the years, but it ends tonight. This gala? This midnight dance? It's the last façade you will ever display."

Penny squatted next to Nella's head. She followed the wire to where it nestled behind Nella's ear in a cluster. Needle-thin metal prongs split apart at the end and embedded themselves in the pores of her skin.

"Don't touch it." Master turned to Penny before she could try to remove the wire.

"Don't touch *her*!" Cricket followed Master's movements with the gun.

"Stop! Both of you. Stop." Master lifted his arms like he could command them with his movements. "This has gotten out of control." With long strides, he walked around the table. Cricket trailed after him, the pistol now pointed at Master's head. "Leave the girl alone." Master grabbed Penny's shoulders as if to yank her away. With nothing left to lose, Penny swung her fist at his jaw. She was pretty certain it hurt her more than it hurt him—her knuckles felt fractured upon impact—but it did knock him back a couple of steps.

With teeth bared like a wolf, Master swiped his hand across his mouth and tried a new tactic. He lunged at Cricket and twisted his nephew's arm until the pistol fell on the floor. Penny dove toward the gun, smacking her head on the table leg as her fingers grasped the handle.

"Penny, watch out!" Cricket shouted, and she rolled over. Her back was now to the hard tile floor. Master leaned over her, a knife held tight in his grasp, the point aimed right for Penny's throat.

Penny froze. The light glinted off the blade, blinding her, and she didn't know what to do. Options flashed past. . . . She could shield herself with her hands, roll to the side away from him, push back. . . . The gun. She lifted it only slightly. A memory pulled to the front of her thoughts. Beppe asking Master about his leg. Days ago when she overheard them in the sun-drenched hallway.

His leg.

Something must be wrong with it.

A loud *pop* filled the room and Master tripped to the side, falling into the counter. Penny shook with the gun's recoil, her feet pushing into the ground to scoot her back and out of the way as he released the knife and it clattered to the floor.

The metal box crashed to the ground with Master as he collapsed. He clutched at his leg, tearing at his slacks. "You . . . you . . ." The linen scraps spread open and Penny saw it.

Her mouth gaped. His skin had split apart, but instead of blood and tendons and veins, there was metal. His leg was a mass of rods fused together with screws and copper wires that seemed attached to the skin somehow. Penny pushed to standing and backed away. Master dug his fingers into the wires, shoving, as if somehow he could meld them back to the flap of skin hanging there.

Something seared the back of Penny's throat.

Smoke.

Dry, metallic, and heavy, it filled her mouth and she gagged.

"We need to go!" Cricket yelled, motioning her toward the door. Flames hissed from the equipment on the ground. It must have been damaged in the fall. The metal box had darkened to black on one side and wires bounced around, waving back and forth and causing sparks whenever they connected.

Penny coughed and retched as she reached over Nella's prone body to grab at the wire still attached to her head. Hoping she wouldn't further damage Nella's memories, Penny grasped the line and pulled. With a jerk, the prongs all detached from Nella's skin and the wire fell limp in her hand.

The box began beeping an angry, harsh sound, loud enough to wake the dead.

But apparently not loud enough to wake Nella. She didn't even flinch.

"Penny, we have to hurry." Cricket was at her side. A cabinet against the back wall had caught flame, and smoke billowed around them in waves.

Penny grabbed Nella by the shoulders and shook, trying to wake her. Nella's neck was bent at an awkward angle, and Penny lowered her back onto the cot. She scooted farther down, readying to lift Nella in her arms, when something wrapped around her ankle and yanked. Penny twisted to the side, trying not to fall on top of Nella. Her elbow hit the edge of the cot and she tumbled onto the tile floor with a yelp. Master knelt in front of her, his eyes an inky coal as he aimed the knife at her chest.

"You don't understand." He gritted out the words. "I have to make you understand. I have to make you stay. I'm sorry."

Penny tried to move away, but she was unable to get traction on the slippery tile. Master stabbed down toward her leg.

"I'm sorry," he said again. The point pierced her calf and she screamed. He was too weak to put much pressure behind it, but the wound stung as if he'd peeled the skin away, bit by bit, with a serrated edge.

Cricket leapt forward, grabbed Penny under the armpits, and pulled her away from Master. The fire frothed higher along the cabinets, burning the wood and spreading ash. The smoke built, heavy with a metallic tang, only a small portion of it being sucked into a sort of vent in the ceiling. Penny could make out the sounds of people shouting on the floor above them.

"I'm sorry," Master whispered again, his eyes vacant, the knife still in his hand.

"Nella." Penny pushed Cricket away as he tried to lift her. "You have to carry her."

Her own wound gaped, so Penny tore off a strip of the sheet and wrapped it around her leg like a bandage.

"Penelope." Master's chest heaved and his eyelids kept sinking, as if he could barely keep them open. "Please don't go. I must make you understand." She dared a glance in his direction. His gaze caught hers. "I love you. Please." His eyes closed.

Penny forced herself to turn away, to turn toward Cricket. "Let's go."

Using the cot for leverage, she hoisted herself to her feet. Cricket scooped Nella into his arms, and Penny followed, close at his heels. She stopped only to grab the key and cord from the lock, and the box Cricket had dropped outside the door. She didn't bother to spare a glance at Master, still lying on the floor behind her.

They stumbled down the hall and up the steps.

"Please."

It was the last word she heard him speak.

CHAPTER 41

In the main hall, several of Master's men stood at attention, keeping watch over the crowd. Penny ducked her chin, fearful they would be stopped. But the guests were already shoving, pinched for space in the room, as they debated whether to leave or stay for the theatrics. Nobody seemed to want to take the rumor of a fire completely seriously, but Penny and Cricket knew otherwise. They pushed through the throng and out onto the main steps.

"Go," Penny said. "Take Nella straight to Tatiana. And have her look at your forehead." Cricket's wound had stopped bleeding but still looked deep. "I have to find the girls and convince them to leave with me."

Cricket paused and his eyes darkened as he seemed to consider his options.

"Please." Her throat felt raw. "She's my sister. I need to know she's being cared for."

Cricket blinked once, his long lashes dusting the freckles high on his cheeks. He nodded in reluctant agreement. "Don't stay long. I hope they come with you. But it's not worth risking your life if they won't listen. We don't know the extent of the manipulations or if they will leave. Try, and then flee the estate. Quickly."

Penny kissed him on the cheek and nudged him down the stairs. Then she turned and fought her way back through the crowd. Her leg throbbed with each step, but she forced the pain into a corner of her mind, along with the agony and terror she felt at having to separate from Nella. Cricket would take care of her sister, just as he had taken care of Penny all this time.

Penny spotted Primo talking to one of the guards. Her instinct was to flee in the opposite direction, but she forced her shoulders back and ran to him. "Primo. You must help! Master is trapped. He's downstairs in the cellar." Let Primo go to him, attempt to save him.

And rot in hell, too.

Penny turned away, not bothering to see how Primo reacted. With the wooden box clutched to her chest, she ran toward the studio. The girls would've clustered there when the chaos began. She took a deep breath and opened the doors.

"Penny!" Maria and Ana ran and engulfed her in a hug. Penny stood there, overcome with emotion. Perhaps this would be easier than she'd thought. They had to know something was happening. She could tell them the truth and free them from the clutches of the estate.

"Where is Master?" Ana looked over Penny's shoulder. "We hoped he was with you."

Penny's shoulders slumped. She placed the box on the ground. "I haven't seen Master since I left the ballroom." Another lie, but a necessary one. She couldn't tell them she'd left him wounded, at her own hand, in the burning cellar.

"What should we do?"

"I'm worried."

"Is the manor really on fire?"

The cacophony of questions snapped Penny's last thread of patience.

"Enough!" She limped into the group of girls. Ana and Maria closed in behind her, and she found herself standing in a circle. She turned slowly and her eyes flitted from one girl to the next. "We have to leave, now. There is a fire and it's spreading. We're all in danger. Come with me."

"No." Bianca pulled away first, her arms crossing over her chest. "I'm waiting for Master. He wouldn't want us to leave without his permission."

"Primo said to go." The words slipped from Penny's mouth before she realized the genius behind them. She continued on with the charade. "He sent me here to escort you from the manor before the flames spread. We're to exit through the servants' entrance and use the carriages waiting for the musicians and extra staff. That way we won't be trampled as the guests depart through the front drive."

A complete lie, of course. Yet another one. But if she could only get them away from the estate, she could keep them safe until Beppe awoke and helped explain all that was happening.

Maria, Cecilia, Ana, even Sara seemed to believe her as they rushed toward the door. But Bianca remained staunchly in place, her fingers drumming on her arm. "Your little ploy won't work with me. I'm waiting." Her voice rose. "You all need to stay, too. Penelope isn't trustworthy. You heard Master this afternoon. You'll only get in trouble if you leave with her."

The quartet stopped and turned back.

Penny knew then: She had to tell them the truth. She stepped in front of Bianca so they couldn't look into her eyes. "She's wrong. You are all in danger. And it's so much more than the fire." She paused. "You must listen to me. Master has been controlling us. He has a way to change our memories, edit our thoughts and behaviors, even our senses. To what extent each of us has been affected, I don't know. But we have families." She looked around, imploring the girls to understand. "We have *mothers*. They're not dead, as you imagine from your photo albums. Those are fake. Your real parents may be searching for you."

Your sister may be here and you wouldn't even recognize her. Penny paced to Sara. "Think back on your history here. On your experience with the wolves. Look for disconnects, things that don't really make sense or seem hazy. Those are changes in your memories." She spun to Ana and grasped her warm fingers. "You used to adore Cricket and now you hardly know who he is. I can prove it. Come with me now. Beppe will tell you everything."

"Master loves us," Bianca shouted from behind them. "You're upset because he doesn't love you best anymore."

Penny wanted to shake her. "That's not true! He doesn't love us. He wants to control us, make us his toys." And then the truth hit her again like a punch to the stomach. Bianca *knew*. Perhaps not consciously, but in some innate manner Bianca knew—and she didn't care. She enjoyed it. "Bianca. This isn't love."

"You don't know anything!" Bianca yelled.

Panicked shouts drifted toward them from the main wing and Penny smelled the metallic smoke again. The fire was spreading. Time was up.

"I'm leaving. I hope you'll come with me." Penny's chest tightened with grief and dismay, but she turned toward the exit. She had promised Cricket she'd leave if they wouldn't listen.

She reached the doorway. The fantastical mural around it mocked her with dancing fairies, joyful and carefree.

Fairies.

Smascherate la fata.

Beppe's incoherent words echoed in her mind as her eyes lit on a lone fairy painted on the right side of the door. The little sprite sat on a rock, her chin propped in her hands as if to support the heavy dragon mask covering most of her head.

A masked fairy. Penny peered closer. The mask itself was raised from the wall, one of the eyes hollowed out. It was the perfect size for the starburst key she'd tied on her wrist as they'd escaped the cellar.

Could this be the fail-safe the prince had mentioned while dancing the other night at dinner? She wondered if Beppe would have created one for the girls. Penny slipped the key lower so she could grasp it in her fingers and plunged it into the hole.

Nothing.

Not that she'd imagined anything would happen.

But then she heard the gasps and wails from behind her. "Make it stop." Ana bent at the waist. Her hands pulled at her hair. Maria sank to her knees, tears leaking from her closed eyes. Penny glanced back and forth between the key and the girls, wondering what she'd done.

"No. Mamma." Cecilia rocked back and forth on the balls of her feet. Her hands stretched out, as if to grab something . . . or someone.

Is it possible?

Ana's breaths came in little puffs of gasps and her entire body trembled. Penny rushed to put her arm around her. "My head hurts. Make the pain stop. Please." Ana's lips had turned a pale blue and she shivered uncontrollably. "It's excruciating."

Penny recalled her own slicing pain when her thoughts were severed from the device. "It will pass. I promise." Her voice rose as she looked around the room, at the pain carving new masks on the girls' faces. "The pain will ease quickly."

Bianca stood off to the side. She looked uncomfortable, but not in any obvious agony. Then she lunged toward the mural. Penny released Ana and tried to get to the door frame first, but Bianca had already pulled out the key. A maniacal grin lifted the corner of her mouth, and she pocketed the cord.

Penny whirled around, waiting for the girls' faces to relax into the smooth, puppetlike state of control. But several seconds passed and nothing happened. Perhaps there was no way to undo what she'd started. Bianca's removing the key hadn't reverted the memories at all.

"We need to go." Penny turned to Ana, who blinked rapidly and then nodded. Penny grabbed the box and stood in the doorway. She raised her voice to all the girls. "There are carriages out back. I will take you somewhere safe."

Several of her *sorelle* still sobbed from the pain, or perhaps from the knowledge of what Master had done to them, but Penny was able to usher them out the door and into the corridor.

Bianca stayed behind, standing still in the middle of the studio. Her eyes darkened to a deep sapphire color, so blue they were almost black. "I'm going to find Master." She stepped forward, her legs bending in an odd limp, almost as if her center of gravity had shifted. Her shoulder twitched higher as she pushed past Penny and made her way down the hall toward the main wing.

"Let's go!" Ana motioned for Penny to lead the way. The air had turned opaque with smoke, but Penny caught a streak of movement out of the corner of her eye. She bent down to lift Leon with her free hand and led the group of girls down the twisting route to the servants' entrance. Shouts and screams continued to echo from the main wing of the manor. Sara flinched every time a high-pitched wail pierced the foggy corridor. It was as if they walked through the forest mist, surrounded by banshees.

Finally, they stumbled out onto the servants' drive. Already some of the staff milled there in pools of lantern light, disoriented. "We've been ordered to evacuate—now—per Master's request," Penny told them.

Two drivers ushered them into a pair of carriages. Penny leaned in to whisper to the front driver's ear. "Ravinni. The apothecary. We're to find assistance there." She spent a brief moment worrying that she would lead Master's men right to Beppe, but she felt certain they'd be occupied with the fire at the estate.

Besides, she needed to get to Nella as soon as possible. She couldn't worry about detours and deceptions.

Penny squished into a carriage and settled on the bench between Ana and Maria, Leon curled up in the skirt of her costume. Across from her sat Sara and two other girls. They all trembled as the frigid air whistled in through the gaps in the doors and across their exposed skin. Their gala gowns weren't meant for travel. The driver tossed in a couple of heavy fur blankets and climbed on top of the seat. The wheels jerked underneath them and they bounced down the drive.

They'd barely made it out onto the main road when a large explosion shook the carriage and lit the sky brighter than noontime. The estate grounds were a shadow against the fire raging behind the manor. White clouds of ash billowed out into the air and flames licked the sky a burnt-orange color.

They sat there silently, the six girls, watching their home as it turned into an inferno. But it wasn't their home. Not really.

In unison they turned away.

CHAPTER 42

Penny tried to make eye contact with her *sorelle* so she could see how they were doing. She remembered well the first few times her true memories had leaked through, the disorientation and discomfort. She had no idea the extent of their thoughts, or what they would now remember of their childhoods. Ana seemed much the same as before, energetic and ready to find the bright side of things. Perhaps because she was the newest girl at the estate. Or perhaps her memories were easier to live with.

Sara also seemed to be doing well, her eyes clear in the dim pool of lantern light. She kept examining her arms, turning her wrists this way and that. "The scars are gone. But what of the marking?" Sara rubbed her thumb against the tattoo on the inside of her wrist.

"I still have mine." Ana pulled her arm out from beneath the blanket.

Penny nodded. "I do, too. It's the same shape as the key Master wore around his neck. I think it's his symbol. His brand."

At that Maria began to cry, a shuddering, shaking, desperate sort of sob. Penny tucked an arm around Maria's shoulders and pulled her close. "What is it?"

The words came out in bits of broken spurts. "I don't know who I am. I don't . . . I don't understand. I thought I loved him. I thought I was happy. I . . . I don't know if I can do this."

"Of course you can." Penny squeezed tightly. "We're all in this together. Maria, your life is just beginning. You have a wealth of choices in front of you, choices you didn't even know you had. I promise, it feels horrible now, overwhelming and terrifying, but we'll get through this. We'll find your family."

Family. If only she could have gone into the room and pulled out information from the girls' files. They'd surely been destroyed by the fire.

Except . . .

She shifted Leon onto Sara's lap and lifted the box from where she'd placed it at her feet. She removed the lid and peered at the loose pages inside. Adrenaline made her movements frantic as she riffled through the papers.

"Maria. Here!" She shoved the page into her friend's hands. "Look. Right there. Your family's information. They live in Sarigliano. That's not far at all."

The girls leaned in, peering at the handwriting on the pages grasped in Maria's shaking hands. "It can't be. How do you have this?" Tears welled in Maria's eyes again, but Penny could see a small bit of relief shining behind them.

"There was a room in the cellar. Walls of cabinets and drawers full of our belongings and information. I fear the fire destroyed the rest, but Cricket removed these to keep them safe." Penny passed out pages to Ana and the others and then closed the box tight to keep the information safe for her *sorelle* in the other carriage.

The girls read the pages and then began talking over one another, sharing details and asking questions. Penny, exhausted from the day's activities and the pain in her neck and calf, leaned back in her seat and closed her eyes, her thoughts drifting.

To her own family.

To Nella.

Her heart clenched.

She had to be okay.

"We're here." The driver eased the horse to a stop in the alley outside the shop. He hopped down to open the carriage door, but Penny had already pushed her way out and sprinted up the steps to the side entrance. She waved at the girls to join her before pulling on the handle and spilling into the back room. Alidoro had moved out onto the sofa, where he now snored, his arm bandaged in a sling and his feet dangling off the edge. Cricket paced the floor, his fingers buried in his hair. His head jerked up at her arrival, and he ran forward to greet her. He took the box from Penny's hands and handed it to Maria before he lifted Penny and swung her in a circle. Her arms laced behind his neck and her mouth sought his for a brief moment before he lowered her back to the ground.

"You made it," he said, his lips mere millimeters from her own.

"Yes." She beamed up at him and brushed his hair from his forehead, where the gash had been cleaned. "All the girls made it—well, everyone except Bianca. I'm not sure what's become of her." She tilted her head toward the open door as the girls came through, some hesitant and skittish as new colts, some bold and interested and eager. "Thank you for the documents. They are ecstatic."

"Of course. I'm sorry it couldn't have been more. I tried to find information for everyone."

Tatiana burst in through the fringe, eyes wide as she took in the new guests.

"I'm sorry." Penny wrung her hands. "I wasn't sure where else to go."

Tatiana gave her a quick hug. "I'm so glad you're safe. We'll figure out something. Beppe wouldn't want it any other way."

"How is he? And"—Penny's teeth worried her bottom lip— "how is Nella?"

Cricket grabbed her wrist. "Come with me." He led her up the staircase and into Rosaura's room. Beppe stood at the edge of the bed, awake and seemingly fine, but his shoulders hunched over as he took in Nella's prone body.

Penny stiffened, expecting the worst.

Beppe turned toward Penny, and she saw that his fingers encircled Nella's wrist. "Her pulse is steady." He scooted aside so Penny could get a closer look. Nella's eyes were closed and her breaths labored, but her cheeks had regained some color.

Beppe ushered Penny and Cricket down the hall into Tatiana's chamber.

"Will she wake?" Penny asked. She collapsed into an armchair in the corner of the room.

He nodded and eased into a chair beside her. "I have no reason to doubt it. The concern is her state of mind at that time. Cricket said you removed her from the machine, which was most likely in the process of transmitting and editing her thoughts. Since that circuit didn't complete, I'm unsure what memories she will have." He paused. "I also removed the cloaking apparatus, although I hope I did a better job than you." He raised an eyebrow at the stitches behind her ear. "Let me take a look at that."

"And her leg," Cricket chimed in from where he'd moved to stand next to her.

"And her leg." Beppe sighed and shook his head. "Always the difficult one." He motioned for her to lie on the bed and asked Cricket to have Tatiana prepare fresh bandages and salve.

"Now why don't *you* tell me what's happened in my absence?" Beppe began to remove the clotted cloth from the wound on her calf.

While he fussed and fixed, Penny recounted everything. ". . . and then I fell on the badminton court. Cricket's touch snapped me out of my memory distortions for a second time." She winced as Beppe pushed a little too hard on her skin.

"Say that again?" Beppe asked.

"His touch." She glanced over at Cricket, who had just entered the room with the supplies. His cheeks flushed pink, as if Beppe would reprimand him for disobeying Master's mandate never to have physical contact with the girls.

Cricket tried to explain, his words tripping over one another. "I seemed to be able to reverse Master's attempts to mask her thoughts. He manipulated them several times while you were gone, and every time I touched her skin, the true memories returned."

Penny glanced at Beppe. "Is it because they're related, he and Master?"

"No. I think it's perhaps something I did. Your mother." Beppe paused briefly, and turned to Cricket. "She was the first of Cirillo's subjects." Cricket swallowed and blinked hard. It was one thing for Master to throw the comment at him in the heat of an argument. It was another to hear it spoken in regret. Beppe shook his head sadly. "I tried to help her after the surgery that reshaped her mind, but traditional medicine failed. And I couldn't reverse the damage to her brain." He brushed a thick, grainy paste on Penny's leg. "As soon as Cirillo became frustrated with his inability to control her, I feared he'd come after you. So, with Tatiana's help, I prepared what I hoped would be a countermeasure." He pressed a dressing over the wound. "We gave you a course of medicine that would reject the implant if he ever attempted to use it. I wonder if ultimately that caused your touch to react with Penny's memory cloaking."

Cricket looked stunned and a little afraid. "Could I hurt someone?"

"I have no reason to believe so." He turned his attention to Penny and patted her knee. "The leg should heal fine." He glanced at her head. "Do you happen to still have the device?"

Penny pointed at the nightstand, where the metal implant still rested. He must not have seen it when he woke. Beppe gripped the strip carefully between two fingers, twisting and turning it so the different facets caught the light. "Interesting. The edges are black. Almost burned." He glanced up. "Penny, your brain nearly severed the connection even before you removed it. I'm not sure if it's a chemical reaction or time decay. There's a chance you brought yourself out of the memory distortions without anything related to Cricket other than a subconscious desire to know the truth."

He put down the strip and stared out the window for a long moment. "I didn't want to be a part of this. It all escalated so quickly. I should have walked away. But there was this allure to it all. Access to both medicine and technology, and the ability to weave it together. And then Cirillo made the school. I had to stay close to make sure things didn't worsen."

"Was that why you made a fail-safe? Is that what the fairy was?"

He turned back to Penny and examined the stitches behind her ear. "Yes. The key released an electronic pulse that put a stop to the circuitry in the device." He glanced at the nightstand as if to make sure it was still there. "That device served a multitude of purposes, cloaking your old memories and allowing new ones to layer on top. It also manipulated your senses in reaction to specific stimuli. For example, whenever you thought of leaving the estate you found yourself with a headache, and when you were close to the border of the estate, all of your senses kicked in—sight, smell, touch—in order to invoke fear of the wolves."

"The wolves aren't real, right?" Penny asked.

Beppe shrugged. "There are a few that roam the estate, but the visions you saw were a heightened version of them. A living nightmare. They were the first animals Cirillo modified. The stilts came next. He is able to access their minds, simple as they are. He can direct their movement and extract what they see. Anywhere within the borders of the estate."

"Spying on everyone," Cricket said.

Suddenly, Rosaura's broken voice rattled from the guest room. "She's awake!"

It was a mad dash as they sprinted down the hall and tried to squeeze through the door frame all at once. Penny fell back, a sudden knot in her stomach.

Beppe checked Nella's eyes and took her pulse, jotting details in a notebook he kept near the bed. Nella sat very still and stared at him. A frightened, timid expression pinched her forehead and lips.

"I'm going to ask you a few questions." Beppe's voice was warm and soothing. He dipped his pen in the ink and readied it over a fresh page in the notebook. "Do you know your name?"

She blinked, her eyebrows furrowed together as if she sought the information but came up lacking.

Cricket glanced back at Penny, the worry in his eyes mirroring her own fear.

"Nella?" She bit her lip and nodded as if to herself. "Nella."

Penny nearly collapsed against the door frame. Relief replaced panic as Beppe asked more questions and she answered them all correctly. It often took her a few seconds to respond, but she seemed to have her memories intact.

"Excuse me, are we done now?" Nella looked at Beppe. "I'm famished."

"I'll prepare something." Cricket turned to leave the room. Nella's eyes followed him. It was then that she saw Penny. She gasped, her fingers digging into the side of the bed as she tried to sit up.

"Penny."

A sob tore from Penny's throat as she ran into her sister's arms.

"Penny, you finally came home."

⁂

Penny slipped out from under the quilt, leaving Nella snoring softly beside her. The sun had risen, casting a pale glow over the room.

The night had been long, and she was sure some of the girls were still awake, whispering near the hearth or sipping the hot tea Tatiana had made by the gallon. They had all welcomed Rosaura back into their fold, once she'd finally eased her way downstairs. Rosaura chose to remain with them, snuggling Leon to her chest as if she might never let him go, and encouraged Penny to rest with Nella in the guest room.

Now Penny walked downstairs and into the living quarters, which seemed an odd sort of controlled chaos. Blankets and pillows were draped seemingly on every piece of furniture and around the floor. She had no idea where Tatiana had found all the linens.

She settled into a chair at the small table near the kitchen where Maria, Ana, and Sara whispered over steaming mugs. Ana passed Penny a cup of coffee. "Cricket and Alidoro ran to the market to get food. I'm starving! I feel like I haven't eaten in months!"

"It's because you haven't." Penny's stomach growled in agreement.

Maria took a sip from her mug. "How is Nella?"

"She seems fine. How are you all?" She looked at them each in turn.

"Other than starving?" Ana asked. "I'm okay, I think. Anxious to find my family."

"Me, too," Sara said, her voice soft.

"Nervous. Anxious. Afraid." Maria's voice trembled. "I still don't understand how this happened to us."

Penny nodded. "Beppe will talk to you all when he awakes. And unfortunately, he still needs to remove the devices." She pointed to the stitches behind her ear. "I think he'll do a better job than I did, though."

Maria's face blanched. She reached over and took Penny's free hand with hers. "You are so brave. Not only for removing that thing, but for coming back to the estate and trying to save us. I know it wasn't easy. I truly can't thank you enough."

The other girls chimed in to express their gratitude.

Penny shook it off. "You're all brave. I happened to have my memories malfunction first. You would have done the same. I just know it."

Cricket swept in through the fringe from the front shop, Alidoro only a step behind. The boy's arm was still wrapped and held stable in a sling, but with his free hand he carried a bag bursting with fruit and a loaf of bread. Ana jumped up and began to help them unload the pastries and nuts, fresh meat and cheese. Penny snatched a pastry and leaned into Cricket's side. His fingers brushed her waist and sparks seemed to race over her skin. He kissed her nose and pinched off a bite of the *sfogliatelle* before she could shove it all in her mouth.

"Any news?" Penny murmured.

He nodded toward the back door and laced her fingers through his, his bare wrist against her tainted one. They walked across the room. Cricket shoved open the door and they stepped out onto the small porch. Side by side, they leaned against the rail and looked out on the narrow alleyway below. Building after building stretched across the horizon. A pair of young children rolled hoops down the street before disappearing around the corner.

Cricket waited until the kids were gone before he spoke. "The back wing of the manor was severely damaged in the explosion, but I believe much of the dormitory and Master's wing were unscathed. The guests made it outside and they were able to get the fire under control pretty quickly."

Penny pondered this. "I'm sure everything in the cellar was

ravaged in the flames. But if his quarters were spared, there's a chance the equipment in his room survived."

Cricket nodded. "We should talk to Beppe and find out where all the different devices were contained."

"Any word on Master? Primo? Bianca?"

"No word on Bianca. They did find remains in the fire. I don't know that the bodies could be identified, but it has to be Master at least." Cricket squeezed her hand. "You're safe with me. I promise. We'll work through all of this. Together."

He pulled her against his chest. She buried her nose in his shirt and took in the familiar cinnamon scent. His heartbeat was a steady rhythm beneath her cheek. She let the honesty and weight of his words settle over her.

Her mother was gone, destroyed by the man Penny had destroyed herself. But she had her sister, and Cricket, and a new family of friends that loved her for who she was. The good, the bad, the past, and the future.

"Are you okay, *mia farfallina*?" Cricket asked, his voice soft in the silence of morning.

"Yes," Penny said, her lips curving in a smile.

And she was. Corrupt as her memories were, distorted as her past had been, they made her who she was today. They gave her strength. They made her whole.

They make me . . . me.

✤ ACKNOWLEDGMENTS ✤

The Midnight Dance is a story of strength and self-discovery. Writing and publishing this book was a lengthy and personal journey, and there are so many people to thank for its success.

First off, an overwhelming and heartfelt thank-you to the team at Swoon Reads and Macmillan. My amazing editor Kat Brzozowski, who also served as mentor and confidant from nearly the start to finish! Also everyone who touched, edited, read, critiqued, and produced the novel: Emily Settle, Lauren Scobell, Holly West, Jean Feiwel, Jon Yaged, Valerie Shea, Janet Rosenberg, Starr Baer, Nancee Adams-Taylor, and Kim Waymer. To the cover designers, Kathleen Breitenfeld, Carol Ly, and Rich Deas. I absolutely cannot thank you enough for bringing to life the dark and twisted vision of Penny and the estate.

Thank you to Demetra Brodsky, critique partner and friend extraordinaire, for being my rock through this entire journey. It's surreal that we did this together only slightly offset. To my original critique partners, Lisa Cannon and Andrea Ortega, thank you for reading multiple drafts of this novel (and all the others) and for your valuable feedback and support. And to Mary Pearson for leading the first SCBWI breakout session where our little trio met.

Debra Driza, Kirsten Hubbard, Shannon Messenger, Cindy Pon, Elle Jauffret, Gretchen McNeil, James Raney, Robin Reul, and the rest of the SoCal authors I've brunched and chatted with, your laughter and support has been immeasurable! To Jay Asher for your support over the years and the almost Space Camp trip!

Margaret O'Hair and Sue Douglass Fliess, I will never forget my first SCBWI conference with you two! Meg, thanks for approaching me that first morning. Special thanks to the girls from Oasis for YA, the board of YALitChat, and the authors and friends from the WriteOnCon Underbelly. Your encouragement and education over the years has meant the world to me.

My children: Katelyn, Kendall, and Lincoln. Thank you for letting me write and rewrite and revise and edit and cry over this entire process, all with minimal complaints and massive support on your end. To Jason, thank you for your support and encouragement through the years of this insane journey. To my mom, Barb, thank you for reading and editing, for your encouragement and love. To my brother, Kenny, for your endless support.

And finally, to my dad, Ken, for his encouragement and writing. Last year, while going through his personal effects, I found a poem he'd written when he was a young man. It seems a fitting way to end this novel. . . . "To die is but a fancy / for death can be a joy / When people you love most / treat you like a toy / I am a puppet on a string / dancing to and fro / Doing what you want me to / while the depths of my love grow / But you don't know how I feel / and you don't really care / For once I'm gone from your side / someone else is there."